Loyalty
&
Deceit

Loyalty & Deceit

Beanie Sigel & Juma Sampson

C.H.A.O.S PUBLISHING

ROCHESTER, NEW YORK

C.H.A.O.S PUBLISHING

LOYALTY & DECEIT

A C.H.A.O.S. PUBLISHING Book

C.H.A.O.S. Publishing E-book edition/October 2017

C.H.A.O.S. Publishing Paperback edition/October 2017

Copyright (c) 2018 by Beanie Sigel and Juma Sampson

Library of Congress Catalog Card Number: 2017946496

Website: http://www.chaospublishing.net

Author's e-mail: Juma Sampson (jumasampson1@gmail.com)

Editing by: Rahiem Brooks (rbrooksbooks@yahoo.com)

ISBN 978-0-984006-03-8

Published simultaneously in the US and Canada

PRINTED IN THE UNITED STATES OF AMERICA

For Tahirah and Donntoya

Loyalty

&

Deceit

PROLOGUE

PHILADELPHIA, PA

An impulsive grin stretched across Shalik's face as he glanced over to the passenger side of his Infinity QX 50 truck where Sandra sat. He couldn't believe his luck. Not only was she one of the sexiest urban models in Philadelphia, but she also owned a popular clothing line.

Sandra had been making eye contact and throwing flirtatious smiles at him while in Club Onyx all night. Donning an exclusive black lace cat suit that boldly displayed her remarkably curvaceous body, paired with black and gold Guiseppe spiked suede heels, all eyes from both men and women were justifiably on her. Seemingly oblivious to them all, she was fixated on Shalik.

His name was quickly spreading throughout South Philly due to his steady rise in the drug game. He never had a problem when it came to the ladies, but to receive the attention from a woman of Sandra's stature confirmed that he made it to the major leagues.

Shalik casually watched Sandra head to the bar. A moment

1

later, to his surprise, she strutted up to him with two drinks in her manicured hands and offered him one. He accepted. Less than an hour later they were on their way to his house.

"Do you wanna stop and get something to eat?" Shalik asked.

"All I want is some desert." The seductive tone in her voice made her message quite clear.

"I'm sure I can satisfy your cravings." He played it cool and continued driving.

They engaged in small talk and exchanged flirtatious jabs until he pulled into the driveway of a spacious white and tan Victorian style home on 65th and Woodbine.

They eased out of the vehicle and Shalik disabled the alarm system to his home before they entered.

"Is this really your house?" Sandra asked as she stood in the marble floored foyer looking around in shock and awe.

"Yeah, I just moved in a few months ago," he answered proudly.

Her expensive heels clicked against the foreign tile as she stepped closer. He met her advance, embraced her and wrapped his hands around her twenty-six inch waist. Her soft, sensuous kiss caused blood to rush through his entire body. He slowly guided his hands down to her forty-two inch hips, allowing them to caress her plump, round butt.

Feeling a slight rumble in his stomach, he took a step back.

"What's wrong?" Sandra asked.

"N-nothing." He felt the rumble again, but this time it was more intense. "Baby, make yourself comfortable. I think I have to use the bathroom."

Before she could respond he began to trot up the stairs.

Sandra removed her cell phone and sent a text: I'm

here…the front door is open. Hurry up!

She slid the phone back into her Yves Saint Laurent leather clutch and waited patiently.

Within two minutes the door opened. Mack slid inside wearing all black clothing, including black leather gloves. "Did you pour that stuff I gave you in his drink?" he asked in a low whisper.

"Yeah. He's upstairs using the bathroom right now." Sandra answered.

"It's a black Crown Victoria with tinted windows parked four houses down. Get in the driver's side. I'll be there in a minute."

She immediately left and Mack closed the door behind her. He crept up the stairs while removing a massive .357 Python revolver from the holster on his waist. Once the bathroom was located, he knocked lightly on the door.

"I'll be out in a minute, baby," Shalik shouted from inside.

Mack pushed the door open and walked into the bathroom. Shalik looked up in fright at the large, imposing man who stood before him. The menacing rubber-gripped hand cannon was clutched in Mack's huge hand, invoking the fear of a tamed pit bull.

"I sent you a message to get down with SP, and I don't like the response you gave my young bawh."

Unsure of what to do, Shalik raised his hands partially in the air. "Can we talk about this, Mack?"

"It ain't nothin' else for us to talk about. I gave you two options—get down, or lay down. You ain't want to take the first option, so I'ma give you the second one."

"That's my word I was going to get in touch with you. Ya bawh came up to me at the wrong time. I was…"

3

"Nigga, you're full of shit," Mack interjected. "Matter of fact, put ya fuckin' head in the toilet."

"Are you serious? I ain't puttin' my head in the toilet. It's shit in there!"

With lightning speed, Mack closed the space between him and Shalik, raising his hand that held the pistol and sent it crashing down on his face.

Upon impact the heavy steel caused his skin to break, causing blood to escape. He fell off the toilet with his jeans draped around his ankles. Mack repeatedly rained thunderous blows from the pistol until Shalik's face was nothing more than a swollen, bloodied, unrecognizable mess. Mack stood up breathing heavily.

"Fuck you!" Shalik managed to push the words through his broken jaw.

"Oh yeah? I like that. Let me see if your tough ass can take these bullets." He aimed his gun at Shalik's face.

His eyes grew wide as he stared deep into the large barrel. Mack squeezed the trigger three times in rapid succession, smearing the bathroom floor with blood, skull fragments and chunks of brain. His body instantly stilled as his soul was released.

With one final look at his work, Mack left the house and got into the passenger seat of the Crown Victoria. Sandra pulled off without saying a word…

CHAPTER 1

SYRACUSE, NY

Terry, known to everyone else as T-Lova, or simply T, brought his matte black Mercedes CLS 55 AMG to a stop in front of his longtime friend and partner Jihad's house. Stepping out of his newly purchased automobile, he inhaled a deep breath of crisp morning air and stretched his six foot, slim, muscular frame. At nine o'clock in the morning, in the middle of September, the weather was unseasonably warm. The wind blew softly, producing a minute cooling effect. There was not a cloud in the sky to bar the sun's omnipotent rays that made its welcomed presence on the Earth.

The thirty year old, chocolate-skinned, young man casually walked towards Jihad's front door. They had spoken with each other over the phone less than twenty minutes ago, so Jihad was expecting him. He opened the door before Terry was able to knock.

Jihad was also dark-skinned. He had a good grade of hair and perfectly circular waves. He stood at five feet eleven inches and two hundred sixty-three pounds of pure strength. His perfectly even white teeth and generous smile often gave people the misconception that he was a big, gentle, teddy bear. However, a deep look into his dark, piercing eyes revealed a glimpse of the beast that lay within. Because of his muscular composition, people often stereotyped him as not being intelligent. That couldn't be further from the truth. He had no problem using their naivety to his advantage. There were very few who knew the true Jihad. He lived by the adage: The greatest trick the Devil ever pulled was to convince the world that he never existed.

"Wassup, T?" Jihad greeted his friend, extending his hand.

"I'm good, bruh." Terry gave him dap and walked into the house.

Jihad owned a modest three bedroom home. After being released a year and a half ago from doing a four year prison bid for armed robbery, he decided to get money with Terry. They had known each other since they were teenagers. Joining forces with him, Jihad had accomplished more within the past year and a half than he had throughout his entire life.

Terry plopped down on the living room sofa. Jihad took a seat next to him. "Damn, nigga, you act like you're still sleepy. What's good?" Jihad asked.

"Nah, I ain't sleepy. I just got a lot of shit on my mind."

"What's poppin', kid? You know I got a degree in psychology." Jihad grabbed a mango flavored Blunt Wrap off of the coffee table along with a bag of Sour Diesel weed and began to roll up.

"The only degree you could ever get is in Criminology," Terry teased. He knew any issue that affected him affected Jihad and vice versa. So, it was mandatory for him to let Jihad know what was on his mind.

"Every since my man, Jukwon disappeared, shit has been crazy. I went from paying twenty G's for a ki of the best cocaine to paying twenty-seven G's for coke that's been stepped on like crazy. Not only that, I can't even find a steady connect," Terry explained. "One minute they got some work, the next minute they're out. If it keep going like this we could lose our power."

"Come on, sun. You trippin'," Jihad said, exhaling a thick cloud of smoke. "That ain't like you to talk like that. I don't even believe you said that bullshit." He passed the weed to Terry, shaking his head in disgust.

The look on Jihad's face instantly made Terry want to retract what he had said. "Don't get it fucked up though." Terry grabbed the blunt and took a heavy pull of the potent strain of weed. "I'm built for this shit. If I wasn't I would have been broke or dead. Ain't nothin' or nobody gon' stop what I was destined to do." There was no doubt that Terry was dead serious.

"That's what the fuck I'm talkin' about!" Jihad exclaimed. He was happy to see that his partner wasn't losing faith in their operation. They smoked and passed the blunt back and forth in silence.

"Yo, do you remember that Dominican cat we met up in Harlem?"

"Yeah, that short, young nigga we ran into at the jewelry store a couple days ago," Jihad recalled. "Didn't he give you some powder to test?"

"Yeah, he gave me five grams. I cooked it up yesterday and it came back nearly gram for gram. It's better than anything we've had in a long time."

"How much does he want for a brick?"

"He said twenty-eight, but I didn't let him know that we could be buying seven bricks a pop. I'm sure he'll bring the price down once he finds out what we're working with."

"Well, we're good then. It ain't too much to think about." Jihad sounded upbeat.

"The only fucked up thing is we gotta go all the way up to Harlem to see this nigga."

"Fuck it, kid. We gotta do what we gotta do. After we get established with the connect, we'll be able to send a mule down there."

"Let me call him and see if everything's still good." Terry pulled out his cell phone and searched through the numbers until he found what he was looking for. After speed dialing the number a man picked up.

"*Dime lo cantando.*" Holla at me.

"*Cálmate, ¿cómo estás?*" Terry replied. Chillin', how are you doing?

"*Bien, bien.*" Good, good.

"*Mi nombre es T-Lova.*" This is T-Lova.

"Oh, yes, the guy from out of town. You speak good Spanish."

"*Muchas gracias, pero necesito aprender más.*" Thanks a lot, but I need to learn more.

"Did you try on the clothes I gave you?" Flaco asked, referring to the cocaine he gave Terry to test.

"Yes, they fit perfectly. I want to come shopping."

"Okay, when you come?"

"How about today?"

"Today is good. What time?"

"I'll be there around seven o'clock tonight."

"Call me when you get to Harlem. I'll give you directions as to where to go from there, okay?"

"*Si, no hay problema. Hasta la noche.*" Yes, no problem. I'll see you tonight. Terry responded.

"Okay, bye," Flaco said, then hung up.

"What the fuck was that?" Jihad stared at Terry in surprise.

"What was what?"

"Sun, I know you wasn't just speaking in Spanish."

"Yeah, I do a little somethin'," Terry said with a sly smirk.

"Get the fuck outta here." Jihad was both surprised and impressed. "Where you learn that at?"

"Come on, sun. I'm nationally known, world renowned and locally accepted." Terry's eyelids had become heavy, signifying his high from the weed.

"In this game we have to be able to mingle with everybody from white collar business men to Spanish drug connects. It's easier to be accepted by someone if they feel you share something in common with them. Feel me?"

"No question. I gotta step my game up," Jihad acknowledged.

"I learned that from my man, Jukwon," Terry said, paying homage to his friend who seemed to have disappeared off the face of the earth.

"I hear you mention that dude's name from time to time. He must have been a thorough nigga."

"He was one of the youngest, sharpest niggas in the game." Terry's respect for Jukwon was displayed in his voice and eyes. "Juk and his brother Dymond ran Rochester."

"Oh, you talkin' about them dudes D and Juk?" Jihad shot up. "Yeah, I heard about them niggas. Matter of fact, I was up north with Dymond. He didn't speak much. All he did was work out, read books, and take damn near every vocational program the prison offered. I heard that them niggas had Rochester on lock so viciously that when they left, the whole city was in turmoil for months. They said that Juk was in a coma and Dymond somehow disappeared after he came home from prison. I heard a rumor that he got murdered in another city."

"I don't know," Terry responded, not wanting to think the worst. "But what I do know is if it wasn't for Juk, I...we wouldn't have none of this shit. Before you came home, Juk drove up here and hit me with a brick of the best coke to touch Syracuse. He's the only nigga that ever showed me that type of love. After he blessed me with that bird, I never looked back. I went from buying eighths to coppin' seven to ten joints a month because of him."

Terry and Jihad conversed for a while longer. He had decided to give Jihad some insight on how he solidified his spot in the game. Jihad knew that Terry rarely revisited his past, so he honored his openness and listened intently.

As their conversation came to a closure, Jihad received a greater understanding as to why Terry ran his operation in a play-no-games manner. What Jihad didn't know was that Terry's all but easy childhood played an integral part in his present life as well. Terry bypassed that part entirely.

They left Jihad's house and got into Terry's Mercedes. He never transported drugs in that car. He and Jihad cruised around the city making their rounds, picking up the money that their drug houses earned overnight. In totality, they had three spots that served ten dollar bags of crack cocaine, three spots that served twenty dollar bags and two spots that sold ounces of powder cocaine throughout Syracuse, New York.

After collecting the money that each spot made, they drove over to the stash house and packaged up more drugs for distribution. They then got into one of their vehicles used to deliver the drugs, a blue Mazda 6, and replenished the spots.

By 1:30 in the afternoon they had completed the day's work. Terry and Jihad went to the safe house and counted up twenty-eight thousand dollars.

They also had a special vehicle that was used to transport large amounts of drugs. A late model forest green Lincoln Navigator. The luxury SUV was equipped with two separate stash locations. One was in the rear, behind the third row of seats. It was capable of holding up to ten kilos of cocaine. The other stash compartment was in the center console, directly in front of the arm rests. It was designed to raise up by hydraulic pumps to reveal an area customized to hold two large handguns and a few boxes of ammunition.

With the money inside a Nike sneaker box, placed inside of a Foot Locker bag, they got inside the Navigator, onto the expressway, and headed to Harlem, New York.

By the time they reached Lenox Avenue, the sun began to descend, slowly giving way to nightfall. Terry called Flaco.

"Hello?" Flaco answered.

"Hola, papi. It's me. I'm on Lenox Avenue, what's good?"

"Come to five hundred West Forty Fourth Street."

"Aaight, I know where that's at. I'll be there in fifteen minutes."

"Ring the buzzer to apartment 14-B."

"Give me fifteen minutes," Terry said.

"Okay," Flaco said before hanging up.

Terry shook his head and let out a deep sigh. "I'm trying to buy a fuckin' ki and this cock sucka wants me to meet him inside of some apartment building." He complained while heading toward his destination. "He acts like I'ma spend a hundred dollars or something."

"I ain't feelin' that shit either, sun," Jihad admitted after a brief contemplation.

"It's too late to fall back, though. We're here now. We just gotta play it smart. I'ma leave the money in the truck. If I ain't out of the building within five minutes, come in blasting ... no hesitation. Flaco told me to ring the buzzer to apartment 14-B, but it could be a set up. I'm sure they have to buzz me in, so I'm gon' leave something wedged in the door for you."

"I got you, bruh," Jihad assured his partner.

Terry pulled his SUV over in front of the building. With his foot on the brake pedal, he shifted the gear into neutral and activated the hazard lights. By doing this simultaneously, the front console rose revealing two black .50 caliber Desert Eagle handguns. Terry removed one gun and Jihad took the other. Terry grabbed an extra clip and slid it into the back pocket of his Robin jeans. Stuffing the gun into his waistband, he made sure that his Polo pullover concealed it. He, then, tucked his platinum chain with the princess cut diamond laced "T" medallion inside his pullover.

"Five minutes," Terry said to Jihad, looking at his Breitling watch.

"Not four minutes and thirty seconds, not five minutes and fifteen seconds...five minutes."

Jihad looked at the time on his watch, which was a gold version of Terry's.

Terry left the Navigator and walked up to the entrance of the building. To the left of the door was approximately fifteen doorbells. He searched for 14-B and found it. He rang the door-bell.

"Who is it?" the accented voice asked through the intercom.

"It's T-Lova." A few seconds later the door buzzed open. Terry stepped in. Before it closed behind him, he wedged a lighter between the door and it's post to prevent it from closing shut.

On the second floor, near the end of the hall, he located the apartment. After delivering a light rap on the door, Flaco opened it displaying a wide smile. He had his arms out-stretched prepared for a hug. With a smile just as wide, Terry simply extended his hand for Flaco to shake. If he would have conceded to the hug, Flaco could have possibly felt the gun rest-ing on his waist. He accepted Terry's handshake.

"*Entra.*" Come in.

Terry walked inside, scanning the interior layout. Except for sparse furnishings the apartment was desolate. The living room contained a well-worn couch, two old chairs, and a cheap kitchen table. There was no feeling of warmth to the place at all.

Flaco closed the door and locked it. He was a small man standing at about five-feet-seven and weighing no more than one hundred and fifty-five pounds. He was clean shaven and no more than thirty years old.

After the door had been closed and secured, an older Do-minican man with graying hair and rough, stern facial features walked into the room.

Terry eyed the man carefully. "Wassup?" He received no re-sponse.

"You didn't bring the money?" Flaco asked with concern.

"No disrespect, Flaco, but we're dealing with a lot of hard earned money. I need to make sure everything's okay."

"No problema. I understand," Flaco turned to the older man. "Pablo, bucalo la ya-yo." (go get the cocaine). The man left and quickly returned with the drugs. He gave the kilo to Flaco. Flaco handed it to Terry. "Here you go. One kilo of cocaine. The exact same coke I gave you before. Now, everything okay?" Flaco spoke in a calm accented voice.

Terry visually inspected the kilogram. It was in a paper wrapping, then double coated in Saran Wrap. "Yeah," Terry said as he placed the cocaine back into Flaco's hands. "I'll be back in two minutes with the money."

Terry left the building and returned to the truck. Jihad pressed the unlock button allowing him to enter.

"Four minutes and seven seconds." Jihad noted, letting Terry know that he was on point. "What's good?"

"They got the work. I'm gonna cop it." Terry pulled himself into the driver's seat and closed the door. "Hand me the box."

He reached behind him to the second row and grabbed the bag containing the shoe box of money. "Here." He gave the bag to Terry. "Just because you saw the blow don't mean they won't try nothing funny, so stay on point."

"No question. The same rules apply. If I ain't back in five minutes, come in with that ratchet in your hand ready to squeeze."

"Fact."

Terry left the SUV with the bag in his hand. Again, he rang the doorbell. This time, no one spoke through the intercom. The door simply buzzed open. He walked in and jammed the door behind him the same way he did the first time. He made his way back to the apartment and knocked on the door. Flaco opened it and Terry stepped in.

"Good, my friend," Flaco said, with his signature smile that was beginning to irritate Terry. "You bring the money?"

"Yeah, I got the money." He removed the box from the plastic bag and held it in his hands.

Flaco opened the box, revealing twenty-six one thousand dollar stacks of money.

"This is not fake, no?" He looked at Terry suspiciously.

Terry laughed at the man's audacity. "I don't play those games. My chain is worth two ki's." He straightened Flaco out. "My money or jewelry ain't fake."

Flaco's smile subsided and seriousness was etched into his face. He mumbled something to his partner. Terry couldn't recognize the words, but his keen eyes quickly picked up on the older man's reaction to whatever Flaco said. The elder man reached under his button down shirt into the waist of his pants. With his hand on the handle, he began to remove his revolver. Terry, who was younger and faster, rapidly pulled out his hulking triangle barreled .50 caliber and squeezed the trigger two times. The thumb sized bullets smashed through the man's chest sending blood and fragments of his rib cage spewing out of the grapefruit sized hole in his back.

"P-p-please poop—" Flaco's words were cut off by the roaring sound of the gun burst. Everything above his top lip was blown off his body into multiple bloody chunks that splattered across the living room.

Terry rapidly picked up the cocaine and money. Covering his hand with his pullover, to conceal his fingerprints, he opened the door and left the apartment. He then fled down the hallway. He hurried to the Navigator and Jihad opened the door.

"Did everything go all right? " Jihad asked.

Terry started up the SUV and slowly pulled off. "I guess you can say it went better for me than it did for them."

"Watchu mean?"

15

"It was three of us in that apartment, now I'm the only one who's still breathin'."

"I told you, you need to work on your anger management skills. I think you need a hug."

"Shut up."

━━━━━━━━━━

When they made it back to Syracuse, they called Twan to come test the cocaine. Twan was a universal soldier. He was six-feet-one, three hundred plus pounds, and agile for his size. He did it all, from robberies to hustle. He was also very good at cooking powder cocaine into crack. He was so good, he earned the nickname, The Chef. There was only one problem. Twan had narcolepsy: a condition characterized by brief attacks of deep sleep.

He was prone to fall asleep at any given time.

After Twan scrutinized the product, he concluded that it was heavily re-rocked, meaning it contained a lot of impurities. The Dominicans took approximately ten ounces of cocaine and added different ingredients to make it appear to be thirty-six ounces of cocaine.

When Terry revealed to the men that his jewelry was valuable the Dominicans decided to rob him of it. They would have been successful in cheating him out of his money, but their greed cost them their lives…

CHAPTER 2

Jihad cruised down South Salina Street in his champagne tan BMW 645 CSI coupe. The twenty-two inch chrome rims with six inch lips gave the gaudy Beemer a more aggressive stance. Terry sat comfortably reclined in the passenger seat. They took solace in the fact that although they could see out, no one could see inside due to the dark tinted windows.

"This drought is kind of fucking us up, T," Jihad mentioned, referring to the shortage of cocaine in the city.

"Yeah, I didn't think it was going to last this long. It's been over three weeks."

"I was reading the *USA Today* and they said the feds busted a vessel containing over two and a half tons of coke two days ago. That's the second major bust this month."

"We're definitely feeling the effects of it. The entire East

Coast is hurtin'. We're losing a lot of fuckin' money," Terry realized.

"I've been doing the math, and it ain't a pretty sight. We have to get our hands on something else in order to make up for the money we're losing."

"What you got in mind?"

"I was thinking about getting a ki of Boy."

"Heroin?" Terry questioned.

"Yeah, I know this Puerto Rican cat that..."

Terry stopped him before he could finish. "I ain't never fuck with heroin before and I don't wanna start."

"It ain't nothin' to it," Jihad stated matter-of-factly.

"I used to sell heroin back in the day. As long as you got good dope you gon' make good money. The fiends need that shit. They gotta..."

"I said I don't want to fuck with it," Terry shouted, interrupting Jihad.

"Nigga, you yell at me again, I'ma kick yo ass out of my car. Matter of fact..." Jihad slammed on the brakes, bringing the coupe to a screeching halt in the middle of the street. "Get the fuck out!" The cars behind him were forced to come to a stop. They began to honk their horns in frustration.

Terry remained calm despite Jihad's antics. "Nigga, if you don't drive this piece of shit I'ma whoop yo big ass."

Jihad took his foot off the brake pedal and eased on the accelerator. "Ah, I scared the shit outta you, punk!" He laughed. "You thought I was gonna make you get out."

"Yeah, okay." Terry turned the music up and sat back in the comfortable leather seat. His mind reflected back to when he was ten years old.

Terry had just come home from school. He removed the shoestring from around his neck, which held his house key, and opened the door to his home.

He walked into the house, tossing his book bag onto the couch. On his way to the kitchen to get something to drink, he heard the sound of his mother crying.

"You stupid, good for nothing bitch!" Terry senior scoffed at his wife and son's mother, Anita. She was sitting on the edge of the bed when he hit her with a back-hand across her face that sent her sprawling to the floor. He stood over her in dominance with his hands balled into tight fists. "Didn't I tell you to bring me two bags when you got off work?"

"I only made eighteen dollars today, Terry. I barely had enough to get you one bag. It was a slow day at the restaurant," Anita managed to explain between sobs.

Her words fell on deaf ears as he straddled on top of her and began to choke her. "I don't give a fuck what you made, bitch. You better do whatever you have to do to make me happy!" He tightened his grip around her neck, cutting off her air supply.

Anita desperately scratched and kicked in an attempt to get him off of her. "Not in front of little Terry." Anita pushed the words through his vice like grasp.

With his hands still tightly wrapped around Anita's neck, Terry looked behind him. His son stood at the doorway with tears streaming down his cheeks. "He needs to see this so he'll know how to treat a worthless bitch."

"Get your hands off my momma!" Little Terry flew towards his father, throwing a wild haymaker, hitting him in the back of

19

the head.

"Oh, you think you're a man now?" Terry senior rose off Anita and faced his son. "The next time you raise your hands to hit me, you better know how to fight."

"Terry, no!" Anita cried from the floor. "Please don't hit my baby." Her plea came too late.

Terry had reared back and slapped his child with full force across the face. Little Terry stumbled as his bottom lip split open, but he refused to fall down. He was only ten, but he knew better than to fight a battle that he couldn't win. Instead of going with his heart and attacking his father, he went over to his mother and cradled her in his small chest.

"Leave us alone!" Little Terry shouted.

"Look at this shit," Terry said, glaring down at his wife and son. "I got two bitches." He shook his head and walked over to the dresser, grabbing his bag that contained the material he used to prepare his fix, then walked out of the bedroom and into the bathroom.

Five minutes later, Terry senior called out to his son. "Little T, come here!"

Little Terry tried desperately to block the one voice that left a pang in his heart every time he heard it.

"Little T, bring yo ass in here before I have to get up and come get you!"

"Baby, just go see what he wants. He's probably going to apologize." Reluctantly, Little Terry left his mother's side and walked into the bathroom. His father was seated on the clothes hamper. He had on the white tank top and brown slacks that he had wore the previous day.

"Do you want to be like me when you grow up?"

Little Terry shook his head in response.

"I don't speak fuckin' sign language, boy. You got a mouth, use it!"

"No."

"No, what?"

"No, I don't want to be like you," Little Terry said without concealing the anger in his voice.

"Good. I'm gonna show you what makes me the way I am. If you turn your eyes away from me for one second, I'm gon' beat shit down your leg. You hear me, boy?"

Little Terry's first reaction was to nod his head, but he remembered what his father had just told him about using his mouth. "Yes."

Terry removed the belt from his pants and wrapped it tightly around his left bicep. He then picked up the syringe that lay on the sink and held it in the air. "Do you see this? This is what makes me who I am. This is my true wife. Ever since we first met, I fell in love with her. She's a jealous woman. She makes sure that I love nothing or no one more than I love her." He looked at his son whose eyes were transfixed on the needle. "Do you know what her name is, boy?"

"No."

"Her name is Heroin. Now if you want to be like me, then, you fall in love with her. This is how you do it." He stuck the tip of the needle into the vein that protruded down the length of his forearm and injected the liquid into his blood stream.

Little Terry stared at his father with growing hatred towards him and the drug that turned the man that he once loved and admired into the cold, heartless being that stood before him.

Instantly feeling the intense high from the heroin that traveled through his body, he slowly pulled the needle out of his arm. A trickle of blood seeped out of the tiny hole and slithered down his forearm. He then loosened the belt from around his bicep and slouched against the wall. "Now get the fuck out of here," Terry ordered. His eyes stared off into oblivion.

———————————

"Damn, T. Did you hear what I said?" Jihad asked, snapping Terry out of his reverie.

"Yeah, I heard you." He lied.

"What did I say then?"

"You was saying something about how you was tired of paying for pussy and how you can't wait to find a chick that'll give you some pussy for free." Terry joked.

"Oh, I know you ain't talking. You so black, when you put on baby oil, it looks like you used Kiwi shoe polish!"

"Nigga, you so black, you gotta wear white gloves when you eat Tootsie Rolls so you don't bite your fingers off." Terry shot back.

"You so stupid, you thought Cheerios was donut seeds!"

"Fuck you!" Terry playfully jabbed Jihad in the arm. "Ride by the restaurant, let's get something to eat."

Terry owned a soul food restaurant with the help of his mother named, Inspirations. The establishment was well known for its delicious food and relaxing atmosphere. Three nights a week, Anita hired local poets to recite their poetry live, and two nights a week she invited jazz musicians to perform for the patrons while they ate and drank.

Jihad pulled over in front of Inspirations entrance. It was noon. The restaurant did not open until 3:00 p.m. but Terry knew that his mother, along with the rest of the staff, were inside preparing for the day.

Terry stepped out of the BMW handsomely dressed in a coffee hued cable knit cashmere sweater. The solid color was the perfect background for his thirty two inch total diamond necklace and matching diamond laced cross. His black Seven jeans and black alligator and leather trimmed Mauri sneakers rounded everything out.

Jihad was dressed in an exclusive green Retroactive hoodie, blue Japanese hard denim Retroactive jeans and a unique pair of grey and green Retro V Air Jordan's.

Terry reached into his pocket and removed a set of keys. After finding the appropriate one, he unlocked the door and entered his establishment.

Is it a Crime by Sade, flowed through the air as Terry took a sweeping look around.

"Hey, baby. What's up?" Anita came walking from the back where the kitchen was located. She was forty-nine years old with a vibrant look and demeanor.

"What's good, ma?"

"What's good?" Anita asked. "Everything we cook is good. What you talkin' about?"

Terry giggled at his mother's reply. "You know what I mean. How you doin'?"

"Oh, I guess I'm alright. Some asshole came and stole three garbage bags of bottles from out back. I hate that shit. You know old man Leroy comes by once a week to pick up them bottles. I'ma get me a BB gun and as soon as I catch somebody takin' them bottles, I'm gonna shoot 'em right in their ass! You watch 'n see."

"Ma, you trippin'."

"No, I ain't either. You think I'm jokin'!" Anita looked to her right and saw Jihad giggling. "What you standin' over there all quiet for, big boy? You can't speak?" She placed her hands on her hips waiting for a response.

"Everything's okay. How you doin', Ma?" Jihad asked, revealing his pearly whites.

"That's more like it. I'm fine, baby." She turned her attention back to her son. "Did you do the accounting and balances?"

"Yes, Ma. I came in last night and took care of it. I also placed orders, restocking everything we're low on. All I need you to do is sign the paychecks. Everyone's completed work hours and hourly wages are on the computer."

"You talkin' to me like I just learned how to do this." Anita smacked her lips. "You boys hungry?"

"Yeah, but I'm gon' call a few more people over so we can talk."

"Well, you need to hurry up. Ya'll gotta be finished before two-thirty, 'cause you know we open up at three o'clock." Anita turned around and headed toward the kitchen. "Call me when you're ready to eat!" she yelled over her shoulder.

Terry pulled out his phone and sent texts to Haitian, Boogs and Twan. He instructed them to come to the restaurant right away, so they could eat and talk.

Haitian was the first to arrive. He was thirty-two years old and from Brooklyn. His facial features were remarkably similar to the reggae artist Shabba Ranks. He used to constantly travel back and forth from Brooklyn to Syracuse to hustle. However, in time, he became so comfortable that he ended up making Syracuse his permanent residence.

Twan came to the restaurant second.

Boogs hadn't made it in yet. Boogs was originally from Philadelphia. His true nickname was Boogie Man, but over time it was shortened and he stuck with it. At twenty-three years old, Boogs was by far the youngest of the bunch. However, his youth had never been a factor, because he was street smart beyond his age.

Everyone who was inside the restaurant heard and felt the vibration and rumble of heavy bass from outside. They instantly knew the source. Boogs pulled up behind Jihad's coupe. He jumped out of his custom candy apple red BMW X5 M. The SUV was fully loaded with red and black suede interior, two fifteen inch JL Audio sub woofers, and gigantic twenty six inch Lexani rims.

He walked into the restaurant hyper as usual with his large white gold chain and diamond studded cross swaying back and forth. His platinum and diamond Cartier glasses commanded attention. Boogs' skin was the color of creamed coffee. His charming round eyes, baby face and low cut Caesar contributed to his beguiling appearance. "What's up, cannon?" He greeted everyone with enthusiastic handshakes, his Philadelphia accent prominent.

"What the fuck I told you about blastin' that music so loud in front of the restaurant?" Terry scolded.

"Damn, my fault. I had that new Meek Mill in there. That bawh is the truth!" Boogs knew that Terry could never stay mad at him for long. He was the little brother that Terry never had. "Guess what, T?"

"What?" A hint of frustration still lingered in his voice.

"I was chillin' in front of Club Roar last night. When it ended, this bad ass shorty came out. As soon as she saw all that candy and chrome she wanted to fuck...the broad was thirty-five!" Boogs professed proudly. "And I popped a Viagra. I beat that pussy like it owed me money!"

"Yo, you a nut, li'l nigga," Twan said.

"Aaight ya'll. We got some important business to discuss, so let's get down to it," Terry announced, bringing seriousness to the conversation. He called one of the waitresses over to the table. After taking everyone's order, she left.

"Okay, ya'll, we have a slight problem on our hands." The men at the table discontinued their small talk and gave their attention to Terry. "As I'm sure ya'll know, the coke prices are getting higher and the quality is getting worse." The group mumbled in agreement. "It's getting increasingly difficult to keep a steady supply."

"Yeah," Twan said. "The shit you've been giving me to cook up can't take a hit, and still be good enough to put out on the streets. They're cutting it up heavy before they sell it to you."

"Well, one thing we gotta do is cut back on the size of our bags," Boogs suggested. "How can we keep big bags when we paying so much?"

"You're right," Terry acknowledged.

Jihad chimed in. "And we're gonna have to weigh the eight balls up at three-point-two grams instead of three-point-five."

"Yeah, every little bit counts. But this is only going to be in effect while the drought is here," Terry informed his men. "As soon as we find the connect we need, everything goes back to normal."

"I think I might be able to help you with a connect," Haitian said.

"Oh yeah? How's that?" Terry asked.

"My man, Powerful."

"What about him?" Jihad questioned.

"His brother, Justice, got locked up and now he's running shit. They say that nigga got more birds than a pet store."

"Listen, I already had one bad run in. I don't have time to waste, or money to lose based on some he say/she say shit," Terry explained.

26

"I used to buy weight from Powerful before I moved here. He been gettin' money, and his brother had Bedstuy on lock for years. It ain't like these some new niggas that just came around."

"Alright, well, I need you to check it out."

"You ain't said nothin'. I'll get on that expressway tomorrow morning."

"Okay, this is what we gon' do. Haitian, I want you to get in touch with your man, Powerful. I'm gon' give you the money for a bird. If you come back with the work, and it's good, then, we'll fuck with him. Do you really think you can get down there tomorrow?"

"No question," Haitian responded.

"Alright. Let's see if everything pans out. But for now, we're just going to do a little cutting back on the size of our bags and shave off a little on the weight we're selling."

"And I got to get on them niggaz about taking so many shorts. From now on, they can't accept nothing less than nine dollars," Boogs said.

"Yo, Twan, I need you to…" Terry cut his words short when he looked over to Twan and saw that his head was tilted back, his mouth gaped. This was not uncommon due to his narcolepsy. Boogs looked at Twan and released a devilish grin.

"Boogie Man, don't do it," Terry warned, realizing that he was up to something.

Ignoring Terry, Boogs grabbed the salt shaker, removed the top, and poured over half of the salt into the glass of water that was in front of Twan. He then took a bottle of tobasco sauce, twisted the top off, crept up the side of Twan, and poured a generous amount of the fiery liquid into his open mouth.

Still asleep, Twan closed his mouth and began smacking his

lips. The sudden burning sensation brought Twan out of his siesta. Beads of perspiration quickly formed on his forehead as the heat forced him awake. He jumped out of his chair and onto his feet.

"Oh, shit!" He reached for the water in front of him and took two huge gulps. Suddenly his eyes grew even wider as he spit the salty water out of his mouth, causing it to land all over him and the floor.

The entire table burst out in uncontrollable laughter. Twan's angry eyes scanned the table. He instantly knew who the culprit was.

"Boogs, I'ma whoop yo ass!"

"What did I do?" Boogs said, attempting to sound as innocent as possible.

Twan was not going for it. He headed towards Boogs like a bull out of the cage.

Boogs jumped up from his chair as if it was on fire. "T, text me when you're ready for me!" Boogs yelled as he quickly darted past Twan and out of the entrance door, narrowly escaping a severe ass whooping.

———————

The following day Terry met up with Haitian. Just as he promised, a meeting had been arranged with Powerful to purchase a kilo of cocaine. Terry gave him a small duffel bag containing twenty six thousand dollars. He also gave Haitian the keys to the Navigator and instructions on how to use the stash box. Haitian got inside the SUV and headed towards Brooklyn,

New York.

"Uuugh…yeah… It feels good, don't it?" Powerful grunted as his shoulder length dreadlocks danced wildly, and he pumped ferociously in and out of the slim, Latin woman in the doggy-style position.

"Mmm…Hmmm…" she mumbled, unable to say anything else because her face was buried in another woman's pussy.

"Don't be stingy, Marisol," the curvaceous white girl said. "Let me get some of that big, black meat."

Without saying a word, Powerful slid himself out of Marisol and easily moved her face away from the white girl's pussy. Spreading her legs wide apart, he plunged himself deep into her unbelievably tight and moist entrance.

"Oh, God!" she screamed from the sudden burst of pain. After adjusting, her screams turned into moans of pleasure as she worked her pelvis, meeting him thrust for thrust.

Marisol was growing tired of rubbing her own clitoris. She straddled her leg over Amy's face. Her pussy was instantly greeted by a skilled tongue.

Ding-Dong! Powerful heard the sound of his doorbell ring, but there was no way he could pull out. He didn't even allow it to break his rhythm. After ten minutes and five more rings of the doorbell, he felt his orgasm building up.

"Oh, shit…I'm 'bout to cum!" As if on cue, Marisol and Amy quickly turned around to greet his rod. Each one took turns licking and sucking. With a mellow moan, Powerful released on the eagerly awaiting faces and breasts of both women. "Damn," he said with a hint of frustration. "Let me see who in the fuck's at my door."

"Wait a minute." Amy reached out and grabbed his shaft in her hand. "I don't want you to spill anything." Using her mouth, she engulfed his dick issuing long, even sucks to remove the remnants of semen from his penis.

"Damn, baby. You're the best. Ya'll go take a shower." Powerful slid on a pair of jeans and removed a .45 semi-automatic from his nightstand. The chime from the doorbell rang again. "Shit," he mumbled. He stood to the side of the door out of precaution, with his weapon in hand. "Who is it?"

"It's Haitian."

Powerful opened the door. "Come in." Perspiration lingered on his face and chiseled chest.

"Damn, nigga. What was you doin', working out or something?"

"Nah, I was in some pussy until I was rudely interrupted. You're early."

"I'm only an hour early, and I know this money is more important than some pussy."

"Is that the dough?" Powerful asked, gesturing towards the bag that Haitian carried.

"Yeah."

"Hold on a minute." He tucked his gun into the waist of his pants and walked away to the coffee table where a few cell phones lay. After sending a text he waited a moment, then received a response. He then placed the phone down and walked back over to Haitian. "You got twenty-five G's in there?"

"It's all there, counted and wrapped." Haitian reached into the bag and pulled out a few stacks for Powerful to see. He had told Terry that the price was twenty-six thousand. The extra thousand dollars was pocketed. *What the hell*, he thought, *I'm the one doing the transporting and risking my ass for him. I should be charging him more.*

Powerful took the bag. They sat down at the kitchen table while he removed the money and casually thumbed through it. "Who you coppin' this brick for?"

"I'm coppin' for myself, nigga. That's all my paper." He lied.

Powerful chuckled. Doubt was visibly etched on his face. "Nigga, please. You couldn't save up two thousand dollars, now all of a sudden you got ki money? Get the fuck outta here!" He couldn't contain his laughter.

Just then, Amy walked into the kitchen. Her long brown hair accented with blonde streaks was pulled up into a bun. She was wearing nothing but a navy blue bra and matching lace cheekies. "Excuse me." She said it more towards Powerful. She walked past them and removed a set of glasses from the cabinet, opened the refrigerator, and bent over to peer inside for a moment in contemplation of what she wanted to drink.

Haitian could not take his eyes off the beautiful, young, white girl with the slim waist, plump, round butt and thick thighs. He had never seen a white woman with such a shapely figure in person. Powerful noticed Haitian lusting after Amy, but paid it little attention. To him, it was like Haitian was staring at a car he could never afford.

"Yeah, P," Haitian began in a cocky voice just loud enough to be heard by Amy as she poured orange juice into the two glasses. "That twenty-five G's ain't shit. If I like what you got, I'm comin' to get seven more next week."

Powerful stared at him incredulously. "I hear that, big boy." He responded with a hint of sarcasm. Haitian didn't notice it. He was too busy watching Amy's ass sashay from left to right

31

as she sauntered out of the kitchen, heading towards the bed-room.

"Damn, P. She's shaped like Coco. You can't just find nothing like that strolling around. She had to come special ordered!"

Ding-Dong! The doorbell rang. Without saying anything, Powerful got up and left the kitchen. When he opened the door there was no one there, only a backpack. He scooped it up, locked the door, and returned to the kitchen table. Without inspecting its contents, he simply handed the backpack to Haitian. He unzipped it and marveled over the kilo of cocaine. This was the first time he had one in his hands.

"You sure this is straight?" he asked, less out of concern, and more because he simply didn't know what else to say.

The question caused Powerful's anger to instantaneously surface. "Mutha fucka, are you insulting my character?"

"No, man, I was just..."

"Nigga, you just disrespected me in my own goddamned house?"

"Come on, P. It ain't like that," he pleaded.

"Get the fuck out!"

"Man, I..."

Powerful removed the .45 from his waist and laid it on the table. His hand was still tightly wrapped around the handle. The barrel was facing Haitian.

"Do I have to repeat myself?"

"Nah." Haitian eased out of the chair, clutching the backpack and headed toward the door.

Powerful followed. "When you come back, bring some fucking respect with you!"

Haitian narrowly made it out before the door was slammed

behind him. Powerful walked to the living room window over-looking the street just in time to see Haitian scurrying to a Lincoln Navigator, and after a moment, pull off. "Lying ass nigga." He was going to find out who Haitian was buying for later. But for now, he had some unfinished business to attend to in his bedroom.

───────────

When Haitian was within fifteen minutes of reaching Syracuse, he sent Jihad a text message letting him know that he was on his way to the house. Terry, Twan and Jihad were driving together when he received the message. He then drove directly to the spot.

A few minutes later, the Navigator pulled into the driveway. Haitian hopped out carrying the backpack over his shoulder. He trotted to the back door and began pounding. Twan jerked the door open, completely blocking the entrance with his massive frame. "Nigga, what the fuck is wrong with you, banging on the door like you're crazy?"

"I just made it back, T," he stated proudly. "I got the work right here!" He held the bag up as if it was a grand prize.

"Gimme that shit." Twan snatched the bag out of his grasp while giving him a cold stare that crushed his pride. He stepped to the side and Haitian darted inside hoping that Twan didn't use his ham sized hand to smack him in the back of the head as he passed.

Terry and Jihad were in the living room watching a Smack DVD when Haitian stormed in, stopping directly in front of the TV blocking their view.

"I told you I was gonna come through, T. I made it, baby! It wasn't nothin', kid. Everything went like clockwork. Once my nigga, Powerful, saw me, he rolled out the red carpet for ya boy. He was about to start poppin' bottles and…"

"Are you made of glass?" Jihad asked.

"Huh? No, why?"

"'Cause your simple ass just came and stopped in front of the TV like I can see through you. Move the fuck outta the way!"

Haitian briskly stepped to the right. He knew better than to take a chance by arousing Jihad's anger. Terry and Jihad got up and walked past him and into the kitchen. Haitian followed them like a lost puppy.

"Yeah, my man was gon' front us an extra bird, but I told him we don't need nobody to front us nothin'. We got paper."

Twan was already in the kitchen. He began to pull out the materials and ingredients to convert the powder into crack.

"What you think, Twan?" Terry asked, completely ignoring Haitian as he babbled on.

"I'm about to find out right now." Twan sliced open the plastic wrapped kilogram with a box cutter. He removed and weighed exactly ten grams of cocaine on a scale. He then took a bottle of clear ammonia and poured about eight ounces into a small bowl. He dropped the powder into the ammonia. The cocaine fizzed up as the impurities rose to the surface, and the pure powder rocked up into crack. Twan removed the crack rock from the bowl, ran it under water, and allowed it to dry. Once completely dried, he placed the crack rock on the scale. It weighed almost seven grams. He picked up the off white rock and studied it. "It ain't bad. It's over sixty-five percent pure. It's not no helluva good shit, but it will hold enough cut for us to stretch it a little. But it's better than the shit we was getting before."

"Probably better than anything else around here," Terry added.

"I'll probably turn it into a thousand and seventy grams of decent work," Twan said.

"I know you're gonna make magic." Terry had total confidence in Twan's ability. He, then, turned to Haitian. "I have to admit, I'm proud of you. Tomorrow, I'm going to give you a grand. In two days, I'm going to need you to go back up there to get four more. Do you think you can handle that?"

"No question!" Haitian beamed. He was already imagining pouring all that money onto Powerful's table. *He ain't gon' believe it when he see me with all that dough*, he thought to himself...

CHAPTER 3

Now that Terry was once again able to meet the demands of the streets, everything began to run smoother. Everyone within his circle had been replenished with drugs, and in turn, they were taking care of their tasks diligently. Terry was concerned that two of his drug houses had recently been raided by the Syracuse Narcotics Unit. His workers who sold drugs out of the houses had been arrested and charged with sales and possession of cocaine. He had arranged for their bails to be paid, as well as hired attorneys for them. He understood that for every potential to make a gain, there was also the potential to take a loss. Preparation and planning had to be made for both.

At 9 o'clock in the morning, Jihad placed a small bag containing one hundred and four thousand dollars into the secret compartment in the rear of the SUV. He handed the keys to Haitian who was making a mental note to remove four thousand dollars of the money for himself.

"That's the money for four bricks," Jihad said in a low voice while maintaining eye contact with Haitian.

"Make sure you keep your seat belt on, take the same exact route you've been taking, and don't do more than ten miles over the speed limit."

"I know, I know." *Why in the hell do this nigga keep tellin' me the same damn thing every time I make this fuckin' trip?* Haitian thought. He opened the driver's door and began to climb in when Jihad grabbed his arm, stopping him.

"And, don't smoke no fucking weed while you're driving."

"Come on, man. I know."

"Yeah, aaight." He smacked his lips, turned around and walked to his car. The Navigator's engine came to life and pulled off.

———————

Haitian made it to Powerful's apartment with the bag containing all of the money, minus the four thousand he pocketed for himself. He rang the doorbell.

Within a few seconds Powerful opened the door and waved his hand gesturing Haitian to enter.

"Back so soon, cowboy?"

"You already know."

"You said you were comin' for four, right?" He removed the cell phone from the pocket of his Polo sweatpants when Haitian stopped him.

"Well, P…that's what I wanted to holla at you about." He pushed the words out.

Powerful lowered the phone. "What's poppin?"

"I'm sayin'," Haitian nervously shifted from one foot to the other. "Even though other people have been trying to get me to buy from them, I still want to cop from you."

"Nigga, get to the point," Powerful spat impatiently. "What's good?"

"Aaight." He took a deep breath and allowed the words to fall out. "If you front me four bricks on top of the four I'm buying, I figured it would save me a lot of time driving back and forth. You know your money will be good." He stopped when he noticed that his request began to sound more like a plea. Taking a deep breath, he waited for a reply.

"First of all, I never know if my money's good until it's in my hands. Second, if you want me to give you something on consignment, you gon' stop frontin' like you coppin' for yourself and tell me what's really going on."

"Aaight, man. I'ma keep it stack with you. My man, T-Lova is running our crew. We put together a plan to expand our operation to Elmira and Buffalo. But the only way we can do it is if we got more coke. That's where you come in, feel me?"

"Tell me more about ya man, T-Lova."

"His real name is Terry and his right hand man's name is Jihad. He…I mean we, got crack houses spread throughout the 'Cuse…" Haitian spilled his guts about Terry. Of course, he added a couple of lies just to spice things up a little bit.

After hearing everything he had to say, Powerful thought about the request. He was paying twenty-thousand per kilo. By charging twenty-five, he made five thousand in profit off of every kilo he sold. Today alone, he would receive twenty thousand dollars in profit from his transaction with Haitian. "Aaight, this is what I can do. I can front you two ki's." He observed Haitian's eyes widen with excitement, and continued,

39

"but I'm gonna have to charge you twenty seven G's a piece."

"Damn, that's fifty four thousand," Haitian mumbled.

"You mutha fuckin' right that's fifty four thousand! And you got three weeks to come see me or I'm comin' to see you and your boys. Now do you want it, or not?"

"Yeah, I want 'em."

"No problem." Powerful grabbed his phone again and sent out a text. He then emptied the money from Haitian's bag onto the table and did his usual thumb through. "Hundred G's?"

"It's all there." Haitian answered.

Powerful never counted the money in front of a person once they confirmed the amount. He always felt that was disrespectful. Once he was alone, every bill was counted and inspected. The doorbell rang. Powerful got up from the table and walked over. A moment later, he returned with a backpack. He pulled out six kilos and placed them into the bag that once contained the money.

Although he felt as if his heart was going to jump out of his chest, he did his best to remain calm as Powerful handed the bag to him. Haitian grabbed the bag, stood, and Powerful walked him to the door.

"I got you, kid." He gave Powerful a reassuring look as he walked through the threshold and out into the hallway.

"Yo, Haitian!"

He turned around and saw Powerful standing in the doorway. "Wassup?"

"You ain't been gone long enough to forget how I get down, have you?"

Haitian's throat thickened. He fought to swallow before he could answer. "Nah, P, I ain't forget how you get down." He nearly tripped over his feet as he spoke while walking back-wards.

"No more than three weeks." Powerful warned with a chuckle, then closed the door.

I know it's my time to shine, Haitian thought as he cruised down the expressway listening to *Push It To The Limit* by Rick Ross. *I went right in there and talked that nigga into fronting me two bricks. These niggas gon' wish they gave me more respect when I blow past them. When I get myself up to ten bricks I can't wait to see how they jump off T-Lova's dick and hop right on mine's! Matter of fact, I'm gon' be the one supplying T-Lova!* He beamed at the thought.

Getting off at the exit, he followed the normal protocol by sending Jihad a text message, letting him know that he would be meeting him at the house in thirty minutes. He was really closer to twenty minutes away, but he had to make a detour to his apartment in order to drop off his two kilos.

Haitian pulled up in front of his apartment. His eyes darted around nervously. He knew that it was unlikely anyone was watching him, however, he was jittery none-the-less. He turned the SUV off, crawled over the second row of seats to the rear and removed his two kilos from the stash box. Stuffing them inside his jacket, he exited through the rear door and hurried to his apartment. With one hand securing the drugs close to him, he used his other to dig into his pants pocket and pull out his keys.

Boom!

The keys fell from Haitian's hand. He struggled to hold his urine. With eyes as big as marbles and filled with fright, he spun around. They rapidly narrowed to angry slits once he locked in on the culprit of the jarring noise. It was his neighbor's bad ass son, Tye-Tye. He was nine years old, but hood raised and terrible beyond his years.

"Tye-Tye, stop hitting my house with ya goddamn balls. If you break my window, I'ma kick you in ya stomach!"

"My bad, Smokey. I'm learnin' how to throw," the boy said with a devilish grin. "You'll throw it back to me?"

"Hell no! Come get your own dirty ass ball." He bent over to retrieve his keys. "And my name ain't Smokey!"

In disgust, Tye-Tye kicked at an imaginary rock on the ground. "Bitch ass nigga," he mumbled under his breath while walking towards Haitian's apartment to get his ball.

"What did you just say?"

"Huh? Oh. I said…That figures."

"No, you didn't. I'm tellin' yo mamma you cursed at me!"

"Snitches get stitches around here, Smokey!"

Frustrated with the little neighborhood menace, he just shook his head, unlocked his door, and went inside his apartment.

Once inside, he removed the coke. It seemed almost unreal. He went from buying two ounces to having seventy two ounces in one day. He paced around the apartment, desperately searching for a secure hiding place. He settled on burying them under a pile of dirty clothes in his closet.

His nerves were working overtime. He needed to calm them. Haitian sat down on his living room couch. With his mind running in ten different directions, he pulled out a bag of Kush, a Backwood cigar, and rolled the weed up. He lit it up and took a deep pull. The smoke did its job in relaxing him.

"Shit." Haitian reluctantly got up with the blunt still in his hand. He had less than ten minutes to return the Navigator to Terry and Jihad. Leaving his house, he cursed the rain that had just begun to descend from the sky.

Haitian guided the SUV through traffic while continuing to smoke. His mind constantly reverted back to the drugs he had hidden in his home. He now had a new mission: to drop Terry off his truck and coke, then get back to his place, so he could begin his process of breaking down, cooking, and packaging his product.

He had become so consumed in his thoughts of becoming the big dog in his city that he failed to observe the blue and white patrol car parked in an empty lot facing the oncoming traffic.

Noticing the dense cloud of smoke that lingered inside of the vehicle, along with the fact that the driver was not wearing a safety belt, the officer quickly pulled out of the lot and activated his flashing lights, easily catching up to the big SUV.

The brightness of the dancing lights coupled with the high pitched shrill of the siren, caught Haitian's attention. Seemingly out of instinct, he glanced in the rear view mirror while simultaneously reaching over his shoulder to fasten his safety belt. After realizing that the half smoked blunt was still dangling between his lips, he leaned forward to snuff it out in the ashtray, then slightly lowered all four windows in an attempt to remove the pungent odor. The sudden increase in his heart rate caused his forehead to glaze with sweat.

"Fuck!" Haitian cursed himself for not taking Jihad's advice against smoking while transporting the drugs. He never told Terry, but his driver's license was suspended for failure to pay child support.

There was no way he could pull over. He was five blocks away from the projects. If he could just get a one block lead, he would have a chance to jump out and disappear into the confines of the housing structure.

Without giving it a second thought, Haitian mashed his foot on the gas pedal. The officer's car accelerated as well, tightening the gap between the two. Haitian careened in, out and around traffic, wishing that he was in a Mustang.

Surprisingly, he began to increase the distance between him and the pursuing officer. He disregarded all traffic lights and warning signs.

The officer was forced to exercise a little more caution. With a quick glance in the rear view mirror, he saw that another officer had joined in on the chase. He had to get out of the truck before more cops arrived. It was all or nothing.

Keeping his foot firmly pressed on the gas pedal, Haitian barreled through a red light, challenging the heavy intersecting traffic. The oncoming cars blared their horns, skidded out of control, violently collided into other cars, and some came to screeching halts. Haitian made it through successfully, yet the pursuing police were having a difficult time making it through the massive pile up.

Haitian made a hard right onto West Onondoga Street. He could still hear the police sirens, but no longer saw the patrol cars behind him. A weary smile made its way onto his face.

Continuing to push the SUV to its limits, he raced down the side street. Knowing that the projects were less than a block away, he knew what he had to do. He eased off the gas pedal just enough to hit the final corner. As he began the turn, his eyes froze with trepidation.

He recognized a young lady with two kids, one child holding on to her hand and the other in a stroller, crossing the street. The impact occurred.

The enormous Navigator bulled the family over like a bowling ball crashing into pins. The lady and the child holding her hand, were thrown into the air as if they weighed nothing. The true magnitude of the collision became apparent when their fragile bodies slammed into the unforgiving concrete fifteen feet away. The baby stroller flew over the hood, past the windshield, ejecting the infant, whirling her through the air.

Haitian lost control of the vehicle, causing it to slam head on into a utility pole. The driver's airbag deployed, smashing into his face. Haitian saw a bright flash of light, then everything went dark.

"Yo, where the fuck is Haitian?" Terry asked Jihad. The mounting frustration was evident in his voice.

"I don't know, T. He texted me saying he'd be here within thirty minutes. That was an hour ago."

"Call his phone and see if that clown answers."

Jihad picked up his iPhone and dialed Haitian's number while casually strolling through the living room. After four rings his voice mail was activated. The phone remained next to Jihad's ear, but what appeared on TV had completely captured his attention. His mouth fell open and he barely blinked.

"T, come here, sun. Hurry up!" Jihad screamed, putting the phone away.

"Wassup?" Terry walked into the room and stopped in his tracks. His eyes were fixated on the TV showing news footage of a wrecked Navigator with orange cones and yellow crime scene tape stretching across the area of the incident. "Turn that shit up."

Jihad stepped forward and increased the volume. The reporter's voice came to life. "...the victims of this horrible accident haven't been named, as of yet. However, from what we've been able to gather, the woman was a twenty-seven year old mother of two. The mother and her infant daughter have been pronounced dead, and the seven-year old has been rushed to an area hospital where she is clinging on to dear life.

The driver of the SUV has been identified as twenty eight year old, Deshaun Obudalu. The suspect was involved in a brazen high speed chase which has resulted in this unthinkable tragedy. Please stay tuned as we will continue to update you on this breaking news. Reporting live, I'm Michael Whitby of Channel Thirteen News."

Terry paced back and forth in an effort to control his vexation.

Jihad snatched up a Dutch Master from the coffee table and began cracking it open. "Whatever's our next step, we have to make sure it counts. We don't know how bad this is really going to hurt us." He spoke without taking his eyes off the Dutch he was rolling.

"I know they found that work. The truck ain't gonna come back to us, but the police is going to be asking a lot of questions, and I'm not sure if Haitian's strong enough to hold back the answers. We're going to have to fall back until we find out what happens…"

CHAPTER 4

"I don't know who this bitch ass nigga think he's playin' with," Powerful growled after calling Haitian for what seemed like the hundredth time. It had been three weeks since he fronted Haitian two kilos of cocaine. He hadn't heard from Haitian since he left his house, a clear violation. The last thing he was going to allow was Haitian to run off with his drugs.

Powerful was a man of action. He'd been getting his hands dirty his entire life, so his next move was a no brainer. He placed a few phone calls and within a half hour two of his most trusted goons were at his house, prepared to do whatever he asked of them. Powerful informed them about his situation as well as his plans. He armed each man with a gun. Just as quickly as they came, they were leaving out, piling into the luxurious interior of Powerful's midnight-blue Mercedes GL 550.

The ride from Brooklyn to Syracuse took less than five

hours. Powerful knew that Haitian lived and hustled on the west side of the city. He drove around and asked people in the hood if they knew him. It didn't take long before he found out what Haitian had gotten himself into. Luckily, Terry didn't go down with him. He also found out that Terry had a restaurant on South Avenue. The trio didn't hesitate to make their way to his place of business.

Upon entering Impressions, they were greeted with a warm smile by Terry's mother. "Good afternoon, gentlemen. Would you like to dine in, or place an order to go?"

"Um, actually, I just came back in town and I was trying to get in touch with my old friend. His name is T-Lova," Powerful explained.

"Well, I'll tell you what. I'll get Terry on the phone for you under one condition."

"What's that?"

"That the three of you sit down and let me put some food in your stomachs. I can tell that ya'll ain't have no decent meal in a long time. You boys today think you can live off fast food, but you're wrong…come on over here." Without waiting for a reply she began walking towards the dining area.

Powerful and his men had little choice but to follow as she led them to a table. Once seated, they picked up menus.

"Now all of this food is freshly prepared, and it's good for you," Anita told them in her natural, motherly tone. "I'ma send a waitress over to take your order while I try to get Terry on the phone." Again, she scurried off before anyone at the table was able to respond.

The three looked at each other, shrugged their shoulders and began scanning their options. The waitress came with refreshments, they placed their orders, and within a relatively short amount of time they were served.

While they were enjoying their meals, Anita walked over holding her phone.

"I finally got a hold of Terry. I'm sorry, I couldn't tell him who you were because I didn't get your name."

Powerful wiped his mouth with a napkin and accepted the phone. "Thank you," was his only response. He then spoke into the phone, "Hello?"

"Wassup, who's this?" Terry asked.

"This is Powerful, from Brooklyn."

"Oh, what's good?" He answered calmly, but deep down he wanted to know why in the hell was this dude in his restaurant looking for him.

"Not a whole lot, my man. Listen, I need to holla at you."

"Aaight, I'll be there within fifteen minutes." Terry hung up and Powerful handed the phone back to Anita who was still standing there.

"How's the food?" She couldn't have cared less about their conversation.

"It's great."

"Much better than some damn *McDonalds*. You boys eat up, and you better leave a tip!"

"Alright." They all shared a light chuckle.

Terry made it to the restaurant before they finished their meals. He walked directly over to the table, making eye contact with all three of the men. "What's up?" he asked, unsure of which one was Powerful.

"Waddup, sun?" Powerful said, glaring at Terry. "We got a problem, my nigga." He shoved a fork full of greens into his mouth. "You see…"

"Slow down, champ." Terry stopped him from continuing. "This is my restaurant. Unless you got a problem with the food

49

or the service, we need to talk outside."

"Maybe you're right. There's no need to cause a scene in front of these good people." Powerful stood up and his men followed suit.

Terry led the way out of the restaurant. Anita stood at her usual spot behind the checkout counter. "How was the meal?"

"It was good," one of the men answered.

"Great. Now who's paying?" Anita asked.

Powerful reached into his pocket and pulled out a knot of crispy bills. He peeled off a hundred dollar bill and gave it to her. Without waiting for change, they left.

Outside, Terry and Powerful, walked to the parking lot with his henchmen a few feet behind.

"I know you drove a long way to come see me, so what's going on?" They stopped and faced each other.

"My problem is I haven't heard from you niggas since I fronted ya'll them two bricks."

"Wait a minute, playboy. You ain't front me nothin'. I don't need you to front me shit. I buy what I want and that's it." He looked Powerful directly in the eyes while correcting him.

"Yeah? All that sounds good, after the fact. The bottom line is ya'll bought four bricks and I fronted you two bricks. You niggas made me get on the highway for five hours. Either you gon' get me my fifty-four stacks or I'ma blow ya fuckin' face off!" Powerful roared. He slid his hand towards the left side of his waist where his 9 mm rested.

As soon as Powerful's goons stepped up and appeared to be reaching for their weapons, the door to a Nissan Maxima flew open. Twan stepped out, pointing a hulking AR-15 at Powerful and his men. A few cars closer was a Honda Accord. Jihad jumped out aiming his Mac-90 at the men. Across from them,

Boogs hopped out of his shiny red BMW X5 with a black .40 Glock in each hand held high and ready to fire. Twan, Jihad and Boogs slowly approached the men without taking their weapons off their targets. Terry removed his .45 keeping it by his side.

"Listen, gangsta," Terry began in a low, even voice. "I don't know if you thought it was sweet because we're from Upstate New York, or because we was sending that lame ass nigga Haitian to cop for us, but if you tryin' to go to war, then you picked the right niggas. Is that what you want?"

"Nah." That answer was his only viable option.

"I'll tell you what, despite me feeling very disrespected, I'm still gon' take the diplomatic route. Leaving you niggas dead in this parking lot would bring a lot of heat on me, and it definitely ain't gon' get you your money. I don't know if you know, but Haitian got knocked. He only had four ki's with him. That means there's two more ki's somewhere. I'm gonna get to the bottom of this shit, and if your work comes up I'll make sure you get it. You got my word."

Powerful nodded his head, agreeing to Terry's terms. "Aaight, I'ma take your word." He slowly began to step backwards with his hands in the air.

His men did the same.

"One more thing," Terry said. The men stopped moving. "Take out ya guns and put 'em on the ground, slowly. Don't trip, I know you got more where those came from." Terry smiled.

They unenthusiastically did as they were told, got back into the Galendenwagon and headed back to Brooklyn…

CHAPTER 5

Inside of the two tiered pod of the Onondaga County Jail, Haitian sat in a plastic chair watching *The Maury Show* alongside other inmates. It had been over three weeks since he had been arraigned on a long list of charges, including assault, two counts of manslaughter, resisting arrest and criminal possession of a controlled substance in the first degree.

The only time he was successful at pushing his situation to the back of his mind was when he watched TV. Once *Maury* went off, he went back to his cell, sat on his hard, uncomfortable and small bunk, and thought about his case.

Because of the seriousness of his charges, his attorney told him that he would be lucky if a plea for thirty years could be negotiated. Haitian began to think about what he would look like coming home at nearly sixty years old. There was no way he could spend that much time in prison.

He lay back on his bed contemplating his options. It didn't take long for him to realize that there were only two. Either he could plead guilty and hope against odds that the judge would show some leniency, or he could cooperate with law enforcement to have his time reduced. After more than an hour of rummaging through his thoughts, Haitian jumped up, searched his cell for a business card until he found it, then walked down the stairs where the phones were stationed. He picked up the phone and dialed the number as it appeared on the card.

"Hello?" the voice on the other end asked. The jail's automated system instantly chimed in informing the receiver that he had a collect call from jail, and in order for the call to be accepted he had to press the number 5. The button was pressed before Haitian spoke.

"Hello, this is Deshaun Obudalu. Can I speak with Lieutenant Shwarts?"

"You're speaking with him. What's up, Obudalu?"

"Listen, Lieutenant, I know I'm facing a lot of time. If you can work something out with the district attorney to get me a good deal, I'll help you guys get some dangerous people off the streets."

There was a deep sigh on the other end of the phone. "You have some very serious charges against you, young man. The assistance that you provide would have to be substantial, to say the least."

"I can promise you that it will be."

"Let me talk to your district attorney. Of course, I can't guarantee you anything. That will be totally up to her. If she agrees, I'll be down there to talk to you before the week is out."

"Alright, cool." Haitian hung up the phone, went back to the television area, and sat down just in time to catch the beginning of *Jerry Springer*…

CHAPTER 6

For nearly three days Terry had been holed up in his condominium in seclusion while he deliberated what his next move would be. The thought of retiring from the game crossed his mind, but after thoughtful consideration he pushed the notion aside. The sad reality was the more money he made, the more bills he accumulated. There were also a lot of people who depended on his financial support.

When the ball was handed to me, I took it and ran. My hustle is what provided a better way for my mother, Terry mused. *I've accomplished a lot, but I know it's not enough. I have so much more to achieve. I'm not giving up until I get all that I deserve. For every problem, there's a solution. I just have to figure out how I'm going to survive this drought.*

His cell phone rang, breaking his concentration. Terry hadn't been answering most calls or responding to any texts, but once he saw that it was his mother, he picked up.

"Hello?"

"Baby, is everything okay?" Anita asked, getting straight to the point.

"Yeah, Ma. Everything's fine. What's up?"

"Well, I haven't heard from you, and a few people stopped by the restaurant looking for you, too."

"I'm good. I'm just taking a little time away from everything so I can get my mind right."

"It's nothing wrong with that, son, but you gotta let the old lady know. You know it don't take much for me to start worrying about you."

"You're right, Ma. My bad." He chuckled.

"Alright, baby. Just make sure you check in with me every now and then."

"I got you, Ma. I love you."

"I love you, too…oh yeah, some boy called for you early this morning. I think his name is Jukwon, or something like that."

"Are you serious, Ma?" Terry shot up, electrified by the news. "Did he leave a number?"

"Yeah, I wrote it down somewhere. Hold on." He heard his mother rustle through some papers. "Okay, here it is."

He inserted the number into his phone as she recited it.

"Thanks, Ma. You're the best. I'll call you back later." His voice was filled with excitement.

As soon as he hung up with his mother, he dialed the number of his longtime friend.

"Hello?"

"Juk, is this you?" Terry questioned.

"Yeah, who's this?"

"This T-Lova. What the fuck is good, bruh?"

"Damn, what's up, my dude?"

"I can't believe it's really you. I...I thought you was dead."

"Come on, baby-boy. Life is too good to be dead. What's up with you?"

"Keeping it real, things haven't been going too good. I mean, my paper is still alright, but it's been dry as hell for the past couple of weeks and it's hurting me," Terry admitted, referring to the drug shortage.

"I heard about it. That's why I found you. Even though I'm out of the game, I figured I could give you a little help."

"Come on, Juk. You're making me smile right now. What's good?"

"You've always been my nigga, and we've always kept it one hundred with each other. There's a way I can help you. But I'm telling you now, once I open this door for you, you'll be walking into a grown man's game. It'll be nothing like the game you're in now."

"I understand what you're saying, Juk. I give you my word I can, and will, handle it," Terry promised.

"Alright. Say no more. Book a round trip ticket to Phoenix, Arizona, for tomorrow. You'll get further instructions once you get off the plane."

"Juk, I really appreciate what you're doing for me."

"I know, that's why I'm doing it. I'm going to book a flight down there, too. I'll see you when you land, kid."

The two hung up. Terry didn't quite know what to expect, but what he did know was that his life was about to take a drastic change. Although he was enlivened by the sudden change of events, he hoped that he was prepared for what the future held.

━━━━━━━━━━━━

During the flight, Terry was unable to sleep. His mind was too busy running through all of the possible scenarios. He finally relinquished his thoughts as anxiety began to surface.

The plane landed at Arizona's Sky Harbor Airport. He did his best to remain calm despite the butterflies that swirled in his stomach. People ambled through the airport either looking for family and friends or to get on a plane that would carry them to their destination. Terry looked around the huge airport, unsure of where to go.

A short, Mexican man, with black framed glasses, and a thick, bushy mustache walked up to Terry. "Are you Mr. Terry?"

"Yeah," he responded cautiously.

"*Buenos dias, mi amigo*. My name is Speedy. Come with me, please." He turned to leave, forcing Terry to follow.

Outside of the airport sat a brand new Cadillac CT6. Speedy opened the door, signaling for Terry to enter. Once inside, he closed the door and hurried over to the driver's side and slid in behind the wheel.

Terry pulled out his phone to call Jukwon and let him know he had arrived.

"I'm sorry, sir, but I can't allow you to make any phone calls until after the meeting, for safety reasons." Speedy did not turn around until Terry replaced the phone in his pocket. Once he relaxed into the back seat, Speedy pulled off.

Terry gazed out the window ingesting the beautiful Phoenix

scenery as he was being chauffeured to an unknown destination.

Finally, the Cadillac pulled into the parking lot of the Pointe Hilton Hotel. It was one of the most beautiful, extravagant hotels Terry had ever laid eyes on. The allure of the hotel helped to ease his worries. They exited the car, entered the spacious lobby, then boarded an elevator. He remained a step behind Speedy until he stopped in front of a door. Instead of knocking, he removed his phone and sent a quick text. Within seconds, the door opened.

A tan complexioned, middle aged, Mexican man, with salt and pepper hair, and mustache that appeared to be freshly cut stood in the doorway. He wore an expensive maroon silk button down shirt, tan slacks that were tailored to fit, and a pair of brown Bally loafers. "Come in, Terry." The man shook his hand firmly. There was no expression on his face. After the greeting, Terry walked in and Speedy left in silence. "My name is Alfredo Lajas."

"It's nice to meet you, Mr. Lajas," Terry replied as they slowly walked through the spacious, luxury suite.

"I'm sure you know who this young man is," Alfredo said, as they entered the living room.

Jukwon stood up from the couch.

Unable to contain his emotions, Terry ran over to his compadre, embracing him in a tight, lingering hug. They were all smiles.

"Damn, sun. You're big as hell now!" Terry said.

"Yeah, I'm working out. We ain't getting' no younger."

"How's your brother, Dymond?"

"He's good. Trying to buy all the prime real estate in the south. We'll have plenty of time to chop it up, but for now let's not waste Mr. Lajas' time, and get down to business."

Terry agreed. He and Jukwon sat down on the couch and Alfredo sat in a chair opposite them.

"Jukwon was introduced to me by a very good and trustworthy friend. Because of that, he receives a high level of trust from me," Alfredo said to Terry in a no-nonsense manner. "When he asked me to consider taking you on as a business partner, I'll admit that I was a bit skeptical. Let's not confuse skepticism with being suspicious. To alleviate any suspicion, I conduct an extensive background check on everyone I'm introduced to. My concern is if you will be able to handle all that comes with the amount of drugs I can provide you with."

"Mr. Lajas, I can't promise you that everything will go perfect," Terry began. "Because, as I'm sure you know, if something has the possibility of going wrong, then sooner or later it will end up going wrong. But, what I will promise you is that I will handle any situation that needs to be taken care of with diligence and without fear. I will conduct this just like, if not more stringent than, any legitimate Fortune 500 company. I'm honored that my friend recommended me to you. Not only do I have to prove myself to you, but I will be representing Jukwon, as well."

The room grew quiet. Alfredo eyed Terry's demeanor as he sat with his right leg crossed over his left.

"These are the rules," Alfredo broke the silence. "If you ever get arrested, you never tell on us, or anyone else. You deal strictly with the Zeta Cartel. No one else. You don't do anything that will bring heat on us. Finally, you pay the money you owe. Our job is to make sure the shipment makes it to you. After you receive it, the responsibility becomes yours. Do you understand these rules?"

"Yes, Mr. Lajas."

"Do I need to explain what will happen if any of these rules are violated?"

"There's no need. I understand."

"Fine. I will charge you fifteen thousand per kilo, with a minimum of ten kilos. Whatever amount you pay for up front, I will give to you on consignment. This price includes delivery. Here." He gave Terry a smart phone. "This is an untraceable phone. You are not to use this phone for any reason other than to place an order. Your code is: cyote 23."

Terry accepted the phone.

"When you make it home, purchase a microwave, place the money inside and reseal it. Call the number inserted in the phone. You will be given an address to send the microwave. Once the money is received, you will give us a safe address where no drug activity occurs and your shipment will be delivered within six days. This method will be temporary. We have distribution hubs, but things will have to be worked out to include your order and that will take a little time."

"Sounds good," Terry said.

They stood and shook hands.

With nothing left to be said, Jukwon and Terry left the hotel. They spent the remainder of the day enjoying Phoenix and catching up on lost time. The next day, they left for the airport, promised to remain in contact and boarded their separate planes...

CHAPTER 7

Once again, Terry and his men found themselves having a meeting discussing the possible options for their future. They sat in the living room smoking, drinking and talking.

"The good news is that our days of going through any more droughts are over. I got in touch with a longtime friend and he put me on with the illest connect in the world. The bad news is Syracuse is just too small for what I want to do."

"So, whatchu sayin'? You want to leave the 'Cuse?" Twan asked.

"We're always gon' keep our roots in the town, but real soon we'll be sittin' on twenty ki's of raw coke, and our supply is endless. If we try to move that much work here we won't last long. We're all known in these streets. Maybe we should start somewhere fresh."

"Somewhere like Rochester or Buffalo?" Jihad asked.

"Nah," Terry answered. "That's too close."

"What about D.C.? It's a lot of money out there," Twan suggested.

"Yeah, it's money out there, but them D.C. niggas is burned out. You might be cool with them one minute, and the next minute they're putting a bullet in your brain all because they're fucked up off that PCP," Terry explained.

"What about Philly?" Boogs suggested.

"Shit, them niggas is crazy, too," Terry answered dryly.

"Come on, T. You got crazy muthafuckas everywhere you go. You can't avoid that. The real question is can we make a lot of money out there. Now I don't know about other places, but I'm from Philly. It's definitely money out there. My cousin is doing his thing in South Philly. I talk to him all the time."

Terry paid attention to what Boogs was saying. He pondered over the option. "So, you think South Philly is a good place to relocate to?"

"Hell yeah! Do you know how big Philly is? It's like one-point-five million people that live there. Do you know what that means? That means it's a ton of fuckin' money there…money that we could be touchin'." Boogs rubbed his hands together greedily.

"Alright, I'll tell you what. Call your cousin and let him know that we're comin' out there for a little vacation. While we're out there, we'll see if it's a good fit for us."

"You ain't said nothin'. Matter of fact…" he pulled out his cell phone and sent a text to his cousin. Almost instantly he received a response. Boogs produced a bright smile. "He said come on down and he'll pull out the red carpet for us."

"Aaight, say no more. Everybody take care of your business. Just be packed up and ready to go by tomorrow morning. We're going to drive our own cars, so we'll meet up here at ten o'clock."

The next day Terry, Jihad, Twan and Boogs were on the freeway by noon. The drive wasn't a long one. Terry set his navigation system to direct him to the Merriott Hotel. Once they arrived, each man checked into his own room. After settling in, they met up in Twan's room.

"So, what are we gonna do?" Jihad asked.

"Shit, it's only one-thirty. I'm tryin' to see what's poppin' in the City of Brotherly Love," Terry said.

"You know I'm with that. I'm feigning to hit the streets. Let me call my cousin, Reek, and see what's up with him." He pulled out his phone and dialed Reek's number.

Reek picked up on the third ring. "Hello?"

"Wassup, cuz?"

"Who dis? Boogs?"

"You already know. What's good?"

"I'm coolin'. I just came out. Where you at?"

"I'm at the Merriott Hotel near the airport."

"Oh shit. You niggas was serious! Aaight, I'm in South Philly. I'ma be on Taylor Street. If you don't see me, look for my Jaguar. I got a silver XJ. What ya'll drivin'?"

"You'll know it's us when you see us. I'ma call you as soon as we hit the block." Boogs hung up and told everyone that they were going to meet his cousin on his block.

"I need ya'll to be mindful of some things," Terry began. "No matter the city, everybody that hustles have one thing in common: we're all very territorial. If it's niggas on the block, then they're trying to get that money. They ain't going to let a bunch of out of town cats come on their block and take the food out of their stomachs. Especially out here in Philly. They're known for pushin' niggas' wigs back without a second thought. That means when we pull up on that block, niggas is gon' be staring. And we might even get some ice grills thrown our way.

"We got bigger plans than to get into beef with some dudes on the block, so don't be muggin' back. Not only are we trying to get a feel for the city, but we're also campaigning. We need these dudes to see our faces and know that we're big boys. So keep the bigger picture in mind."

Satisfied that everybody was on the same page, it was time to go.

The cloudless powder-blue sky allowed the sun to heat Philadelphia to a comfortable sixty-three degrees. Just warm enough to urge people to put on something nice and go outside. Indeed, that was the case on Taylor Street. The dudes who were on the block hustling made sure their apparel was on point all the way down to the fresh out of the box sneakers. And there were plenty of women out there to admire the hustlers who were shining.

Reek leaned against the driver's door of his Jaguar, while a cute young lady was complaining to him, basically clamoring for his attention. Reek was twenty-four. He stood at five-eight, with a slender frame that was toned like a prize fighter. He had a tan complexion, with full lips and chinky eyes that sat behind platinum and ivory Cartier frames.

The woman was complaining about not getting enough of his time when his phone vibrated. "Hold on a minute, Stacy."

"Stacy?" she said with a shocked and disgusted look on her face. "Nigga, did you just call me Stacy?"

"I was just joking, girl...hold up." He answered his phone. "Hello?"

"Waddup, cuz?"

"Waddup, Boogs. Where you at?"

"We're haded down Taylor street now."

Reek looked down the street. There was a Dodge Charger being trailed by a Camry heading towards him. "Is that ya'll in the Charger?" All he could hear on the other end was laughter.

"A Charger? Nigga, don't you ever disrespect me like that," Boogs shot.

"Then you must be on the wrong block, because I don't…" Reek stopped mid sentence when he saw the candy- red painted X5 followed by the matte black CLS 63 AMG, BMW 645 CSI and Range Rover Supercharged. Each vehicle looked showroom new and was complimented with aftermarket rims. "Pull over behind my car," he said, then hung up.

"So, you're just going to ignore me like that, Reek?" the lady continued.

"Look, shorty, you're drawin' right now. My peoples is here from out of town. Call me tonight." Without waiting for a reply, he left her and walked towards the caravan of luxury vehicles.

Boogs hopped out of his SUV and gave his cousin a big hug. Boogs was dressed in a Polo knit sweater, True Religion jeans and wheat colored Nike ACG boots.

"I know this ain't your whip. You ain't doin' it big like that!" Reek was all smiles.

"Come on, cuz. I'll talk fly to you before I lie to you. It's all mine's." Boogs, then, waved to Terry, Twan and Jihad, signaling for them to get out. They all came over and he introduced them to Reek. Everyone greeted him with a pound.

Their conversations flowed smoothly and everyone felt comfortable around each other.

Although, Terry, was relaxed, he was observant nonetheless. Not only did he notice people slow down to admire the line-up of cars, but he also noticed a few dudes who were using the streets as their place of business, eyeing them suspiciously. It was obvious that they were out-of-towners who were getting money, but beyond that, nothing else could be extracted.

Terry appeared to be engulfed in small talk, but he was actually studying this kid, Reek. His fresh brown Pelle leather jacket, crisp white T-shirt, hard denim jeans and Gucci boots were all new. He always maintained eye contact when talking and never appeared to be nervous. Those were all good signs. Terry needed to find out if he was respected on his block. There was no way he could consider making their mark in this area if their foundation, which would be Reek, was weak.

Several times during their conversation, someone called over to Reek. He excused himself and they went inside of his car for a few moments, then he came back as if he never left. None of this escaped Terry's vision. The men that approached Reek did not appear to be addicts, and he knew that some type of transaction was going down.

"What you sellin', weed?" Terry asked casually.

"I got some Piff if you want to burn somethin', but I don't sell weed. I sell eight balls." His words were music to Terry's ears. If he had been making his living selling weight on the block, he had to have a decent level of respect from the other hustlers.

"Let me holla at you real quick, Reek," Terry said.

They stepped away and began to walk towards the Jaguar. Boogs smiled. He already knew what the conversation was going to be about.

"Wassup, T-Lova?"

"I wanna ask you a couple of questions, if you don't mind."

66

"Nah, it's cool."

"How many grams are you coppin'?"

At first, Reek was hesitant, but with one look into Terry's eyes he knew that the question came from a man of business. "I'm buying eighths a hundred and twenty five grams."

"Who's the big boys in this area?"

"Shit, it's a few niggas gettin' money, but the bawh, Mack, and them SP cats is doing their thing. They're the brick layers," Reek informed Terry.

"Yeah? So, what's up with them niggas? Are they thorough like that?"

"I'ma keep it real, the bawh, Mack, is a nut, and he got some certified cannons on his team. If somebody tries to take it there, they better be ready for war."

"I take it that the streets is loyal to this kid, Mack, huh?"

"I ain't gon' say all that. The streets is loyal to whoever has the power. There's niggas that don't like him, but they still respect his gangsta. Plus, he keeps that work, so niggas ain't got much of a choice other than to see him. Shit, I cop from him."

"How much you payin' for an eighth?"

"Coke is scarce right now, so I'm payin' forty-two hundred."

"How's the quality?"

"It aint' the best, but it's enough to keep niggas comin' back."

"I got one last question for you. Is your loyalty with Mack and his SP crew?"

Reek brooded over the question for a moment, then gave Terry his answer. "My loyalty is given to those who want the best for me, and those who are loyal to me. I'm not a grimy nigga, so I'm not against SP or anything like that, but I understand that the relationship we have is strictly business."

"I'ma keep it real with you. I'm thinking about coming down here to Philly and making a few moves. Boogs speaks highly of you. We can easily take your game to a higher level, but I need to know two things: if you want more for yourself than what you're getting right now, and if you're scared of these SP niggas?"

"I ain't in this game just to float above water, I'm tryin' to navigate the ship. And as far as being scared of Mack, SP, or anyone else, there's nothing wrong with fear, anger, or any other emotion. Fear inhibits action. I'm far from a sucka. If I take action, muthafuckas gon' die."

Terry was beginning to take a liking to Reek. Spoken like a true G. I'm going to give you a chance to navigate that ship..."

CHAPTER 8

Haitian had successfully reached a deal with the State. He provided information on Terry and a few other people throughout Syracuse. According to his deal, he had to play a pivotal role in leading to their arrests and convictions. The stipulations of his release was for him to call in every forty eight hours. He also had to assist in a successful bust within seventy two hours of his release.

He knew that he had made a deal with the devil the moment he signed the agreement. He was also aware that his only chance at having a second shot in the streets would come at the cost of his only true friend's demise.

"Fuck it," Haitian said out loud as he sat on his couch staring at the two kilos of cocaine that he stashed before his arrest. "I gotta do what the fuck I gotta do." He picked up his phone and dialed Terry's number.

"Hello?"

"What's good, T?"

"Who dis?"

"This is Haitian. What's poppin'?"

"Oh, shit, what's poppin', my G?" Terry said excitedly.

"Ain't nothin'. I just got out. I need to see you."

"How in the fuck did you get out of jail, my dude?"

"You know the kid is gonna make moves," Haitian boasted. "My grandfather put up his house and twenty G's for my bail. Now I can fight the case from out here. I know I'm gonna have to do some time, though, so I gotta get my money right. That's why I need to holla at you. I got this—"

Terry quickly cut him off. "I'm out of town right now, kid. I'll see you as soon as I come back."

"When are you coming back?"

"In about a week or two."

"Aaight, kid. I'll see you then." They hung up. "Shit!" Haitian tossed the phone onto his well-worn couch in frustration.

He removed the wrapper from one of the kilos, shaved off about thirty grams and put it into a sandwich bag. After concealing the drugs in a safe place, he left his apartment and got into his six year old Honda Accord. Haitian rolled down the driver and passenger window to remove the stale air, then pulled off. The subtle and slightly chilly breeze also helped to clear his mind.

It was hard to believe that after all that occurred, he was once again a free man. He thought about the ill-fitting orange jail uniform that he was forced to wear, and the terrible trays of slop that he was given to eat. He, then, reflected on the price he had to pay in order to be freed from confinement. Haitian shook his head at his circumstances. A somber look made its way onto his face. He selfishly made the choice to become what most people despised.

He exhaled a long, stress filled breath. With one hand on the steering wheel, he used his free hand to grab his cell phone. He punched in the newly memorized numbers and the phone was immediately answered.

"Shwarts speaking."

"What's up Shwarts. This is Deshawn."

"How ya doin', kid?"

"I'm okay. Listen, I can get you an arrest for a few guns today."

"A few guns? I guess that'll be good to get your feet wet. What time?"

"Whenever you're ready."

"Well, come down to the building and we'll get everything on paper, and set up."

"Alright, I'll be there within an hour."

———

The meeting was over within thirty minutes. Haitian informed Lieutenant Shwarts of who the men were and what types of guns they could expect to retrieve. He acquired this information because he had just left the house late last night.

Shwarts assured him that his officers would be in position and waiting. As Haitian was preparing to leave the building, Shwarts placed a pudgy hand on his shoulder, causing him to turn slightly. Their eyes met. "Good job, boy. You're doing the right thing."

His milky colored skin contrasted with his silver-streaked black hair that was more prominent on the sides of his head than the top. His thick, black mustache hung just above his thin lips. He wasn't obese, but the years of being in great shape were behind him. His brown, beady eyes cast a deep, direct look at Haitian, causing him to look away.

"Thanks Lieutenant." Haitian forced a weary smile upon his face, turned and left the building. He made it to his car engulfed in an influx of emotions. He was angered that this son of a bitch, Shwarts had the audacity to act like they were friends. Shwarts despised him and he knew it. Haitian was disappointed in himself. His stupidity and weakness caused him to switch sides. Now that he worked for the enemy, his friends were no longer safe around him.

Finally making it to Lincoln Avenue, he pulled over in front of a small two story gray house that was desperately in need of some TLC. Pulling out his phone, he sent a text: *Waddup Butter. R U at the crib?*

He received a response within seconds: *Yeah, I'm here.*

Haitian reached under his seat, grabbed the sandwich bag of coke, and shoved it into his pocket. He, then, closed his eyes and took a few deep, collected breaths in order to calm his nerves. With a now-or-never frame of mind, he got out of the car, walked up the battered wooden steps onto the front porch and rapped on the door.

"Who is it?" a voice from inside yelled.

"It's me, Haitian." A moment later the door opened.

Butter's girlfriend, Tasha, stood at the door. Wassup, Haitian?" she spoke evenly.

"What's good, girl? Damn, you gettin' big." Tasha was dressed in a simple white T-shirt, pink sweat pants and house slippers. The bulge in her stomach was evident. He stepped inside and closed the door. "How many months are you?"

"Seven." She gazed down at her stomach, giving it a gentle rub. "I'm having the baby shower next month. You comin'?"

"No question," he lied. "Where's your man at?"

"Same place as always. In there with his stupid ass friends playing them stupid ass video games." Her face clearly showed her disapproval. "Go on in there. I'm going back upstairs."

"Aaight. You better stop being so mean, girl. Your baby's going to come out talking shit to the doctor."

"Shut up." For the first time, she smiled.

The pleasant smell of weed hit Haitian as soon as he walked into the living room. Butter and the rest of his friends were lounging, smoking, and playing Playstation.

"Waddup, Butter?"

"Waddup, kid?" Butter said, not taking his eyes off the flat screen. His concentration was on the game he was playing.

Haitian, then, spoke to everyone in the room. They greeted him back.

"Let me hit that." Haitian extended his hand out to Pook, who sat on the couch. He casually passed the Dutch and Haitian took a much needed pull. "Listen, my dude, I ain't got a lot of time," he began, taking another drag of the blunt. "I got a big come up, but we gotta move quick."

"For what?" asked Butter.

"For two ki's and at least twenty thousand."

Haitian's reply caused Butter to pause the video game and redirect his attention. "Are you serious?"

"Mothafuckin' right." He pulled out the bag of coke. "This out of town nigga heard I fuck with T-Lova and started showing off. I saw the work and mad money. He just gave me all this." He raised the bag of drugs as evidence to solidify his story.

"Who is the nigga?" Pook asked.

"This older cat from Yonkers. It's four people in the house, and it ain't no problem for me to get in. All we gotta do is hold everybody down and take all the work. Ya'll tryin' to get this money?"

Everyone was hyped up and willing to move out. However, Butter seemed a little reluctant. "I don't know about this shit. It sounds a little crazy."

"It is crazy. That's why we gotta get them before somebody else gets them," Haitian said convincingly.

No one in the room had ever had more than two ounces of cocaine at one time. The prospect of having kilos and thousands of dollars was alluring.

Butter thought about his current financial struggles. The fact that those struggles were likely to increase in the next two months when his first child would be introduced to the world was the deciding factor.

"Fuck it. Let's do it."

"That's what I'm talking about!" Haitian exclaimed. "How many guns do we have?"

Butter had a .357 Magnum revolver and a sawed off shotgun, and Pook had a .380 semi automatic, which meant there were three guns between the four of them. "Aaight ya'll, let's go and get this money."

Butter went and grabbed the guns, giving one to his friend and keeping one for himself. They went over the plan, then left the house. Haitian got into his car and the other four men jumped into a separate car.

Haitian dialed Lieutenant Shwarts' number and put the

phone on speaker so that the occupants of the other vehicle wouldn't notice him on the phone.

"This is Lieutenant Shwarts."

"It's me, Shwarts. In ten minutes, you're going to see my car followed by a maroon Dodge Magnum wagon with four dudes in it. They got the guns. We'll drive down South Salina Street."

"Alright. We'll be ready to pull them over as soon as they pass us."

Haitian pulled off. Butter followed. The Magnum was completely silent. Dreams of no longer having financial worries occupied their thoughts. Little did they know that a few miles ahead of them, their wonderful dreams would come to a startling halt. The nightmarish reality would hit them when they were dragged out of the car at gun point, arrested, and sent to prison.

Ten days passed since Haitian had been released from the county jail. Over that time he had set up two successful busts. They were both low level, so he wasn't too worried about it coming back to haunt him. He also made more money in the past ten days than he'd ever made. He moved about a ki and a half in the streets. With over seventy thousand dollars saved up, and his cell phone constantly ringing, he finally knew what it felt like to be the man.

Haitian believed that the time to take control over Syracuse had come. But, in order for him to do so, he would have to think smarter and on a higher level. Instead of working for the police, he was going to change the tides and make them work for him.

Anyone he deemed to be a threat or competition, he'd simply feed them to Lieutenant Shwarts, then take over their area once they were out of the way.

Nightfall had cast its dark shadow over the city. The different spectrums from the street lights, cars, store fronts and homes contrasted with the navy-blue skies to create an attractive ambiance. Haitian was on his way home from Destiny USA Mall where he spent a good chunk of money on expensive clothes. "I'm gon' shut the club down tonight!" he shouted in a sudden outburst over the music as he drove to his apartment.

With less than a half kilo left, the time to purchase more drugs was fast approaching. He owed Powerful fifty-four thousand dollars, and he had no intentions of paying him. He knew someone else who could supply him the amount of coke he needed. Haitian had already made plans on using a portion of the money to buy a Camaro.

He pulled over in front of his apartment building, directly in front of a tan Yukon XL with tinted windows. His jovial mood caused him to pay little attention to the SUV. With bags in each hand, he used his hip to close the car door. With the music from the car stereo still lingering in his head, he bopped his way to the front door. In order to free his hands and single out his house key, he sat three bags down.

"Here. Let me get that for you, homie." The familiar voice slithered into Haitian's ear, causing the hairs on the back of his neck to stand. He turned to see Powerful's dark brown and red veined eyes, bored deep into him. He tried to swallow, but his throat instantly tightened, making it nearly impossible. Sensing the presence of more men, Haitian half spinned in the opposite direction only to come face to face with Powerful's two goons.

"P-Powerful, wassup, bruh? I-I was just gonna call you, my nigga."

"Yeah, I know," Powerful responded sarcastically.

"Come on, let's go inside."

Haitian did his best to remain calm, but his trembling hands revealed the truth when he struggled to insert the key into the lock. Finally, it went in and he opened the door. Once inside, Haitian dropped the bags onto the floor, and placed his keys on the coffee table. "Have a seat. Ya'll want..."

Powerful rapidly delivered a hard, right hand to Haitian's mid section, pushing all of the air out of his diaphragm. His legs went limp, and he fell to his knees, struggling desperately to inhale.

The two goons grabbed each arm, and stood him up. One of them gave Haitian a thorough pat search. Making his way down to his pants pocket, he tossed Powerful a stack of cash and a cell phone. Once he reached Haitian's ankles, he stood up and looked at Powerful. "He's clean. No wires."

Powerful dropped Haitian's phone onto the floor and stepped on it, digging his heel into the screen. The crackling sound of the glass ensured that the phone was no longer operable.

Haitian wasted no time. "Powerful, listen, man. I got knocked. Everything got taken by the police. T-Lova is out of town. As soon as he gets back we're going to get everything together and straighten you out. That's my word."

"That's your word?" Powerful asked harshly.

"Yeah, we know we still gotta take care of you. We got you."

"Man, sit your bitch ass down!"

Haitian was too scared to protest. He stumbled over to the couch and plopped down, holding his stomach.

Powerful pulled out his cell phone and dialed a few numbers. "Waddup? ...No question...Yeah, he right here...Hold on." He handed the phone to Haitian.

With a bewildered look on his face, he accepted. "Hello?"

"Waddup, my dude?"

"T-Lova, wassup, bruh?" The sound of relief was heard in Haitian's voice.

"Listen, I know you working for the police. The only chance of leaving that house alive is if you tell me the truth. You got one chance, nigga. I'm gonna ask you one time. What did you tell 'em about me?"

"I didn't tell them nothin' about you. I told them about some other niggas." Haitian instantly wished he could retract his words. "The things I told them wasn't even true. It was just enough for them to let me out." He did his best to minimize his actions.

"You know what, for some strange reason I believe you. Let me holla at Powerful and try to convince him."

"T, I swear to God I'm not lying to you. I would never do no shit like that. You're like my brother."

"I know," Terry responded. "Give Powerful the phone."

Haitian wanted to say more. He wanted to be sure that Terry was totally convinced, but there was nothing more to be said. Reluctantly, he handed the phone over.

"Yeah...Aight...You already know...Peace." Powerful said, glaring at Haitian.

"Did he tell you that he believes me?" Haitian asked wide eyed.

Powerful stuffed the phone into his pocket and drew a black .40 caliber Glock, aiming it at Haitian, who sat frozen with fear on the couch. "Nah. As a matter of fact, he told me to make sure that your mother has to give you a closed casket funeral."

"Please..."

"The gun burst ripped through the air. Instinct caused Haitian to flinch. Because of the life saving move, the bullet grazed his temple, ripped his skin, producing a light flow of blood. He jumped up from the couch and darted towards the door. He grabbed the handle and turned it as soon as the next bullet was released. It tore through the back of his head, causing his body to fall like dead weight.

Powerful stood over him and pumped three more slugs into his skull. Blood spewed from the holes in Haitian's lifeless body, permeating the cheap carpet.

"Hurry up and see if we can find the blow," Powerful ordered.

It didn't take long. The money and remainder of the drugs were in the closet. They planted the drugs under the cushion of the couch so that his murder appeared to be a drug deal gone bad. The trio, then, hurried to the Yukon and left Syracuse...

CHAPTER 9

It didn't take long for Terry and his crew to learn the ways of South Philly. Reek had become his liaison to the streets. He introduced Terry to some thorough hustlers. Because of his new cartel connection, he was able to supply them with the best coke at unbeatable prices.

Jihad, Twan and Boogs also began networking in the streets. They weren't flamboyant with their hustle, nor were they aggressive towards others. This method made other hustlers more willing to gravitate towards them. They also began setting up drug distribution houses.

███████████████

Sunlight reflected off the chrome twenty-two inch Giovanni

rims as the ice blue Mercedes CL63 eased to a halt against the curb on Capital Street. Mack slid his brawny, agile frame out of his coupe. He shook off a slight chill from the fall wind and adjusted the navy-blue Retroactive velour track suit. The white on white Buscemi sneakers were as exclusive as his outfit.

Approaching the sidewalk, he was immediately greeted by the crew of the young men hanging out in front of a row home.

"I smell it, so let me inhale it," Mack said, referring to the blunts being smoked by his SP comrades.

Without hesitation one of the men passed a blunt to him. After taking two pulls, he blew the smoke out and looked at the blunt in disgust. "What the fuck is this? Ya'll know I'm allergic to regular weed." He pulled out a sandwich bag containing light green, fluffy buds. "Roll up some of this Lemon Skunk." Mack handed the dude a nice sized bud and replaced the bag into his pocket. "Shawn, let me holla at you, cannon." The two stepped off to the side.

"What's up, Mack?"

"Are you finished with that work, yet?"

"Man, it's been slow as hell. I only moved about four ounces in the last couple of days. Niggas ain't been coppin' no weight," Shawn explained.

"What the fuck is goin' on? It's Saturday afternoon. None of the sack spots sold out, and you hardly moved anything. Either the fiends stopped smoking or somebody else is getting the money."

"The bawh, Fruit, came up to me this morning telling me about some niggas from out of town who sold him an eighth of powder for thirty five hundred."

"That nigga is lyin'. As dry as it is out here, can't nobody afford to sell coke that cheap." Mack shook his head at the news.

"Not only that, he said it was the best coke he had in years. I don't think the bawh is lying. Think about it. Within the last couple of weeks money has been coming in slower and slower."

"Find out who these mutha fuckas is," Mack demanded.

"I already asked Fruit. He said the bawh's name is T-Lova."

"I want to know everything about him. What he's sellin', who he's running with, and where he stay. We're going to have to show him how SP gets down."

"Get down or lay down." Shawn said with a sinister grin.

"Nah. He's doing too much. This might be a special case of lay down and stay down…"

CHAPTER 10

Terry sat recumbent in the passenger seat while Jihad piloted his coupe through the lively streets of South Philadelphia. The mild temperatured, bright day slowly began to descend as evening approached.

"I can't believe that everything is going so good for us out here," Jihad said, focusing on the road.

"Yeah, Philly is making it a lot easier for us to do our thing and stay below the radar."

"Boogs and Reek is movin' that work like it's nothin'. I gotta see them again before the night's out."

"We've been grinding since we came here. It's time for us to have a little fun. We'll get back to work tomorrow," Terry stated.

"I'm with that. I heard a lot about Club Roxy. You wanna go there?"

"Yeah. They say that jawn is live. Let's go pop a few bottles."

Jihad drove over to South Street and pulled over in front of Dr. Denim, an urban, high-fashion boutique that was becoming his favorite place to shop. About thirty minutes and over two thousand dollars later, they left with a couple of bags filled with high-end apparel. They tossed their bags into the trunk and got inside the car. Then, an ice blue CL 63 pulled up on the side of them and parked. A brown skinned, bulky man got out, gave a quick glance at the BMW, and then headed towards Dr. Denim.

Damn, that Benz is official. That nigga gotta be gettin' money," Jihad said.

"That color is crazy. He put that jawn together right," Terry said as Jihad pulled off.

Later on that night, Terry's gleaming Mercedes eased into the large parking lot surrounding Club Roxy, followed by Jihad. Vehicles were pulling in by the minute. Terry stepped out of his car dressed to impress in a powder blue Burberry sweater with its iconic print covering the elbows, blue Seven jeans, and sky blue Prada sneakers. His diamond studded chain and Hublot watch rounded out his attire.

Jihad sported black Tom Ford frames, a black Gucci sweater, black fitted Rock & Republic jeans exposing the shiny golden buckle of his Gucci belt, along with a pair of black Tom Ford loafers. A gold Cuban link chain and Audimoire watch contrasted perfectly against his outfit.

They made it into the prodigious, lavish club. The festive atmosphere and upbeat music, combined with the well-dressed men and women, created an exceptional atmosphere. Terry and Jihad strolled around, visually ingesting the club as D.J. Flow kept the crowd active with his selections.

Jihad stopped by the large bar and ordered two bottles of Ace of Spades. After paying for the champagne, they found a table on the outside of the dance floor and took a seat. Jihad noticed a crew of men in the VIP section popping expensive bottles as if they were going out of style. "Who's them niggas in the VIP?" Jihad yelled over the loud music.

"I'm not sure, but I think its them SP cats," Terry responded.

A few minutes later, D.J. Flow's voice blared through the speakers. "Shout out to the bawh, Mack, and the whole SP squad. They see you, but they can't be you...it's levels to this shit!" He, then, played the song *Levels* by Meek Mill. Mack stood up and raised his shiny gold bottle into the air, acknowledging D.J. Flow's salute.

"Yo, that's the kid who pulled up next to us at Dr. Denim," Jihad said.

"That's our competition," Terry said.

"We might have to eliminate him before he becomes our problem."

"We ain't ready to go to war with him, yet. Right now, we're outnumbered, and out gunned."

"It won't be a war, it'll be a hit." Jihad took a swig from his bottle. "The advantage is in our corner. If he don't have a clue that we're plotting, it's impossible for him to prepare a defense."

Terry leaned back and bobbed to the music, doing his best to memorize the faces of everyone partying with Mack. Not wanting to devote too much time to his potential opposition, he shifted back to party mode.

Women constantly passed Terry and Jihad's table, throwing

them flirtatious glances of approval. They loved the attention, but the night was still young. There was still plenty of time to select a candidate worthy of leaving the club with.

"I gotta take a piss, then, I'm going to get us two more bottles." Terry got up and walked to the restroom. Inside, he saw two men who appeared to be scheming on something. Paying them little attention, he went directly to the urinals. The men were oblivious to him. They continued on with their conversation in barely audible voices.

"I'm telling you, we gotta get that nigga, Mack, tonight. He murdered Shalik, and we're out here actin' like everything's all good."

"Yeah, but you was plotting on Shalik yourself," the other man said.

"So, what! That bitch ass nigga is eatin' too fuckin' much anyway. Come on, we gon' catch him when he go to his car." They shook hands, and then left the men's room.

A moment later, Terry exited and headed towards the bar. After replaying the two strangers' conversation, he spun around and walked towards the VIP section. Once there, he approached the heavy-set man who was enjoying himself. "Pardon me, is your name, Mack?"

The stranger's question caused Mack's demeanor to shift instantly. "Do I know you?"

"Nah, you don't know me. I just came to give you a warning. I overheard two dudes in the bathroom plotting on killing you."

"What?" Mack responded stone-faced. He leaned in closer, not wanting to miss a single word.

"They're going to be waiting by your car when you leave the club, so be on point." Before Mack could ask any additional questions, Terry slid off, disappearing into the thick crowd.

Mack decided not to reveal the news to his comrades. They were all intoxicated. If he told them that someone was plotting on his life, they would surely react out of anger. He was aware that if moves were carried out in anger, mistakes would be made.

He pulled out his phone and sent a text to Sandra: *I miss my two babies. I need to see them ASAP. You know where I'm at.* Replacing his phone in his pocket, he continued enjoying himself as if he didn't have a care in the world.

At around 12:30 a.m. he received a text. After reading it, he told his crew that he had to go. He gave them dap, strolled through the club one final time, and then left.

As soon as he stepped outside, Mack was greeted by Sandra. He gave her a hug as she tucked two royal-blue .40 caliber Glocks into the waist of his pants. He pulled his Armani sweater over the handles to conceal them.

"Thanks, baby." Mack kissed Sandra softly on her lips. "Go home. I'll be there soon."

"Are you sure?" She looked up at him puppy eyed.

"I'll be there within the hour." As he spoke to her, he surveyed the parking lot. It was desolate. Everyone was inside enjoying themselves.

"Okay baby. Be careful." With a quick kiss on the cheek, Sandra walked to her car and left.

Mack, then, began to wobble in the direction of his car as if he was inebriated. "SP for life!" he shouted, slurring his words. "I'm the mutha fuckin' boss. I got money to blow!" He continued, walking with unsteady feet.

"Aye Mack!" a voice yelled out aggressively.

The drunken swagger immediately disappeared. Mack spun around with a semi-automatic gripped in each extended hand. The blaring gun shot and bright flash caught Mack's eye.

He responded by firing multiple .40 caliber rounds at the source. The windows of an Escalade that Mack was crouched behind were blown out from the shooter's return fire.

Mack dropped down flat on the pavement. Looking under the parked cars, his eyes locked on two sets of feet scurrying in an attempt to get closer to him. He raised his gun and fired a single shot into the air. Just as he expected, the feet paused. He, then, repeatedly squeezed the triggers sending eight slugs beneath the cars, striking the men in their legs. Loud shrills pierced the air as the attackers collapsed in agony.

With astonishing agility, Mack, rose to his feet and trotted over to the shooters-turned-victims. Without coming to a complete halt, as soon as they were in range he began firing bullets into their bodies. The Full Metal Jacket slugs dismantled their organs ensuring death.

Hastily, Mack made it to his Mercedes. After a quick and careful scan for potential witnesses, he pulled out of the parking lot.

———

Taylor Street was active as usual. Pedestrians were en route to their destinations and the hustlers did their best to meld in, while simultaneously being on alert for both customers and the police. Reek sat in his Jaguar casually thumbing through the stack of money that was given to him by the young man in the passenger seat. "You sure this is straight? It's a lot of counterfeit money floating around."

"I heard about that. That's why I double check everything that touches my hands," the young man responded.

Reek reached under his seat, pulled out an ounce of cocaine

and handed it over.

The buyer quickly stuffed it into his jacket pocket.

"Alright," he said, looking out the window instinctually, "I'll be calling you for more before the day's over." With that said, he slid out of the car and blended into the streets.

Shortly after, a black on black Jeep Wrangler Rubicon swerved to the curb in front of Reek's car. Mack hopped out, walked directly to the passenger side of the Jaguar and got in.

"Wassup, cannon? I ain't heard from you in a minute. You stopped hustlin' or something?" Mack said, while delivering an imposing look to Reek.

"Nah, I'm still gettin' money," Reek confessed.

Mack shook his head and chuckled. "I help you get on your feet and this is how you repay me?" His temper was clearly rising.

"It's not that I cut you off. My cousin and his man's came up from New York with that work. They fronting me a half a brick at a time. How can I turn that down?"

"Do one of them drive a BMW coupe?" Mack asked, remembering the car he parked next to at Dr. Denim's with the New York State license plates. He thought about the accent of the man who gave him the warning at Club Onyx. Mack described him to Reek, who reluctantly confirmed. "What's this nigga's name?"

"Come on, Mack. You know I ain't with that. I can't give you information on him. Snitching is snitching no matter how you look at it."

Mack's first thought was to pull out his gun and smash it into Reek's face, but after consideration, he had to respect the kid's thoroughness. "I'll tell you what, call him and ask if he hollered at me at Club Onyx. If he say yes, then tell him I want to talk to him."

"Alright, I'll do that."

"Now!" Mack demanded.

Feeling the pressure, Reek grabbed his phone and dialed Terry's number. He spoke to Terry momentarily. Upon Terry's request, he handed the phone to Mack.

"Hello?"

"I would ask you what's good, but seeing that I'm talking to you today, I see that life is good," Terry said.

"Yeah, life is definitely good. Listen, I appreciate you giving me that heads up. I've been hearing a lot about you, and I created a perception of you based on that. It wasn't a good one. Last night, you did something that you didn't have to do, and that changed everything. If you don't mind, I want to have a talk with you."

"That's cool. We can talk."

"Do you know where Warm Daddy's restaurant is?" Mack asked.

"I think so. It's on...Delaware Avenue and Reed Street, right?"

"Yeah. Can you meet me there within a half an hour?"

"I'll be there."

They hung up. Mack gave the phone back to Reek.

"So, where does that leave us?" Reek questioned.

"You'll know after I talk to the bawh." Mack left Reek, hopped into his Jeep, and then left.

Reek sighed and slid the compact 9 mm he had concealed in his left hand back under his thigh, relieved that he wasn't forced to use it.

———————

Inside of the restaurant, Mack took a seat next to the window. From that location he was able to see everyone who neared or entered. The waitress delivered his order of marinated grilled steak, scrambled eggs with cheese and seasoned home fries. He wasted no time tearing into his food.

A moment later, Terry stepped inside, Mack waved him over with the fork still in his hand.

He approached the table and extended his hand to properly greet Mack. "Wassup, bruh? I'm T-Lova."

His greeting was accepted with a handshake. "I'm Mack. Have a seat." Terry sat down. "My bad for ordering before you came, but I'm a big boy. I can't be around food without eating."

"It's alright." Terry chuckled. He signaled for the waiter who immediately came over and jotted down his order of baked turkey wings, macaroni and cheese, and greens.

"I'ma get straight to the point. I asked you to meet me, because you made the decision to give me that warning last night. That decision might have saved my life, but it definitely saved yours."

"Is that right?" Terry responded without displaying too much emotion.

"It's some niggas out there looking for you as we speak." Mack popped a slice of steak into his mouth and chewed while his comment lingered like a dense cloud of smoke. "You see, I don't have a problem with you gettin' money, but I do have a problem with you taking money out of my pocket." Terry remained stone faced. "Under any other condition, I would have allowed your life to be taken. Consider my warning a returned favor."

"So, you're telling me that I have to stop hustling in South Philly?"

"Yeah," he answered plainly.

"I appreciate the warning, but packing up and running away is not an option for me."

"You'd rather get killed in a city you barely know than leave?"

"I'd rather kill than get killed. But I'd rather die as a G than live as a coward."

"I gave you the warning. Once this conversation is over, it ain't no turning back."

"I respect that," Terry said, "but you have to respect the fact that I'm not out here hustlin' because it's cool. I'm providing a way for me and mine's...just like you. We're more alike than you think, Mack. Let's not be like these other niggas and kill each other over a block when we don't even own the buildings on them. Money is gon' continue to be printed whether we live or die. It's enough money for everybody to eat. If we come together, we can run this city."

"For one, what makes you think you can catch me slippin', and rock me to sleep?" Mack asked, no longer concerned with the food. "And two, what sense would it make for us to get together when I already have South Philly on lock, and you're just trying to get your foot in the door?"

"To answer your first question, no one is bullet proof. You never know, I could have the drop on you right now."

"And, it could be a gun pointed at you as we speak," Mack countered.

"It could be," Terry acknowledged. "As for your second

question, there is something valuable that I can bring to the table. I have a Mexican connect. I'm paying fifteen stacks a brick and he fronts me whatever I buy."

Mack's eyebrows rose with interest. "Are you serious?"

"No question."

"Damn, I'm paying double that for a jawn. I'm making this Dominican muthafucka rich, knowing he's stretching the coke."

"The birds I'm getting is untouched and my plug is cartel connected. Like I said, I'm not in this game because it's cool. My ultimate goal is to make enough money to switch my hustle and make the same amount of money, or more, legally."

"I've been brain storming on the same thing," Mack admitted.

"You see, we're more alike than we are different."

"I can tell that you have morals and integrity. I don't see any deception with you. With loyalty, we will become monumental. With deceit, we will be nothing more than memories."

"I'm not driven by greed, Mack. In this game, greed only brings a long prison bid, or an early death."

"I like the way you talk. We're both thinkers. If we get together and hustle with a common goal, not only will we reach it, but we will run circles around all these niggas out here," Mack stated confidently.

"Do you smoke weed?"

"No question."

"Let's bend a couple of corners and see if we can put a master plan together."

"Aaight." Mack slid his Beretta Pico .380, he held under the table at Terry, back into his pocket.

He stood up just in time to see Terry sliding his Kahr Arms compact .380 into his pocket. "What was you doing?"

"Nothing that you wasn't doing," Terry responded as he stood up, pulling out a stack of bills to pay for their meals.

"You're right." Mack issued an approving smile. "We are more alike than we are different…"

CHAPTER 11

Creating a merger turned out to be an extremely wise and lucrative decision that catapulted Mack up the ranks. With the understanding that although the distribution of cocaine was illegal, it was a business nonetheless. They created a controlled structure for their enterprise.

Mack and Terry were the bosses. They dealt directly with the connect, oversaw the entire operation and made all vital decisions.

Jihad was the president. He supervised and controlled all of the street activity on a higher level.

Shawn was the vice president. He took care of any business Jihad was unable to.

They basically worked together as a team to ensure that every hustler who purchased a kilo or more never ran out, and did business exclusively with them.

Reek and Boogs managed the streets. Reek sold everything from three-point-five grams to one hundred twenty-five grams of cocaine. Boogs made sure that all of the drug houses that sold ten and twenty dollar bags ran properly. If a house was raided by police, or bringing too much heat, he was responsible for finding a new place and migrating the customers.

Twan made sure that all of the drugs were cut, cooked and packaged properly. He knew the amount of drugs everyone on the team was to receive and, he made sure that they had their product on time.

Sandra was the secretary. She gave notice to every SP member about all meetings. She also kept a guarded list of addresses and numbers of everyone in case there was a need for urgent contact.

Within eighteen months they had amassed enough capital to finance a legitimate venture. They decided to establish a luxury rental car service that catered to sports stars, entertainers and affluent businessmen visiting the

city with a desire for high end, temporary transportation.

The growth of Dynasty Luxury Rentals exceeded their expectations. What began with ten high end vehicles expanded to over forty premium cars with a line up consisting of Lexani Executive vehicles. Bentleys, Rolls Royces, Ferraris, Lamborghinis, and more.

Their business also provided them with the opportunity to meet and become acquainted with very prominent and influential people, including the Mayor of Philadelphia. Because of their immediate success and the introduction to people who could become paramount to their continued elevation, they were forced to maintain a lower profile in the streets, allowing Jihad and Shawn to become the faces of their illegal enterprise. This not only gave them more time to focus on marketing and promotions for Dynasty Luxury Rentals, but they were also readily available to attend celebrity parties and corporate functions. This was important not only for putting faces to their brand, but also for promoting and connecting with other entrepreneurs.

Their short journey together had been exceptional, and with the mindset that if they're going to be thinkers, they must be big thinkers. Their room for growth was limitless.

Their success or demise would come as a result of their choices and actions...

CHAPTER 12

MANHATTAN, NY

A gentle kiss stirred Marty Frankel out of his sleep. His mouth formed a smooth smile as his eyes adjusted on Kate's comely figure, his wife of just over a year.

"Good morning, Princess," he said in a raspy voice, yawned, and then wiped crust from his eyes.

"Rise and shine, lazy bones. You have to be to work in less than an hour." Kate stood over him in a jasmine colored, silk nighty. Her honey-blonde hair rested on the shoulders of her petite, shapely frame.

"That means I have time to give you the best ten minutes of your life." Marty reached out and grabbed her by the waist, trying to pull her closer.

Kate's emerald green eyes twinkled as she smiled and softly pulled away.

"Sorry, lover boy, but you have to take a shower and I have to make you something to eat. Didn't you say that you had an important meeting today?"

Marty swung his feet over the edge of his California-king sized bed and sat up while running a hand through his hair. Her question sparked the realization that this was a day he was not looking forward to. His wife knew that the meeting was significant, but she had no clue that it could cause his ruin. "Yeah," he answered flatly.

Kate dismissed his drab response. "Well, get yourself together and I'll make breakfast. It's much harder to focus on an empty stomach." She whirled around and scurried down the stairs of their ultra-luxurious apartment.

He stood, stretching his six-feet-two-inch, toned frame. At forty-three years old, Marty relied on a strict diet, and rigorous exercise to help combat the signs of aging. It also felt good to know he didn't look out of place when out with Kate, who was nine years younger than him.

Marty staggered to the bathroom and pressed number two on the wall mounted key pad. Instantly, water of his preferred temperature streamed out of the multiple shower heads, and Def Leopard's *Pour Some Sugar On Me* blazed through the surround sound speakers. He undressed and stepped into the spacious walk-in shower. The steaming water massaged his muscles while the music invigorated him. His mind traveled through all the possibilities of what lay ahead. He chased away the pessimistic thoughts and committed himself to handling the day in the same manner he did when confronted with burdensome situations of the past.

Marty descended the spiral stairs and walked into the palatial kitchen dressed impeccably in a tailored navy-blue Ralph

Lauren Purple Label suit, white Egyptian cotton shirt, a red silk tie, and brown leather Ferragamo shoes. He sat down to a plate of poached eggs, lightly buttered wheat toast, and a bowl of oatmeal. Mastering the art of multi-tasking, Marty ate, engaged in a light conversation with Kate and scanned through the *Wall Street Journal*.

After a quick glance at his Rolex Sky Dweller watch, Marty stood, and kissed Kate on her forehead. "I'm sure the car is out front waiting on me. I'm going to stop by the gym after work, but I'll be home no later than four."

"Ashly and I are going to an art exhibit in New Jersey, so I may not make it in until after six."

"I'll take it that means we'll be going out for dinner?"

"It's either that or you can whip us up something," Kate said.

"Not a chance, young lady. I'll make reservations. Try not to spend too much on those paintings. You're still developing your eye for art."

"I'll try," Kate responded.

Marty left his penthouse, boarded the elevator, and exited in the lobby of the ritzy Dakota Building. Walking out of the doors, he inhaled a deep breath of crisp, morning Manhattan air. Although it was only six-thirty in the morning, the New York streets were bustling with people and cars in a hurry to reach their destinations. Parked directly in front of the building rested a gleaming, black Rolls Royce Phantom. The chauffeur stood near the rear and opened the door as Marty approached.

"Good morning, Mr. Frankel."

"Good morning, Larry." Marty eased into the back seat, pulled out his phone, and checked his emails. The driver navigated the grand sedan to the Goldman Sach's Building.

Marty Frankel had worked tirelessly for Goldman Sach's for

100

over eight years as a commodities trader. He engaged in high volume, risky trading of natural gas derivatives. He essentially made bets based on the future direction and unpredictability of the price of natural gas. His base salary was four-hundred-thousand dollars per year, however, he earned millions of dollars in bonuses and incentives. He was extremely talented in his field, and did whatever was asked of him by his supervisor, Jack Goldberg.

Jack was the head trader in the Commodities Derivative Group. He was responsible for Goldman's strategic decisions and trades. In addition to being at the helm of trades, Jack managed Goldman's commodities trading strategies and ensured that Goldman's trading books were accurately valued each day.

Jack used his unrestrained market power to manipulate the prices of natural gas and futures contracts. The higher-ups turned a blind eye towards his actions. Their main concern was him becoming sloppy and that millions of dollars would not continue to pour in.

As prudent as Jack was, a thorough review of Goldman's trades by a major accounting firm led to the discovery of Jack's mismarkings. It was also discovered that despite Goldman's full access to Jack's trading records, Goldman's risk management and supervisory systems failed to intervene. Three months ago criminal and civil charges were filed against the company and selected employees.

The elegant Rolls Royce Phantom slowed to a stop in front of the building. Briefcase in hand, Marty got out and hustled inside. He boarded an elevator that took him to his desired floor, greeted his secretary, and then entered his office. In less than five minutes of his arrival, his phone was ringing.

"Goldman's Sachs, Commodities. This is Marty Frankel. How can I help you?"

"Good morning, Mr. Frankel." It was Jack's secretary. "Mr.

Goldberg would like to speak with you concerning an urgent matter."

Marty used is index finger and thumb to massage the bridge of his nose. "Thank you, Maggie. I'll be there in a second."

Once again, he boarded the elevator, getting off at the top floor. After releasing a deep breath, he knocked on the thick mahogany wood door.

"Come in," Jack yelled. Marty opened the door to see his supervisor pacing back and forth in the thick carpeted, massive office. "Have a seat."

Marty sat down in a maroon leather chair opposite Jack's desk. Although Jack was a slender, active man, his sixty-four years of living was evident by the gray hairs that wrapped around the sides of his head, and the slight sagging of skin under his eyes and chin. However, his piercing steel gray eyes were as alert as a twenty-five year old soldier's.

"I received a call from my attorneys this morning," Jack said as he stepped closer to the bay windows, offering a magnificent view of Manhattan. "There has been a new proposed settlement."

"Does this one still involve me?" Marty questioned.

"I'm going to be honest. Yes, it does."

"Jack, you know I only want the best for you, but I can't destroy my life, my marriage…my future for you."

"This is much bigger than you and I. You work for one of the largest trading firms in the United States. You've witnessed first-hand the amount of press coverage this mess has received. If you were to get fired, there's no other firm in this country that would risk hiring you."

"Fire me for what? I've done nothing wrong!" Marty shouted defensively.

Jack turned around staring intently at Marty. "Goldman's a very big ship. If it goes down, many people will drown." His words hit like stiff punches, causing Marty to slouch in the chair at the thought of him losing his job. "But there is a way out of this. It's possible that you can come out of this with an even more powerful position at Goldman's." Marty sat up, correcting his posture, giving Jack his complete attention. Jack continued, "My attorneys informed me that the new proposed settlement contains a 'neither admit, nor deny' provision. The only way that the prosecutor will approve of this is if there's an acceptance of responsibility by someone actively involved in trading. A minimum of thirty-two million dollars in disgorgement, penalties and interest. Arguably, as much as the SEC might be able to recover if they were to prevail at trial against us. In essence, we need you to be the face of this settlement, and, in doing so, you can decline to admit to the allegations against you by the SEC. There will be no criminal conviction."

"What about the forfeiture money? How will we pay them?"

"We can't just write you a check for thirty-two million dollars. That would make everything obvious to the point of really pissing the SEC off. It will certainly remove the deal and they will force us to criminal trial."

"There's no way I can come up with that type of money on my own."

"Your net worth, including your assets, is thirty-one point six million dollars, Marty."

"No...no fucking way!" Marty stood in anger. "You're asking me to give up everything I've worked my ass off for. I can't do it...I won't do this!"

"It's everything to you, but it's fucking peanuts to us, and you know it!" Jack screamed, standing face to face with Marty. "Look, kid. This is how it's going to work. Once you forfeit your money, the SEC will get off our backs and find someone else to screw. You will get back every dollar that you gave up. And for your loyalty, you will also receive this office and the position that comes with it, including a seven-figure signing bonus."

Marty was aghast by the promise that was made. When...I mean, how can you be sure that everything will go as you're saying?"

Jack reached into his desk drawer, removed a gold business card, and handed it to Marty. "Here. These are our attorneys. They are the best and they will represent you in this matter. When you go to your office, I want you to call our boss and confirm all that I've said regarding the promotion and compensation that you will receive, contingent on your assistance."

"I will call them both immediately." Marty accepted the card.

"If you receive this confirmation, do we have a deal?" Jack asked.

"Yes, but I need you to understand that I'm placing my entire life in your hands, Jack."

"Trust me, I understand. And I promise you that even though this is difficult for you, it will be the best decision of your career." They shook hands and Marty left.

With a huge sigh of relief, Jack dropped down into his chair, picked up his phone, and punched in a few numbers. "How are you doing, boss?...I sealed the deal. He's going to do it...they don't call me Jack the Ripper for nothing...I'll see you for lunch." Jack hung up the phone, interlocked his fingers with his hands behind his head, and smiled proudly...

CHAPTER 13

Julio sat at the small, cluttered desk of his vehicle repair shop on Hunting Park Avenue in North Philadelphia smoking a Marlboro. At 10:09 in the morning his office phone rang. He quickly raised the receiver to his ear in anticipation of the call. Just as expected, it was Norfolk Sutherland train station. A Kia Sorento that was purchased from an online auction had arrived and was expected to be picked up by his company.

After informing the caller that he was on his way, he logged onto Norfolk Southerland's website and re-checked the estimated delivery time for the Kia. He had been on the site numerous times over the past few days, however, a great sense of relief set in knowing that the vehicle was ready to be picked up at approximately

the same time that was posted on the site. If Julio would have received the phone call over an hour later, he would have followed the orders given to him and denied the SUV.

He snubbed the cigarette into an ashtray brimming with ashes and butts like tombstones in a cemetery. He yelled out for his cousin, Miguel, to accompany him on the drive to pick up the Kia.

At the train station's service desk, Julio filled out and signed the paper work, placed his dealer's tags onto the vehicle and then headed back to his shop. Once there, he called Mack and Terry. Within fifteen minutes they pulled into Julio's large, warehouse-styled garage.

Miguel locked and secured the building behind them. He and Julio went to work using an assortment of electrical tools to remove body panels and engine components from the vehicle with the skill of seasoned surgeons. An hour later, forty individually wrapped kilos of cocaine lay on the concrete floor, and the Kia was little more than a frame with an array of parts strewn around the garage.

Mack removed ten large Zip Lock bags containing compact stacks of U.S. currency from the trunk of his Dodge Charger. He handed them to Julio with instructions to conceal them in the panels of the truck before reassembling it.

Terry opened the glove box of his car and pulled out a small pouch that contained ten thousand dollars, placed it into Julio's hands and thanked him for his services.

With the drugs safely tucked into the Charger's hidden compartment, Mack and Terry carefully drove out of the garage and merged in with the traffic. Muddled feelings of uneasiness and excitement always occurred during their drive, despite having done this numerous times.

"We should drop ten jawns off to Twan right now, so he can break them all down," Mack said, putting an end to the silence. He kept his eyes on the road.

"Aaight. Then after that all we have to do is take the rest to the stash house and the risky work will be done."

Terry gave Twan a call, letting him know they were on their way. It didn't take long before Mack pulled inside Twan's two-car garage.

A white, late model Dodge Caravan with tinted windows sat five houses down from Twan's home. Two men sat inside chain smoking Newport cigarettes for the past two hours. They were contemplating on grabbing a quick bite to eat when a black Charger cruised past them.

"Oh, shit. That's that nigga, Mack, right there!" the man on the passenger side exclaimed.

"Damn, he was right. He's about to drop off some work to the bawh, Twan," the driver said.

"Aaight. Let's stay and wait until he leave. We don't need him now. We'll get his fat ass later."

The familiar rumble of the Hemi engine penetrated the walls. Twan walked into the garage as Mack turned the engine off.

"Pizza delivery!" Terry joked, easing out of the passenger side.

"Do it look like I need some damn pizza?" Twan asked, rubbing his rotund belly.

Mack got out and pushed the button on the wall causing the

garage door to close. "Hell no, you don't need no pizza. You need some Hydroxycut!"

"I know your super-sized ass ain't talkin'. Your body's shaped like a conversion van!" Twan shot back.

Mack looked down at his frame for a quick second.

"Nigga, I'm the slimmest fat boy you ever met." They all laughed. Mack went back to the Charger, activated a series of switches revealing the secret compartment, and opened the trunk. He and Terry removed ten kilos, closed the compartment, and went inside.

Terry placed the drugs on the living room table and took a seat. Twan grabbed a vanilla Blunt Wrap, a bag of high quality indica and rolled it. The potent strain of weed delivered immediate results as it was smoked and passed around by the trio.

"Damn, that weed got me high as a muthafucka." Terry slouched back in his chair with his eyelids nearly touching.

"Me, too, but we can't stay too long," Mack said, refocusing. "We need you to cook up two birds. Give one to Reek and one to Boogs. Re-rock the other eight jawns and stretch them to ten. Give Jihad five bricks and give the other five to Shawn."

"Aaight, I'ma get right on it. As a matter of fact…" Twan pulled out his cell phone and sent a text. "I just told Reek to come over. He's been hitting me non-stop since yesterday. That li'l nigga is a hustle-holic. Don't trip. I'll make sure everybody gets their package by this afternoon."

"Good lookin', Big Boy." Terry stood up to leave. "Call me after you've seen everybody." They gave each other dap, then Mack and Terry left.

Twan wasted no time pulling out all of the needed material to cook up and re-rock the cocaine. He took a seat at the table, used a box cutter to slice through multiple layers of plastic, revealing the pearl white cocaine. Just as he removed the packaging, his narcolepsy set in. Twan's body went limp in the chair. He abruptly began to snore, falling into a deep sleep.

———————————————

The Charger exited the garage, backing out of the driveway, then, drove down the street, fading out of view.

———————————————

"It's show time, cannon," the man in the passenger seat said. After double checking their guns to make sure bullets were chambered, they tucked them into the waist line on their pants, placed the stocking caps on top of their heads, and then jumped out of the van.

They trotted to Twan's house, rolling the stocking caps down over their faces. The bigger man used all of his strength to deliver a strapping forward kick to the door. It loosened but was still secured to its posts. The second kick caused the wood to splinter. He then used his shoulder to ram the door, busting it open.

———————————————

The skin splitting impact jarred Twan out of his sleep as blood trickled from the fresh wound across his forehead. He looked up in shock staring at two massive barrels of semi-automatic handguns being held by masked men.

"Yo, what the…"

One of the men pressed the cold steel against Twan's cheek, silencing him.

"You're too big to be playing with, Scrap. Put your hands behind your back."

As bad as Twan wanted to take a chance and rush one of the men, he knew that it would only end in his death. He released a sigh of defeat and did as he was told.

The second robber pulled his large hands behind the back of the chair and cuffed him. He, then, gathered the drugs that lay on the table and dumped them into a black garbage bag.

The first robber kept his gun trained on Twan. "You can make this a lot easier on yourself and tell us where ya boys keep their work stashed at."

Twan smiled. "Suck my dick, nigga!"

"Oh, you think this shit is a game, huh?" He tucked the gun into his waist, then, threw a powerful right hand punch, smashing his fist into Twan's face. He absorbed the blow, but swelling quickly began above his left eye. "I'ma ask you again…where the bawh, Mack, keep his fuckin' work stashed at?"

"And I'ma tell you again, suck my fuckin' dick!"

He threw another punch, hitting Twan square in the mouth.

Twan smiled, showing blood stained teeth. "You better kill me, muthafucka!"

"Go and search the house," the robber ordered his partner, before turning his attention back to Twan. "Don't worry, as soon as I get everything I want out of you, I'ma blow ya fuckin' head off!"

"Bitch ass nigga, you ain't getting' nothing out of me!"

Twan's anger was boiling over as he began to struggle to break free. His massive frame shook the chair violently. The strength that Twan displayed caused the robber to draw his gun and aim it at Twan's head.

The deafening shot echoed off the walls. To Twan's surprise, it wasn't the robber's gun that was discharged. Twan opened his eyes and saw the contents of the robber's head splattered over him. The dead body hit the floor with a thud. Reek stood there with a black .44 Bulldog in his hand.

"What the fuck is going on?" Reek slid behind Twan and wrestled with the handcuffs in an effort to free him.

"Two dudes just tried to rob me...hold up. The other one is still somewhere around!"

Reek looked up just in time to see the bright flash escape from the barrel of a 9 mm. Three bullets struck Twan in his upper chest, stopping his heart instantly. Reek raised his revolver and squeezed the trigger two times. At the same instant, three bullets tore into his stomach, ripping through his small intestines. One bullet lodged into his spinal cord. Shock abruptly set in, but there was little pain. Paralysis removed all of the feelings from the lower half of his body.

The robber grabbed the garbage bag containing the drugs using his good arm. The other was of no use because of the extensive damage that was done by the large slug embedded in it. He escaped out of the house leaving a trail of blood.

Reek managed to pull his cell phone out of his blood soaked jeans. He dialed Terry's number. His heart rate increased as the blaring sirens of the police cruisers grew louder.

"Hello?" Terry answered.

"H-h-help..." Reek's words trialed off into silence. He lost blood rapidly. The phone slipped from his grasp as his muscles relaxed and consciousness escaped him.

Three squad cars with bright flashing lights came to a screeching halt in front of Twan's house. The front door was slightly ajar.

"Police! We received a report of gunshots inside this house. Is anyone there?" the chief officer yelled, standing to the side of the door for protection. There was no answer. "Police! We're coming in!"

The first officer entered with his gun firmly in position and ready to fire. The other officer flanked in behind him. Reaching the dining room, their eyes were pulled toward the three bullet-riddled bodies.

"Cover and secure the rest of the house," the chief officer commanded, reaching down to check the vitals of the victims. The heavy-set man who was slumped over and handcuffed to the chair had no pulse. The young man who lay on the floor had a pulse, however it was extremely weak. There was no need to check the third victim. Over one third of his masked face had been blown off. Using his two-way radio, he called for paramedics and homicide unit.

The ambulance was the first to arrive. Paramedics were forced to cut the clothes from Reek's body in order to locate the bullet's entry points. Recognizing the extent of his injuries, they did their best to reduce the bleeding, wasting no time strapping the young man to a gurney. They rushed him to Albert Einstein Medical Center.

Moments later a tan Chevrolet Impala pulled up behind the Crime Scene Unit's van. Todd and Latrice Reed, a brother and sister, homicide detective team, got out of their car. They approached the crime site, ducking under the yellow tape used to cordon off the scene.

"Good afternoon, Detectives," the chief officer said as he shook their hands.

"Good afternoon, Thomas. Can you brief us on what happened?" Latrice asked, getting directly to the point.

"Yes. Follow me."

The trio walked into the house. Photographers were busy placing numbered cards next to every item of evidence as they recorded and snapped pictures. The chief officer explained in detail all that he and his men had observed upon entering the home.

Once in the living room where the two corpses were, along with the remnants of clothes left behind by the lone survivor, Todd shook his head in disdain. "More lives lost prematurely." He spoke more to himself than to the others. He kneeled over one of the bodies. There was no way the body could be identified by his facial features. Blood began to congeal on what was left of his stocking cap, hardening it, and a small puddle of blood formed under what was left of his grotesquely disfigured head. Everyone seemed impervious to the copper smelling stench of spilled blood that accompanied death.

After one of the photographers snapped multiple pictures of the handcuffs at different angles, Jonathan Welch, the pathologist, removed them with great care in order to preserve any possible finger prints or DNA, and then placed them into an evidence bag.

"Another case of senseless killings," Latrice mumbled. Her mind instantly transgressed to that dreadful day when she was thirteen years old and Todd was eleven. It was Christmas Eve and their father was preparing to take them out to dinner. While Latrice and Todd were putting on their coats and boots, their father went outside to brush the light snow off of his car. Todd opened the door and saw a masked man pointing a gun at his father. He and Latrice ran out of the house screaming at the robber, who turned the gun on them.

"Here. Take the money and leave!" their father screamed.

In the midst of all the commotion, the robber snatched the wallet, looked at their father for a split second, and with trembling hands, he pulled the trigger. He then fled.

The two children huddled over their father, cradling him and crying while the life drained from his body. The murderer was never captured, which became the driving force behind them pursuing careers as homicide detectives.

"So, what do you think, Jonathan?" Todd asked. Latrice took a step closer, eager to hear his assessment.

"This was a robbery gone awry. The front door shows evidence of forced entry. The paraphernalia on the living room table, along with traces of cocaine, leads me to believe that it was a larger amount there at one point. The big guy," Jonathan paused for a second to take a look at his notes, "Antwon Green, lived here. I believe that he was tied up and beaten for information."

"From the looks of it, he was reluctant in giving it up." Todd commented.

"This is where it gets crazy. The masked man, whom we haven't identified, was shot in the head from behind. Because of the large exit wound, I believe it was from the .44 that Tyreek Simmons had in his possession."

"Is that the kid rushed to the hospital?" Latrice asked.

"Yes. His weapon was discharged three times. Once into the deceased. There was one recovered round which was lodged into the wall, but the third round is unaccounted for."

Jonathan took a few steps, heading out of the living room, and then pointed down to the carpet. "Those blood stains appear to travel in a particular direction..."

"Out of the house," Todd finished.

"Exactly."

"We have someone out there with a huge slug in him, and we need to find him," Latrice commented.

"There was also a phone in Tyreek's hand when the officers discovered him. The phone was on and a call was processed."

"We'll get a copy of his phone records. Let's hope that he survives. He should be able to shed some light on this mess." Todd jotted down a few things on his note pad.

"Let's get everyone identified, the evidence organized, and crack this case," Latrice said to her brother/partner.

"I'll notify every hospital in the tri-state area to be on the lookout for someone with a large caliber gunshot wound."

"Then comes the hard part," Latrice said.

"Yeah, notifying the victim's family," Todd said. "The only thing that'll make me feel better is catching those who are responsible..."

CHAPTER 14

The last two weeks had been hell for Marty Frankel. He had no idea that his bank accounts would be frozen the day after he agreed to the offered plea. Kate had the embarrassing misfortune of finding out first, shopping with her friends. The credit cards on their joint account had been declined.

After explaining her ordeal to Marty, he was forced to confess everything to his wife. The most difficult part was getting her to understand that he had to forfeit his coffers.

Kate was livid at the situation he landed himself in. How could he be so selfish not to consider her and her well-being in his decision?

A brutal argument ensued, creating distance between them. Marty made numerous attempts to reconcile, but to no avail. She simply refused to accept that their assets would be replaced shortly after the tribulation was over.

The alarm chimed stirring Marty out of his sleep. He sat up and gazed angrily at the clock, as if it were aware he fought half the night to fall asleep. He didn't know if his inability to sleep was due to him being forced to stay the night in the second bedroom alone, or because in a matter of hours he would be in a courtroom taking a life altering plea.

Tiny beads of perspiration formed on his forehead as anxiety hit him. Marty took a few deep breaths, and then stood. He trodded to the bathroom and got into the shower, hoping that the hot flow of water would help ease the tension.

After showering and donning his favorite Tom Ford charcoal gray suit, he peeked into the master bedroom to check in on his wife. The room was empty and their bed was made. *She must be downstairs*, he thought. *Let's see if she decides to stand by my side and come to court with me.*

"Kate!" Marty yelled out, walking down the stairs. There was no answer. "Honey!" he called out again. Confused about her whereabouts, he slowly walked into the kitchen. His eyes focused on the refrigerator. A yellow piece of paper was held to the door by a magnet. Removing the note, he read it carefully.

*Marty, you have shown me that you are not
the man I fell in love with and married. You made
it clear by putting your job before us. Your choice
destroyed all that we had. I'm filing for a divorce.*

Kate

Continuously shaking his head in disbelief, he refused to accept what was written on the paper. His hands began to tremble. "Kate, honey, you just don't understand," he said. "Everything is going to be fine." He rushed to the phone and dialed

Kate's cell number. His call went directly to her voice mail. After leaving several messages, he reluctantly gave up. He leaned against the wall. Still feeling unsteady, he slid down to the kitchen floor, dropping his head into his hands, sulking in utter disbelief. During one of the most trying times of his life, he found himself without the love and comfort of his wife…alone. He was forced to fight this battle by himself. The only thing that left him with a fraction of stability was the promise from the CEO of Goldman Sachs, Jack, and their attorney.

Thirty minutes elapsed before Marty gathered the strength to rise to his feet. "Once this ordeal is over, you'll see that everything will be better than ever."

Marty called his lawyer who had already made it to the federal building. He gave Marty instructions to meet him in the lobby. Marty grabbed his briefcase, cell phone and keys, and left his apartment. The unexpected chill from the crisp morning wind caused Marty to put a pep in his step. He quickly got into his awaiting Phantom.

The chauffeur came to a stop in front of the federal building. The sedan was instantly swarmed by a slew of hungry press. Caught completely off guard by the crowd that surrounded his car, Marty darted out of the Phantom and barreled toward the building. Pushing forward microphones were shoved into his face, bright flashes of light from snapping cameras made him wince, and so many questions were thrown at him that they were indecipherable. Refusing to respond to anything, he continued to march forward until he reached the entrance.

Inside of the building, on the opposite side of the metal detectors, stood his attorney, Tom Paranillo. After passing through, Marty stormed toward him.

"What in the hell is that out there?" he questioned.

"That's called the media," Tom answered flatly.

"Why in God's name were they on me like a pack of hungry wolves?"

"Are you kidding me?" Tom chuckled. "I don't know if you've been under a rock for the past couple of weeks, but this story has been steadily gaining media coverage."

"I know that, Tom, but my identity was supposed to remain undisclosed." Exasperation had become evident by his demeanor. In response to Marty's pitch rising, Tom consciously lowered his.

"I have no idea how the media acquired your name. Evidently someone leaked it to them."

"You think?" The sarcasm in Marty's escalated voice bounced off the walls, causing a few people who were passing by to turn their heads. "I'm ruined!"

Jack walked up, interrupting them. "Don't be ridiculous, Marty." He shook their hands firmly, then continued. "There's no such thing as bad publicity when it's of this stature. We may be human, but Goldman is immortal. Trust me, you're doing the right thing. After today, your future will be secured. Your face will be synonymous with ambition and power."

Tom glared at his watch. "We were supposed to be in court five minutes ago. We have to go." He spun on his heels and headed toward the courtroom.

Jack gave Marty a strong pat on the back. "Come on, son. Let's get the last day of your old life over with."

They followed Tom into the courtroom where the judge and U.S. attorney anticipated them. Butterflies churned in Marty's stomach as the proceedings began...

With the deal finalized and on record, Marty walked out of the courtroom feeling completely drained and disconnected from life.

"Marty, I want you to take this weekend off. You have too much on your mind to worry about work. By next Monday the buzz surrounding all of this should be gone, then we can move forward. Maybe you and your wife should go on a vacation."

Jack's comment caused a surge of emotions to materialize. "It's quite difficult to go on a vacation when you have no money, Jack."

Jack displayed a sly grin. "Come on, Marty, I know you've set up a nice safety net."

"What are you talking about, Jack?"

"You know our investigators have noses like bloodhounds. Just under two million dollars had been incrementally removed from your account over the past three weeks. But the only problem they're having is figuring out where it was hidden. That's not a bad thing at all for you, because if they can't find it, then the feds shouldn't be able to."

"Jack, I have no idea what you're talking about."

Marty's perplexed expression appeared genuine, however, Jack was skeptical.

"I can understand if you don't want to touch your money right away." Jack pulled out his checkbook and a pen. He filled it out. "Here's a check for fifty thousand dollars. It should hold you down momentarily." Marty was left with no other choice but to accept it. "I'll see you next week," Jack said, then left.

Marty trudged through the mob of awaiting press, taking a sigh of relief once he was safely in the confines of his Phantom. The driver immediately pulled off and headed toward Marty's apartment building. As the car approached the Dakota Building, Marty's eyes zoomed in. He was grateful not to see any press laying in wait for him. Once inside the building he boarded the elevator, got off on his floor, and entered his apartment.

Although everything looked the same, the place felt different. The feeling of coming into a home was no longer there. Without Kate, their apartment was nothing more than a place to stay.

He walked to the bar and poured a generous amount of Scotch into a glass. After throwing it back, he placed the glass on the table, and picked up the bottle. He took a huge gulp and headed into the living room with the bottle in hand. The alcohol intensified all of the feelings contained within him. Marty sat on the sofa and continued to drink.

After devouring a quarter of the bottle, his thoughts travelled to his wife. He pulled out his phone and did his best to focus enough to dial her number.

"Hello?" Kate answered.

"Kate, honey, I need to talk to you," he pleaded with slurred words.

"Marty, there's not much to talk about at this point. You did what you felt you had to do, and I've done what I had to do."

"No, baby. We…we can make this work. It's only…"

"Why are you still talking to him?" a male voice said in the background to Kate.

"Who - who was that?"

"I think you should be more concerned with what's on CNN. Good bye, Marty." The phone went dead.

"Kate…Kate…Kate!" Marty yelled desperately into the receiver. She was gone. He threw the phone violently against the wall, causing it to shatter upon impact. Everything that he cherished in life began to dissipate before his eyes. Who in the hell was the man in the background? What was on CNN? He scrambled for the remote control and turned on the TV. It was already on the news channel.

Marty's eyes grew wide as he saw the CEO of Goldman at a press conference. He repeatedly apologized for the exposed scandal. He informed the press that investigators had been hired by the company and Marty Frankel was responsible for the manipulation of the gas contracts. He went on to say that Marty accepted responsibility for his actions, however, deceiving the American people would not be tolerated. And, because of that, Marty Frankel's employment was terminated immediately.

This backstabbing surprise hit Marty like a ton of bricks. He didn't know if he should scream in anger or cry from the hurt. He laughed. He laughed at the fact that his loyalty was repaid with deceit. He picked up the bottle of Scotch and drank. He drank until he was numb. His dependency on alcohol was born. His life had taken a tremendous turn for the worse, and he was not willing to experience a second of it sober...

CHAPTER 15

"I'm not letting this shit ride, T," Mack warned. They sat in the plush living room of Terry's condominium smoking blunts of their own.

"I don't want to let them niggas get away with this shit either, but we can't just run around killing muthafuckas on some nut shit. We've got more to lose now than we've ever had."

Mack was well aware of all that was at stake. The last thing he wanted was to destroy the empire that was being built by Terry and himself. The problem was he had recently become a businessman in the legal field, but he had lived the street life since an adolescent.

One rule of the streets was if someone waged war against you, either back down or take them to war.

"Everything we have is because of the streets. We're not ready to leave the streets alone, yet. If we don't do nothing, you better believe we're going to be the next in line to get hit."

"Maybe we should wait it out and let the dust settle before we turn it up," Terry suggested.

"Fuck that, cannon. Don't let this money make you soft. If we don't react, we're going to open the door for anybody to test us. This is part of the game, my nigga. They violated us. If they want war, then war it's gon' be!" Mack paused for a moment to take a long drag from his blunt. "I know how you felt about Twan. We have to bury him. Reek will never be able to walk again. My man might have to do a prison bid in a fuckin' wheel chair! I don't know about you, but I can't live with myself knowing I didn't do nothin' about this. This shit is personal. I'm going to handle it...with or without you."

Silence consumed the room as they continued to smoke. "You're not doing nothing by yourself, my nigga. We're in this together."

"I found out that the nigga who Reek killed was muscle for the twins," Mack revealed.

"Who the fuck is the twins?"

"Kahdeem and Quadir. They get money in North Philly. I had to punch Kahdeem in the mouth at a concert a couple of months ago, but it wasn't nothing too big, or at least I didn't think so."

"Oh, I know who you're talking about." Their images became clear in Terry's mind as Mack spoke. "They own that car wash at Broad and Lehigh Avenue, right?"

"Yeah, that's them," Mack answered. "They knew Twan was with us. I guess now that they're touchin' some money, they think they can try to run down on us."

"Fuck it, let's get them niggas out of the way."

"I'm gonna show 'em what happens when they play chicken with a Mack truck."

The electric-blue Audi RS7 pulled into Pit Stop Car Wash and Detail Shop, stopping in front of the office door. Quadir stepped out of his car into the brisk air, shaking the chill off. He was five feet nine, with a medium build and caramel toned skin. His well-kept shoulder length locks was the only distinction between him and his twin.

As usual, he was the first to arrive at the shop. It was 10:00 in the morning. The shop wasn't scheduled to open for business for another hour. With a little time to kill, Quadir decided to smoke his morning blunt. He wasn't quite finished rolling up the weed when he heard a light rap on the door. He got up to see a young, Hispanic woman on the other side.

He cracked the door partially open, and asked, "Can I help you?"

"Do you wanna buy this truck?" she asked. Her words were filled with attitude.

Quadir looked out the door's window and saw a clean white and tan Suburban equipped with chrome twenty-eight inch rims. "It's definitely nice, but I wasn't looking to buy a truck at the moment."

"You give me an offer and I'll take it. I'm sick of this *puta*," she ranted. "I do everything for him, and he gets that dirty bitch pregnant? Oh, hell no. I'll give this fucking truck away before he gets back in it!"

It was evident that the lady was emotional because of a failing relationship. If the Suburban looked as good on the inside as it did on the outside, there was no question he could get it for a steal. "Do you have the title?"

"Damn right. I legally own this truck." She spat.

"How many miles does it have?" Quadir asked.

"I think it has around thirty thousand miles," she said. "You can check the truck out for yourself. I just want to get him and all of his shit out of my fucking life. I don't want anything that reminds me of his no good ass." She folded her arms and continued to rant in Spanish.

Quadir stepped outside and walked toward the Suburban. Before he was able to reach it, he felt the searing pain of fifty thousand volts erupt into his body. He went rigid and immediately fell to the pavement.

Unaware of what was going on, his mind raced to find clarity. Before he was granted that opportunity, he was tazed again, for a longer period.

The excruciating pain completely immobilized him. A pillowcase was thrown over his head. His hands and feet were securely bound. He was picked up and tossed into the rear of the Suburban by the two men who attacked him.

"Lock up the shop and take his car. Put it in your garage. I'll be by to get it later," the man instructed her. He, then, jumped into the SUV and pulled off.

The uncomfortable ride lasted less than twenty minutes. Quadir was rustled out of the SUV and carried into some type of confine. Once placed into a chair and tightly secured to it, Jihad and Shawn left him...

CHAPTER 16

The light winds caused snowflakes to dance through the air before landing. Mack drove around the city in his Jeep, enjoying the warmth his vehicle provided, despite the blustering temperature outside.

Turning down Sigel Street, he saw a kid bundled up in a black Northface coat, skully and Nike ACG boots. Even the frigid weather couldn't deter him from manning the block and chasing his dream of reaching financial freedom by selling drugs.

The sight of him caused Mack to reflect back to his teenage years. He was the first person on the block hustling, and the last one to leave. While everyone was out partying and chasing women, he was on the block chasing money. That ambition played a pivotal role in him rising above the ranks.

As he drove nearer, the kid began to wave his hands in an

attempt to get Mack's attention. He recognized who the kid was and pulled over. The kid eagerly ran over to the driver's side, and Mack lowered his window.

"Wassup, ole head?" the kid asked through nearly numb lips.

"Wassup, Keith? What you doin' out here?"

"Shit, I gotta get this money. My stomach ain't gon' feed itself."

"I can dig that."

"You heard anything about the bawh, Reek?" Keith asked.

"It ain't lookin' too good right now. He's still in the hospital, and in custody," Mack informed him.

"Keepin' it real, it ain't been the same for me since he been gone. That nigga kept me with that work, and he was really gon' bless me...then, that shit happened. It's like my luck will never change for the better."

"Stop believing in luck. Believe in taking advantage of opportunity once it presents itself. You wanna go for a ride?"

Keith's eyes widened. "No question!" He didn't hesitate at the chance to cruise the city with a hood star. He darted around the Jeep, jumped inside, and adjusted the seat.

"Roll something up for us." Mack handed him a bag of high grade weed and a vanilla Blunt Wrap, before pulling off.

Mack drove around the city giving Keith much needed advice, which had become a rarity. Either the elders were reluctant to offer counsel, or the younger generation was unwilling to accept it. However, Keith appeared to absorb his words like a sponge.

During their conversation Mack was able to get a greater insight into Keith's mindset. He respected the young man's intellect and lack of naivety. He understood his hunger and eagerness to gain a greater position in the drug game.

Mack watched Keith grow up and he knew that Reek had him under his employ. He vaguely recalled a conversation when Reek told him he considered giving Keith an elevated position, but he wanted to be certain that Keith's loyalty was absolute first. Mack's phone rang, interrupting their discussion.

"Hello?"

"Wassup, Mack? I need to holla at you," Shawn said.

"Is everything taken care of?" Mack asked.

"Nah. I only talked to one of them."

"What the fuck you mean you only talked to one of them?" Mack's voice had risen. "Do you understand how important this is to me?"

"Come on, man. You know…"

"Come on, my ass. Don't fuckin' call me again until you talked to the other one!" Mack ended the call and banged his hand against the steering wheel in frustration. "Bitch ass twins," he mumbled to himself.

"Mack, I ain't tryin' to get in your business, but are you trying to get in touch with the twins from North Philly?" Keith asked.

He looked over at Keith, unsure of whether or not he should answer. "Why?"

"It ain't nothin' for me to get in touch with them niggas. I'm fuckin' their little sister. And he used to front…" Keith paused, looking over at Mack, unsure if he should continue.

"Go ahead and finish what you were saying," Mack demanded.

"He used to front me whatever I bought. But I only used to fuck with him when I couldn't catch Reek. I wasn't playin' both sides of the fence." Keith made sure to throw that last part in.

Maybe he was, or maybe he wasn't dealing with Reek and the twins at the same time. At the moment, that wasn't important. He had to make a decision as to if he should involve Keith in this situation. The bottom line was the button had been pushed. One of the twins had already been kidnapped and the clock was ticking. The other twin had to be captured within twenty-four hours or everything could go awry.

"How do you feel about the twins?" Mack asked.

"I don't give a fuck about them niggas. They know I'm out here struggling, and they never offered to put me on. Ever since they got on some Take Over the City shit, they stopped frontin' me work. And they want straight money. They don't give a damn about how much paper I bring them. On some real shit, I've been plottin' on getting them niggas."

After a moment of driving in silence, Mack looked over at Keith and asked, "You ready to get this money with SP?"

"I've been ready. All you gotta do is give me the ball and watch what I do with it."

"Aaight, here's what I want you to do…"

━━━━━━━━━━━━━

Keith called the twin's sister, Quianna, and convinced her that he wanted to spend the day with her. She gave him a little attitude because she hadn't heard from him in nearly a week, but after a few choice words, she gave in.

He was given eight thousand dollars, then dropped off at Quianna's place on Indiana Avenue. Keith approached her apartment and rang the doorbell. She opened the door dressed in a pair of gray, cotton, stretch shorts and a white T-shirt. Quianna was one size beyond thick, but her curvy figure remained intact. Keith couldn't help but notice her semi-hard nipples pushing against her tight fitting T-shirt, as a smile appeared on her face.

"Watchu want?" she asked with a false attitude, standing at the door with her hands on her hips.

"I want you." Keith answered.

She stepped to the side and he walked in. After removing his coat and getting comfortable, he rolled up a blunt and they smoked. It didn't take long before they were high and horny. After a few minutes of foreplay and teasing each other, Quianna grabbed Keith by his hand and led him to her bedroom. They pleasured each other until they were both sexed out.

"Boo, I'm going to take a shower. You comin'?" Quianna asked.

"Shit, I can't even move because of you. I'll take one later." He reached for his pants and removed a pack of Newports.

"Don't smoke that in here. You know I hate the smell of cigarettes."

"Aaight. I'm going in the living room."

She left to wash up. Keith popped a cigarette into his mouth, slid on his boxers, grabbed a lighter, and then went into the living room. He removed a burn out cell phone from his coat, lit his cigarette, and then called Kahdeem.

"Hello?" Kahdeem answered.

"Wassup, bruh? This is Keith."

"What's going on?"

"I need to see you."

"Aaight, give me a number."

"Eight."

"Eight what?" he asked skeptically.

"Eight stacks, my nigga."

"Are you serious?"

"Yeah, I'm at Quianna's crib. Come through."

"I'll be there in twenty minutes." They hung up.

Keith then called Mack. "You got fifteen minutes. Make sure you're ready." He turned his phone off, removing the large stack of money from his inside coat pocket. Never before had he held eight thousand dollars in his hands.

Some saw money as the root to evil. Keith saw it as a solution to his problems. Only if all the money he held was actually his. The cash had been given to him as a backup plan. He sat on the couch and thought about the possible direction his life could turn toward.

Quianna walked into the living room wearing nothing but a powder-blue thick cotton robe and matching house slippers. "Keith, where did you get all that money from?"

He quickly snapped out of his thoughts. "This is why you haven't heard from me in a few days," he lied. Keith stuffed the money back into his coat pocket. He had to come up with a way to keep Quianna busy for at least the next half hour. "Boo, I'm starving."

"Whatchu want to eat?"

"I want some fried chicken wings, macaroni and cheese…and some mashed potatoes and gravy."

"So, you just plan on fucking, eating and leaving?" Quianna crossed her arms across her full breasts.

Keith stood and walked up to her. His nose took in the sweet smell of green apple body wash that lingered on her skin after the shower. "Actually, I was thinking of making love to you throughout the night, and waking up in the morning with you in my arms." His words instantly softened her.

"That sounds nice." She blushed, revealing pretty, white teeth as she smiled, and then leaned in for a kiss that Keith was happy to give her. "Let me start preparing the food." She reluctantly stepped back.

"Hurry up before I change my mind and eat you." He smacked her on the butt. She giggled and turned to leave.

Keith rolled another blunt of weed and stood by the living room's window, peeking out into the streets while smoking. Within ten minutes a white Audi Q7 parked against the curb in front of Quianna's place. Keith's heart began to race. Kahdeem was early. It was too soon for Jihad and Shawn to be in position.

If Kahdeem made it to his sister's house, Keith would be forced to give him the money and the mission would have to be aborted. Kahdeem could not be kidnapped leaving his sister's house after doing a deal with Keith. There was no question he'd be the main suspect.

Kahdeem got out of his Audi and Keith cursed to himself as fear of the plan unraveling set in. His eyes grew wide as he saw two men run up on Kahdeem with their guns drawn. One of the men took Kahdeem's keys, the other pressed a gun to his chest, and forced him into the back seat of the Audi. The Audi pulled off with all three men inside.

Keith was spiked with adrenaline, watching the kidnapping take place. He scanned outside to see if there were any possible witnesses. The wintry streets were desolate. Confident that everything went smoothly, he walked into the kitchen and took a seat at the table.

"That chicken smells good, baby. How long before we eat?..."

CHAPTER 17

During the next two days, Keith continued with his regular routine. He was mindful not to do anything out of the norm to avoid any type of suspicion. Unsure of the twin's fate, combined with not hearing from Mack, Keith became nervous because of his role in the kidnapping.

After washing up and getting dressed, he grabbed a sandwich bag containing fifty ten-dollar bags of crack, his 9 mm Rugar, and left his apartment. He secured the door. When he turned around, he stopped in his tracks, and locked eyes with Mack who sat in the passenger's seat of Terry's new Mercedes S550.

"Wassup, cannon? You gon' get in, or you gon' stand there and stare at me?" Mack asked.

A sly smile crept onto Keith's face. He jumped in the back

seat, happy to know Mack was safe. "Nigga, why you ain't answer your phone?"

"I've been real busy, but I tried to call you this morning."

Keith pulled out his phone and looked at it. "I ain't even turn it on, yet."

"Keith, I want you to meet my man, T-Lova." Terry turned partially in his seat and gave Keith some dap.

"I heard a lot about you," Terry said. "You wanna ride with us for a while?"

"Yeah, but I'm dirty. I got some work and my gun on me. Let me run back in my crib and put it up. Plus, I gotta get ya money, Mack."

Keith got out of the car and rushed into his apartment. A few minutes later, he was back in the Mercedes. Terry pulled off. Keith tossed a brown paper bag over Mack's shoulder. It fell on his lap. "That's the eight stacks you gave me."

Mack removed the money from the bag. "Are you sure it's all here?"

"Yep," Keith said proudly.

"If I count it, and it's not all there, then what?"

"Then, I'm responsible for whatever's missing."

Mack twisted in his seat and handed the cash back to Keith. "That's the right answer."

"Huh?" Keith slowly extended his hand to accept the money, but his facial expression displayed confusion.

"When a soldier does wrong, he must be disciplined. When a solder does well, he must be rewarded. This is your reward."

"Damn. Thanks, Mack." Keith marveled at the money differently knowing that it now belonged to him. "How can I ever be disloyal to someone who wants me to do good?"

"Stay loyal to us and the sky's the limit," Terry added.

"It's not every day that we allow someone in our circle," Mack explained. "So, I think we should celebrate. You ready to spend some of that bread?"

"Hell no! I want to flip this bread. I never had this much money at one time before."

Terry and Mack looked at each other and laughed. "As long as you do the right things, you may have some problems, but money won't be one of them," Terry assured Keith.

"I'll tell you what, if you can blow those eight bands tonight, I'll give you another eight bands in the morning," Mack challenged. All Keith could do was smile. "Let's go to King of Prussia Mall, then tear Atlantic City up tonight."

"Shit, you just gave me an offer I can't refuse. Let's do it." Keith sat back in the comfortable leather seat.

After everything they said settled in, he leaned forward. "Ya'll know I'm only twenty, right?"

"So? What's that supposed to mean?"

"I'm not going to be able to get in the clubs out there."

Terry giggled. "When you're with SP you have diplomatic immunity." They eased into the mall's huge parking lot, got out, and entered.

"We ain't goin' shopping for hoodies and boots, li'l nigga," Mack joked. "You gotta be on your grown and sexy shit tonight."

They strolled into Nieman Marcus and Keith ran around the department store like a puppy taken off the leash. Within ten minutes, he came back to Mack and Terry holding a Prada knit sweater and a pair of Polo cotton slacks.

He displayed the outfit that he had picked out, waiting for

their approval. They simultaneously shook their heads in disdain.

"You goin' to the gambling spot on 32nd and York wearing that?" Mack cracked.

"Put that shit back on the sale rack, and come with us. We gon' get you right, young bawh," Terry said.

They left the mall carrying bags containing tailored button down dress shirts and slacks by Giorgio Armani, Hugo Boss and Salvatore Ferrogamo. They chose different designer hard bottom shoes that matched their outfits.

As evening approached, Mack picked up the champagne tan Maserati Levante SUV, which was pre-ordered specifically for Dynasty Luxury Rentals, before they boarded the highway.

Once Atlantic City, New Jersey, became visible, Keith couldn't contain his excitement. The young man was captivated by the larger than life casino hotels and beautiful bright lights that accompanied them. Never had he been afforded the opportunity to travel outside the State of Pennsylvania. He was inside the most luxurious vehicle he'd ever saw in his life, with more money than he'd ever had in his life. And he was in the company of two of the richest men he'd ever met. Mack and Terry had single-handedly changed his quality of living. In such a short period of time, they had become amongst the most important people to him.

"Oh, shit!" Keith blurted out. "That's the Borgata Hotel and Casino right there!"

"You heard of that place before?" Mack asked.

"Damn right. That's where all the stars go," Keith shot back.

"Well, since we're hood stars, then that's where we need to be," Terry suggested.

Mack navigated the Maserati into the parking lot. Once inside the grand hotel, Terry used one of his credit cards to rent three indulgent and expensive suites.

With bags in hand, they retreated to their quarters. Less than two hours later, the trio reunited at the hotel's main lobby. People who crossed their path had little choice but to take notice of the impeccably dressed men. Their demeanor and attire cast an aura of prestige.

Keith was very perceptive. He quickly came to the understanding that he had to take control of his youthful energy and emulate the laid-back swagger of Mack and Terry. He remained in step with them as they strolled to the casino.

Their first stop was the blackjack table. They sat down and began to play, and the cards were not kind to them. In a short amount of time, Mack lost six thousand dollars in chips, Terry had lost a little over four thousand, and, Keith, who had been playing conservatively, was down nine hundred.

"This muthafucka is raping us." Terry gave the evil eye to the dealer. "Let's hit the craps table," he suggested.

"Alright. This is my last hand." Mack placed six thousand in chips on the table. The dealer dealt him two cards, a jack and a ten. Mack had twenty points. The dealer's two cards was an eight and a seven. "Yeah!" Mack jumped to his feet with a confident smile. "I'm good. Hit yourself," he instructed the dealer.

The dealer removed a card from the deck and expertly flipped it. The card was an ace. With only sixteen points, he was forced to hit himself again. Removing another card, he turned it over. The card was a five. The dealer now had twenty-one points. Mack's smile vanished as he stared at the cards in disbelief. The dealer glanced at Mack, then swooped up his chips and the cards.

"What the fuck you lookin' at me with that stupid ass expression for?"

"Sorry, sir," the thin, older white man said nervously.

"Sorry? You just took more money from me than you make in a month and all you can say is you're sorry? Don't be sorry, be a dealer, and deal me another fuckin' hand!"

"P...please place your bet on the table, sir." The man was afraid to look Mack in the eyes.

"Come on, bruh. If you stay you're gonna be chasing the money you lost all night. Let's try our hands with the dice." Terry stood up, and Keith followed suit. Reluctantly, Mack got up from the table, as well. He glared at the dealer while he stood to his feet. The dealer's eyes remained on the table.

"H...have a good night, gentlemen," the dealer pushed the words out.

"Shut ya ass up!" Mack snapped.

It didn't get much better for them at the craps table. Mack was on the dice and he couldn't hit his numbers.

"Mack, let me get the dice," Keith suggested.

"Aaight, hold up." Mack rolled a six. After placing three thousand dollars in bets, he rolled the dice again. The numbers on the dice added up to seven. Terry was just as upset as Mack, because he was betting on Mack's shot.

"Mack, I'm telling you, let me get the dice," Keith pleaded.

"Here, man." Mack relinquished the dice in frustration.

Keith placed a one hundred dollar bet and rolled a seven on his first shot. He won.

"Beginner's luck," Mack mumbled.

"You told me not to believe in luck, remember?" Keith shook and threw the dice onto the felt lined table. The dice landed on...eleven. He won again. "Yes!" Keith exploded, throwing his hands in the air victoriously.

Terry saw that Keith was hitting his numbers at an alarming rate. He placed a three thousand dollar bet on Keith's roll. Keith rolled and Terry won. That made Mack a believer. By now a small crowd had gathered to watch the spectacle. Roll after roll, he barely missed. Because of Keith's hot hand they won all that was lost at the blackjack table, plus a lot more.

Noticing that he was a few thousand dollars richer, Keith dropped the dice as quickly as he initially picked them up. He began to gather his chips.

"Whatchu doin'? Terry asked confused.

"I'm done." Keith was now organizing his chips.

"You can't be done. You're killing 'em," Mack said.

"Let's quit while we're ahead," Keith stated flatly.

"Fuck this money. We're always going to be ahead," Terry shot.

"It may be nothin' to ya'll, but this is everything to me. I've never had this much money before and I ain't gon' lose it as quick as I got it." The look on Keith's face gave them a clear view of just how important that money was to him.

After looking at the situation through Keith's eyes, Mack smiled. "Say no more, cannon. Let's go."

"What it do, Mack?" Everyone turned around to see who was the source of the southern accented voice.

"Oh, shit. Wassup, 2 Chainz?" Mack walked up and greeted his friend with a pound and a hug.

Terry gave him a pound as well. They had been introduced to 2 Chainz through a mutual friend who recommended their rental car service to him. 2 Chainz instantly took a liking to them. Just like him, they were brought up in the streets, and now working towards creating a legitimate lifestyle.

"I'm on my way to HQ. I'm performing there tonight. Ya'll comin' through?"

"You know we can't miss that," Terry said.

2 Chainz reached into his pocket and pulled out three tickets. "Here, these are VIP tickets. Only the best for the best."

Mack accepted the tickets. "Thanks, man. We'll see you later on." They shook hands and 2 Chainz left.

Keith remained frozen in the same spot holding a shocked expression the entire time.

"Damn, this night keeps getting better and better." Mack tucked the tickets away with a generous smile spread across his face.

"Do ya'll know who that was?" Keith finally spoke up. Before anyone had a chance to respond, he continued. "That was 2 Chainz in person!" Keith was talking more to himself than to Mack or Terry. "My favorite rapper was just in front of me. I gotta get his autograph." He spun around in the direction that 2 Chainz left.

Mack quickly reached out and was able to get a hold on Keith's arm. "Slow down young money. You'll see him again tonight," Mack promised.

2 Chainz's performance was electric. The crowd remained in a frenzy even after his show was over. The intense energy that he cast to his audience was undeniable.

Moments later he joined Mack, Terry and Keith in the VIP section, a slightly elevated area above the dance floor, separated by a waist high wall. The tables were adorned with chilled bottles of Ciroc, Ace of Spades, Conjur and D'Usse'.

2 Chainz, Mack and Terry sat back, relaxed on the comfortable couches with bottles in their hands, enjoying the music. The combination of alcohol and youthful energy had Keith too

wired to remain seated. He diddy-bopped to every song while waving his bottle of Ace of Spades Rosé in the air.

"Yo, Mack!" a man yelled out from the floor. "Mack, wassup, nigga? Can I get in VIP with you?"

Mack looked to see who was yelling his name. It was Raheem, a stocky man, medium height, with a Caesar cut. He was wearing a black T-shirt, black fitted jeans and three large gold chains. Mack used to serve him weight, but he hadn't dealt directly with him in about a year.

"If I could, I would...I'm a guest myself, Scrap," Mack shouted over the music.

"Nigga, you actin' funny 'cause you with 2 Chainz? Stop dick ridin'. He ain't the only nigga with money!" Raheem pulled out a pocket full of bills and flung them into the VIP section.

Mack's anger had risen in a heartbeat, but before he had a chance to react, Keith grabbed a fresh gold bottle from the table and hopped over the divider. The champagne bottle glistened as the club's lights reflected off its shiny surface. In one fluid, swift movement, Keith raised the bottle in the air. He was so quick, Raheem could only raise his hands to block what was surely coming. His reflex wasn't enough. Keith's momentum caused the bottle to come down with brute force, splitting Raheem's forehead. The impact buckled his knees. Keith swung again, connecting. That blow dropped Raheem. Keith straddled him, raining blow after blow to his mug. The thick bottle never broke as it was continuously bashed against Raheem's face, causing distorting damage.

Mack and Terry rushed over to pull Keith off Raheem. Blinded by anger, he struggled against them to get back at his victim. The club's security came and quickly dissolved the situation by escorting everyone outside.

"Yo, what the fuck's wrong with you?" Terry scolded Keith.

"Man, fuck that. Ain't nobody gon' disrespect ya'll in front of me. I don't give a fuck who it is." Keith looked Terry in the eyes as they stood outside the club, feeling the crisp bite of the night's weather seep through their expensive fabrics.

"You know what, I gotta respect that," Terry admitted reluctantly. "But you can't always react out of anger. People judge us by our actions. You've heard the saying a million times: Real G's move in silence. You gotta keep the gangster and the gentleman separated. No one should be able to pull the goon out of you, but you."

"You're right," Keith acknowledged.

"What's done is done. We're not gon' let that shit spoil our night. It's still early. I'm about to text 2 Chainz and tell him to meet us at the Borgota casino. Let's see if we can knock off some broads..."

CHAPTER 18

Detective Todd sat in his congested cubicle on the second floor of the 35th police precinct at Broad and Champlost Streets. There had been a spike of murders over the past week, and the additional cases that were being assigned to him were beginning to take a toll. He and Latrice decided to work close, long and hard to bring closure to some of the open cases.

For the moment, their focus was on the triple shooting/double homicide that occurred at 1463 Upsal Street. They discovered that Antwon Green, from Syracuse, New York leased the house where the shooting occurred. According to the landlord, he had lived there for seven months. The second murder victim, the man who was believed to have been killed while trying to rob Antwon, was identified as Cornell Watts. He had an extensive record, including drug possession, armed robbery and assault. Cornell was also a suspect in an unsolved robbery/homicide that occurred two and a half years ago.

Reek had undergone his third surgery. The hospital contacted Todd earlier that day to inform him that although his condition was still listed as critical, he was stable and coherent enough to endure a brief conversation. So far, Reek was their biggest hope to solve the crimes.

Latrice walked into her brother's cubicle carrying a small stack of papers. "The records to Tyreek Simmons' cell phone came in."

"Great. Let's see who was so important that Mr. Simmons felt compelled to call him while shot."

"I already checked it out. The call was placed to a man named, Terry Maddox."

"Okay. I'll run his name through the database to see what comes up."

"I did that too," Latrice gloated.

"Well, damn, sis. What do you need me for?"

"Batman had a sidekick. I guess Wonder Woman needs one, too."

Todd sucked his teeth at her snide remark. Latrice took a seat, placed the paper on the edge of his desk, and thumbed through them until she found the printout.

Latrice's eyes were fixed on the paper as she spoke. "His record isn't too bad. He had a criminal sales of a controlled substance when he was sixteen. He received a youthful offender adjudication for that. He was arrested for attempted murder five years ago, but the charge was eventually dismissed."

"So it's either he's not doing much now-a-days, or he's been slipping through the cracks," Todd commented.

"I'm leaning more towards the latter. I dug a little deeper and found that he's the co-owner of Dynasty Luxury Rentals."

Todd's eyebrows creased while trying to put the few pieces

together. He Googled the company, then visited its website. "Wow." His eyes widened as he took in what the monitor displayed. "This isn't some nickel and dime business. Every car that they rent is exotic. Someone invested some major money into that place." Todd clicked through every page of the website. "It's located on Passyunk Avenue in South Philly."

"I think we need to have a talk with this guy," Latrice said.

Todd shut the computer off. "The last one to the car has to drive." Without saying a word, Latrice shot out of the cubicle and dashed toward the elevator.

━━━━━━━━━━━━

Todd pulled the Chevy Impala into the parking lot of Dynasty Luxury Rentals. The police-issued cruiser stuck out like a sore thumb among all the other beautiful automobiles. Latrice and Todd exited their sedan, and casually examined a few vehicles. They did their best not to gawk, before they walked inside the building.

The lavish waiting room complimented the theme of the business. Bright white walls were adorned with artistic paintings of beautiful cars and an eighty inch, flat screen smart TV. Plush, black, Italian leather chairs were strategically placed around the room. An elegant glass table held an assortment of car and luxury magazines. It didn't take long before an attractive, young white lady approached them.

"Welcome to Dynasty Luxury Rentals. My name is Kerri. How may I help you?" she asked with an infectiously polite and upbeat attitude.

"I'm Detective Latrice Reed, and this is Detective Todd Reed. We're homicide detectives." Latrice produced her badge, then placed it back on her waist next to her holstered firearm. The cops maintained eye contact with Kerri as her smile dissipated. "Is Mister Terry Maddox in?"

Kerri took a half step backwards, looking at the detectives as if they had morphed into a pair of scary creatures. "Y-yes," she stammered, "one moment, please." Kerri turned around and walked off.

It didn't take long before Terry emerged from his rear office impeccably dressed in a charcoal gray Brooks Brothers suit. "Good afternoon. I'm Terry. How can I help you?" He shook hands with the detectives.

The detectives introduced themselves. Todd was the first to speak. "We're investigating a double homicide and shooting that occurred on Upsal Street. Do you mind coming down to the station so we can ask you a few questions?"

"I don't mind you asking me a few questions, but is it a must that I go down to the station? I'm the only one in charge who's here at the moment."

"This really won't take long. It's standard procedure to conduct any in depth questioning of possible witnesses at the station." Latrice did her best to make her explanation sound harmless.

"So that everything I say can be recorded?" Terry asked, but it came across as more of a statement.

"Well, yes," Todd answered truthfully.

"Okay. Let me make a call so I can get someone to take over while I'm gone." Terry walked over to the secretary's desk and called Mack. He explained what was going on, and asked him to come down to the business. After hanging up, he returned to the detectives who appeared not to have moved an inch since he first left them. "Are you guys ready?"

"Sure."

They walked casually to the police cruiser. On the outside Terry appeared to be cool and calm. However, on the inside, he was as nervous as a fat man on a tightrope. Along the ride to the precinct, Todd and Latrice created casual conversation. Terry interacted seamlessly with them, but the core of his thoughts were on the interrogation that lay ahead. He was a prominent drug dealer in Philadelphia. He had used the proceeds from his joint drug operation with his friend and partner, Mack, to create a lucrative legitimate business.

But Terry knew that their main focus would not be on how he obtained the business. After all, they were homicide detectives.

Worry settled in as the vision of the twins' murders, he and Mack committed played through his mind. A homicide detective's job was to uncover evidence. He sensed that he wasn't dealing with a pair of rookies. What did they know?

The ride came to an end, along with the conversation. Terry was escorted inside the building and into a small room that had a cheap metal desk and three uncomfortable metal folding chairs. The despair of the room begged for any visitors to hurry and leave. They left him in solitude for awhile, but Terry knew he wasn't completely alone in that chamber. Nestled in the upper corner of the wall was a tiny video camera. Without making direct eye contact with the camera, Terry removed his suit jacket, placed it on the back of the chair, and waited patiently.

Todd entered the room carrying a few files. Latrice was behind him with two cups of steaming coffee in her hands.

"Would you like some coffee?" she asked.

"No. Thank you," Terry declined.

"Cigarette?" Latrice asked.

"No, I don't smoke."

"Okay, Terry." Todd let out a deep sigh and took a seat opposite him. Latrice followed suit. "Let's get to why you were asked to come down here. We're investigating the murder of Antwon Green and the shooting of Tyreek Simmons. Can you tell us what, if anything, you know about this?"

"Antwon was a good friend of mine that I've known since I lived in Syracuse. I met Reek through Twan. He's a cool, young man that I took a liking to."

"Do you have any idea why they were targeted?" Latrice asked.

"No."

"What are the streets saying?"

"I don't know. I'm not in the streets."

"Come on, man. I'm not convinced by the expensive suit and your fancy business. Those guys were in the street life and I know you have ties to the streets as well. Do I look like I was fucking born yesterday?" Todd's voice escalated, signifying his mounting frustration.

"Listen, Mr. Reed. If you want to ask me about what happened to my friends, feel free. But if you brought me down here to accuse me of all this other bullshit, you'll have to do that while my lawyer is present." Terry's words came out even and filled with confidence. His face showed no signs of intimidation.

His reply was a strong gush of wind pushing Todd back in his chair.

Todd was unable to conceal his vexation. "Do you know that Tyreek tried to call you while shot?"

"Yes."

"Why would he think to call you, as opposed to the cops, or even his mother?" Latrice asked.

"He really looked up to me. I let him hang out with me at my business over the past couple of weeks. I wanted to show him my way of life. I promised that if he proved he wanted to work, I would give him a job. I know he thinks highly of me. That would be my only guess as to why he tried to call me."

The questioning continued, but they obtained little to no additional information to aide their investigation. There was no doubt in their minds that Terry knew more than he was willing to tell. The problem was there was nothing that could be done about it. Todd handed Terry his card and asked him to give him a call if he heard anything. Terry falsely promised that he would. They offered him a ride back to his business. He respectfully declined and called a friend to pick him up.

"So, where do we go from here?" Todd asked.

"To the hospital. Let's see what Tyreek has to say."

The Reed detectives entered Einstein Hospital, spoke to the doctors who were responsible for the care of Reek, and the security. Afterwards, they entered his room.

Tyreek was conscious, but it was evident that prescribed medication had him heavily sedated.

Latrice approached the bed looking at the slender, baby-faced, young man who lay helplessly in the hospital bed with nothing but a thin white hospital gown partially covering his body. A sense of sadness came over her. She just couldn't come to grips with why young men and women risked permanently damaging, or losing their lives, chasing a dream that would never be caught.

The doctors had informed them that Reek lost approximately ninety percent of the use of his lower body. It would take months, possibly years, of rehabilitation before the likelihood of any noticeable signs of improvement would occur.

"Good morning, Mr. Simmons," Latrice said.

"Morning." Reek mumbled. He turned his head and cracked his eyes open just enough to get a peek at the two figures standing at the side of his bed.

Todd delivered his routine introduction, then asked if it was okay to question him.

"Law-yer," Reek forced the word out.

"It's too late to play the tough guy role, son. You can't be a tough guy rolling through prison in a wheel chair doing life for murder."

"Lawyer!" He raised his voice, then relaxed his head back on the pillow. He winced from the pain caused by the sudden, and subtle movement.

"Okay. That's fine with us, Mr. Simmons," Latrice said politely. "Have a good day, and I wish you the best." She grabbed her brother by the arm and ushered him out of the room.

"What in the hell are we going to do now?" Todd growled through clenched teeth.

"The same thing we've been doing, continue digging."

"It'll be senseless to ask the DA to charge him with murder. There's no way any warm blooded jury would convict him based on what we have. Especially when they see that he's paralyzed."

"I'll call the DA and talk to him. At the least, we can charge him with illegally possessing the gun," Latrice said.

Todd spun around toward his sister, wide eyed. "I have an

idea…let's go to the office."

———

Back at the police precinct they continued to work on the case. Things weren't going too well on Latrice's end. She talked to the district attorney. As expected, he refused to charge Reek with murder, explaining that it would be too easy for him to prevail with a claim of self-defense. He agreed to charge him with unlawful possession of a weapon.

Todd's prudence proved to be beneficial. According to his theory, if someone had been shot with a large caliber gun, there was no way he could avoid going to the hospital without dying from complications. He called every hospital in Pennsylvania, with no success. He then took a shot by calling hospitals in the tri-state area. Thirteen exhausting phone calls later, he reached out to Cooper Hospital in Camden, New Jersey. To his relief, he was informed that a patient was released from the hospital three days earlier who sustained a .44 caliber bullet to the shoulder. The patient claimed to be the victim of a random robbery in Camden. His name was listed as Kevin Singleton.

Todd ran the name in the NCIC database. Not only did Kevin have a lengthy criminal history, but he was also from Philadelphia. Releasing a triumphant smile, Todd called the Homicide Task Force, relayed all the information he had obtained on Kevin, and requested they bring him in on suspicion of murder.

———

Two days later, Todd and Latrice received a phone call from Homicide Task Force informing them that their suspect, Kevin Singleton, had been brought into custody. They raced back to the police precinct. Kevin had been in the interrogation room for an hour where he nervously waited for someone, anyone, to enter the room. He felt a slight sense of relief when the two homicide detectives walked in.

"So, how's your shoulder doing, Kevin?" Todd jumped right in.

"Huh? Uhhh…it's okay."

"Where were you shot?" Todd continued.

"Right here." He pointed to his left shoulder.

"Not where on your body!" Todd stood, placed his hands flat on the desk, and leaned forward. "Where were you shot at? What fucking location?"

"On…in, um…New Jersey, sir," Kevin stammered.

Todd sat down and relaxed in his chair, calming down. "Now we're getting somewhere," he smiled to Latrice, who nodded her head in agreement. "You see, I get to ask you a question, you get to lie to me, then I get to charge you with the two murders, and an attempted murder that happened on Upsal Street," Todd explained matter-of-factly.

The mention of the murders hit Kevin like a bolt of lightning. He sat straight up in his chair. "Man, I ain't kill nobody! I don't know what you're talking about." He rolled his eyes and folded his arms across his chest defiantly.

"You didn't?" Todd asked with one eyebrow raised. "Well, I'm going to tell you what I know. I know the bullet that was lodged in your shoulder has been sent off to forensics to see if it was discharged from the same .44 that was found on one of the victims." Todd slowly slid a brown folder across the desk.

Kevin cautiously opened it. His eyes locked on the beaten

and bloodied body of the large man who was tied to a chair. He gave his attention to each photograph. The final picture was of his friend, Tah, who lay contorted on the floor with a gaping, blood-soaked hole in his head. Beads of perspiration began to materialize on his forehead.

Todd noticed that Kevin was paying particular attention to that picture. He decided to continue. "I also know that we're going to take a blood sample from you – whether voluntarily or by obtaining a warrant – and it will be compared to the blood samples that were taken from the scene of the crime. Lastly, I know that when both the ballistics and DNA results come back, you will never have the luxury of freedom again. You're going to begin a new life with Fishbone. Do you know who that is?"

Kevin shook his head no.

"Fishbone is a three hundred pound, muscle built, balled headed black dude who likes to knock fake tough ass dudes like you out and take their virginity." Todd couldn't suppress the chuckle, but it was obvious that Kevin was more concerned with the evidence that was being compiled against him.

"Make no mistake about it, honey," Latrice chimed in, "You're in a hell of a lot of trouble, but you can certainly lighten the load on yourself. Give us something to work with and we may be able to negotiate a favorable deal with the district attorney on your behalf."

Kevin remained quiet.

Latrice sensed that he was weakening. She had to take advantage. "Listen, baby, I know this is hard on you. You're in a horrible position, and you're scared. Believe me, I understand. Whatever you do, don't dig your hole deeper than it already is. Your best option is to minimize the damage. Try to right your wrongs. That's the only way we can help you, Kevin."

"I'm...I'm scared." Kevin broke down and sobbed.

"I know you are, honey. Talk to me and let me know what's going on."

"None of this was supposed to happen. It wasn't supposed to turn out like that." Kevin cried into his hands. He wiped the tears from his face and stared down at the table before continuing. "The twins sent us to rob Twan, and the shit went bad. Now the twins are dead."

"Are you talking about Khadeem and Quadir Wilson?" Todd asked.

"Yeah."

The charred remains of the brothers were found inside a stolen Suburban that had been set on fire.

"If he found out that they were the ones who ordered the robbery, he probably already know I had something to do with it. He's gon' try to kill me, too." Kevin rambled on, brimming with fear.

"Who are you talking about? Who do you think killed the twins?"

"It was Mack and his man T-Lova…"

CHAPTER 19

Winter had receded and the welcomed spring temperatures eased in. The vibrant afternoon sun energized the entire Manhattan.

That brightness, however, was barely able to penetrate the drab, rundown one bedroom apartment Marty Frankel inhibited. His tiny domicile was sparsely furnished and unkempt. The putrid smell of alcohol, spoiled takeout food, and stale air infested his living quarters. A far cry from the clean, lavish home and high-end lifestyle he once enjoyed.

A matty haired, scruffy bearded Marty had finally awakened. He trudged to the bathroom like a zombie to relieve himself. Hung over from the night before, his balance and aim was off.

Urine splattered all over the toilet and he didn't care to clean his mess, or even give the toilet a flush, for that matter.

He made his way to the kitchen and opened the refrigerator door. There was a single can of beer inside. He grabbed it. There were a few drops left. His need to consume alcohol intensified. He searched around the sink's countertop, which was cluttered with old liquor and beer bottles for one that contained alcohol. They were all empty. He inspected the bottles that were strewn around the living room floor along with piles of *Investment Business Daily* and *Wall Street Journal* newspapers. Nothing.

With less than one hundred and seventy dollars, and uncertain of when or how he would receive any money, he threw on a ragged pair of blue sweat pants, his old Harvard college sweater, and a worn pair of New Balance sneakers. He then took ten dollars and walked to the liquor store.

Moving through the congested New York City streets, Marty paid little attention to anyone. While on his mission, his mind remained blank. That had become his method of dealing with life's issues.

He had been abandoned by his wife, betrayed by the company he worked for, and outcast by his friends.

It was him against the world, but unfortunately he was losing the battle by a wide margin.

Not focusing on where he was going, Marty collided into a man who hurried out of a bistro, nearly causing him to drop his lunch, and spill the drinks he balanced in both hands.

"Hey, watch where you're going!" The young man checked his tailored suit to make sure no contents were spilled on it, glaring at the disheveled man who bumped into him. The weathered person looked extremely familiar. He took a deeper look. "Marty?...Marty Frankel? Is that you?"

There were plenty of rumors circulating about the condition of Marty. It brought surprising pain to see that there was truth to the stories which were told at the Goldman Building.

"Sorry about that, Vincent," Marty mumbled. He proceeded to walk away until Vincent grabbed him by the arm stopping him.

"Hold on a second, Mr. Frankel. I just want you to know that your hard work at Goldman's was not in vain. You've taught me things that no one else would have been able to. Hell, even if they had the knowledge, they wouldn't have been willing to share it."

For the first time, Marty raised his head high enough to look Vincent in the eyes. He continued, "Since you've been gone, my position was elevated. Now I work for the Capital Markets Group. In all honesty, it's you that I have to thank for that. I modeled myself after you," Vincent explained.

"Thank you, Vince." Marty placed a hand on his shoulder. "You have always been a hardworking and intelligent kid." Marty glanced over to the street where a pristine navy-blue Mercedes S550 Maybach Edition was parked. Jack, Marty's former supervisor, and the cause of his current situation, sat in the back seat of the large and luxurious automobile in repose. He seemed oblivious to them as they conversed, with pedestrians walking around them. Feelings of anger and hurt that was deeply buried abruptly resurfaced. "Have you ever heard of a king snake, Vince?" Marty asked.

"Uh, I think so. Why?"

"A king snake can easily co-exist with it's own species, but it will not hesitate to devour another one if the need arises. Be careful, son."

"Mr. Frankel, you have too much knowledge in that brain of yours. Please don't let it go to waste. If you leave the alcohol alone and get back on track, I'm certain there's something I can do for you. Here's my number." Vincent pulled out a business card from his inside coat's pocket and handed it to Marty. "If you ever need any help, give me a call."

Marty accepted the card, thanked Vincent, and walked off.

Vincent got into the back seat of the Maybach with Jack. The parable that Marty had given him lingered in the back of his mind.

As Marty walked down the busy street, he mentally sank lower and lower. Disgusted by the ragged clothes he wore and his appearance, he knew that the time to change was upon him. He had come to the conclusion that the hardest part of life was living through failure. The very first time life had knocked him down he couldn't muster the strength to get back up. He had quit. The old, ambitious Marty was still somewhere inside of him, he simply needed to be pulled to the forefront of his existence.

With an unprecedented surge of inner strength, Marty decided to walk past the liquor store. Instead, he walked a few blocks further to Starbucks…

CHAPTER 20

While surfing the Internet, Terry came across a nicely-sized, defunct car dealership available for lease in New York City. The opportunity to expand Dynasty Luxury Car Rental immediately came to mind. He wanted to see the property in person.

Keith was making great strides in the relationship he was building with Terry and Mack. He had proven to be a good hustler by quickly and efficiently moving the packages that were being fronted to him.

He also proved his commitment to SP when he pistol whipped a local hustler into unconsciousness on the corner for talking disrespectfully about Terry and Mack behind their backs. However, all of this was done while they were in relatively close range. Terry wanted to test Keith to see how he would act knowing the bosses were not in the city.

Terry informed Keith that they were going out of town for a

few days. He gave Keith the keys to his new Tesla along with a few instructions.

Terry scheduled an appointment with the real estate agent, then he and Mack made the trip to New York City. They were financially capable of expanding their luxury rental car service. Mack agreed with Terry that Manhattan was an ideal location for their business. Before meeting with the agent, they stopped at Starbucks.

"I was thinking...we have to work on creating a more diverse portfolio," Mack mentioned to Terry.

"Yeah, we have to start investing our money into some different things. We gotta start making our paper grow from more angles. We're getting beyond the point of working for our money. We have to start making our money work for us."

"I agree with you, bruh. Did you have something in mind?" Terry asked as they stood in line, waiting to place their orders.

"I was thinking about purchasing stock in Facebook," Mack answered.

"I don't know about that. I read somewhere that they just started turning a profit, and who knows how long that's going to last. What about Twitter?"

They turned around at the same time due to the snickering of a disheveled, middle-aged man who stood behind them in line. With a roll of their eyes, they continued their conversation.

"Twitter might be worth investing in. Shit, I'm always tweeting," Mack stated.

The chuckles turned into outright laughter from the man who stood behind them in line.

"What's funny, my man?" Terry had become agitated.

"You two ding bats," the man replied, smirking.

"Us?"

"Yeah. Typical guys making typical mistakes. You work your butts off to accumulate some money, then you want to invest in the first company you heard about on TV. And as soon as your investment sinks, you're back to square one," Marty began laughing at the thought of it all.

"Can you believe this?" Mack asked. "We're getting advice on investing from this dude who can't even afford a decent outfit." They looked at Marty and burst into a laughing fit of their own.

Marty took offense. "I've given away more money than either of you could spend in ten years. I'm still shitting out food that you idiots can't pronounce! You got one of those smart phones, Google my name, it's Marty Frankel." He spelled it for clarification. "I've made people more money than they could have ever imagined." His rant captured Mack and Terry's attention. Marty was usually a reserved person, but the absence of alcohol in his system had him on edge.

"Maybe you was somebody back in the day, but right now all I see is a washed up old man," Terry spat, wanting to put an end to the back and forth.

"That's your problem. While you're focusing on one area, you're missing the bigger picture." Failing to realize they were next, Marty side stepped them, and placed his order.

Mack pulled out a few bills and paid for the man's drink. Marty gave him a simple nod of acknowledgement. "So, what do you think is a good stock to invest in?"

"None," Marty said flatly, sipping his espresso. He winced from the heat of the coffee which was much different than the liquid his body had grown accustomed to.

"Why do you say that?"

After forcing down another swig, Marty said, "Stocks have

been a major investment opportunity for years, but there's going to be a major shift in dominance of the electronic market."

"What does that mean?"

"That means a huge opportunity for Market Access Holdings, which is an electronic trading system for bonds. Your invested funds could receive a five year average return of twenty-nine point two percent versus twenty-one point five percent for the Standard and Poor's."

The man's knowledge of financial investing intrigued Mack. "Thanks for the advice, Marty." The two shook hands.

Because of Mack's sudden change of attitude, Marty decided to give him a piece of advice. "Listen, young man, if you're looking for some quick money, purchase shares of Western Union. It'll jump eight point eight percent in the next three weeks. Once it reaches its peak, sell your shares." With that said, Marty turned and left.

"Do you think pops knows what he's talking about?" Terry asked skeptically.

"Hell no. What I look like listening to him? If he knew so much about investing, he wouldn't look like he's a day away from being homeless. He's burnt out." Mack responded. His words may have come out with confidence, but deep down he wasn't so sure. An old adage came to him: *The wisdom of the teacher is much more important than his appearance.* They brushed their encounter to the side, ordered their drinks, and then left Starbucks.

The meeting with the real estate agent went well. They explained to the realtor that the property needed major renovations to suit their needs. She contacted the owner and he was willing to negotiate reasonable lease and price terms. With a fair offer on the table, Terry and Mack promised to make a decision and get back with them relatively soon.

Terry and Mack remained in New York City for Friday and Saturday. They were back in Philadelphia by early Sunday evening. Mack drove directly to their lounge house on the eight hundred block of Price Street. Once there, Terry sent Keith a text telling him to come to the house. He was anxious to see if his new car had been taken care of.

Mack grabbed a Blunt Wrap, removed a bright green, sticky nugget of Berry Kush from the Tupperware bowl that was filled with the exotic strain of marijuana, and rolled it up. They smoked and talked about what business needed to be handled. It was time to collect their money from the streets, which amounted to a little over one hundred and thirty thousand dollars. Their shipment of cocaine was expected to arrive within the next two days. The money needed to be counted and packaged in advance so it could be quickly inserted into the panels of the delivery vehicle after the drugs were removed.

Terry picked up his cell phone and called Jihad.

"Hello?" Jihad answered.

"What's shakin', sun?"

"I'm chillin'. Where you at?"

"I'm at the cool out. Come through, I need to holla at you."

"Come through? Nigga, I'm in Miami."

"Yo, what the fuck you doin' in Miami?"

"You know Wiz Khalifah invited us to the party he's throwing at King of Diamonds."

"Nigga, we said we wasn't going!" Terry shouted.

"Nah, you said you wasn't going. Me and Shawn is down here, playboy."

"We got a ton of work to do up here, and you gon' bounce out of town like that?" Terry growled into the pone. "So it's fuck us, huh?"

"T, you buggin' the fuck out. We bust our asses every day for ya'll...for the movement. But, damn, my nigga, we need some time to enjoy ourselves, too."

"How in the fuck are you gonna decide when to bounce out of town without at least taking care of your business first?"

"You know what? You're right, boss," Jihad said sarcastically.

"What? Don't fuckin' play with me, nigga! Who the..." The line went dead. "Hello?...Hello?" Realizing that no one was on the other end, Terry cursed Jihad aloud in frustration. He was so entrenched by the argument that he didn't notice Keith enter the house.

"Wassup?" Mack asked Terry.

"Jihad and Shawn are down in Miami partying."

"What? Oh, them niggas think they runnin' shit now?"

"Yeah, they're getting too big headed."

"Here, T." Keith disrupted the momentary silence. He tossed Terry the keys to the Tesla along with a paper bag.

"What's this?" Although Terry's anger was still present, he was simmering down a bit.

"That's twenty stacks," Keith answered. "The bawh, Khabir, pulled me over while I was in the Tesla, thinking I was you. I remembered you saying something about you fronting him some work. So when he asked me 'bout you, I just told him to give me that money he owes you."

Terry couldn't help but smile as he pulled the rubber band wrapped stacks out of the bag. "At least we got somebody who's loyal to the team."

"Keep taking initiative like that and you'll keep rising." Mack patted Keith on the back. Just then, his cell phone vibrated. "Wassup wit' it?"

"Wassup, Mack? This is Boogs."

"What's goin' on? I was just about to call you."

"Shit, I probably wouldn't have answered. I had a long night with two bad bitches I took home from Club Roxy last night."

"Goddamn, cowboy. Next time call me before the fun, not after." Mack kidded.

"Don't trip, I got these shorties from Reading, that I'm working on. They model material. Aye, you know Reek is gettin' out, right?" Boogs said, changing the subject.

"When?"

"It might be in a week or two. They have to take care of all the paperwork."

"Who you hear that from?"

"He called me yesterday. They didn't indict him on the body. He only got a gun charge. They're going to let him out on conditional release so he can go to a rehabilitation center. My nigga is able to stand up on his own already." The pride in Boogs' voice was unmistakable.

"Damn, that's wassup. Yo, I gotta take care of something important, li'l bruh. I'ma call you back."

"Aaight, bruh. Later."

Mack ended the call and looked at Terry with a blank expression.

"What's good? You look like you saw a ghost," Terry said.

"Not, yet, I might be seeing one soon." Mack shook his head. "Reek is about to get out of jail."

"Get the fuck outta here. How's that possible?"

"Boogs said all he got is a gun charge. They gonna let him out so he can go to a rehabilitation center. Damn...I know my nigga ain't fold," Mack mumbled.

Terry walked over to his partner. "You know we gotta find out what's up with him, right?"

"No doubt."

"You also know what has to be done if he turned into a rat, right?"

"Come on, T. Don't disrespect my gangsta. Any nigga that shows weakness in our circle must be eliminated. It ain't nothin' else to it."

Keith listened to their conversation, nodding his head in approval...

CHAPTER 21

After a night of mingling with a few of his white collar associates, Mack was pleasantly surprised by the amount of fun he was capable of having with them. He enjoyed being introduced to new forms of entertainment. He left the function inebriated and in a jovial mood. Instead of going home, he went to Sandra's house.

Mack pushed a button in his Bentley Flying Spur. "Call Sa—." Before issuing the command, he de-activated the call assist.

Since Sandra had been texting him throughout the day and he never responded, he figured it would be in his best interest to see her face to face. That way it would be easier to dodge any potential argument.

He eased the Bentley into the driveway, got out, and activated the alarm system. He rummaged through the numerous keys on his chain until he located the right one. The effects of the alcohol caused his balance to be slightly off. He stabilized himself enough to insert the key into the lock. With a few unsteady twists, the lock's bolt receded. He turned the knob, opened the door, then stepped inside.

To his surprise, Sandra stood at the entrance wearing a red silk robe adorned with Oriental markings. Her hands were on her hips. Her face displayed a mixture of agitation and anger. Nonetheless, she was alluring.

"What are you doing?" she asked, holding her ground.

"Watchu talkin' about?" Mack flashed an easy smile in an attempt to reduce the tension.

"I've been calling and texting your ass all day. Now, all of a sudden, you want to show up at three o'clock in the morning?" Noticing he wasn't quite himself, she leaned in to get a better look at him. "Are you drunk?"

"Nope...I only had a little." The slur in his words contradicted his reply.

"Mack, are you serious?" She shook her head in disgust. "I'm not going to keep going through this." Sandra fought hard to hold back the tears that desperately wanted to escape.

"Going through what, babe?"

Sandra contemplated telling Mack everything that she knew. Things he wasn't aware of himself. Should she let him know that she was aware of the multitude of women he was sleeping with while she remained faithful to him? Should she let him know that one of the women he had given himself to was her first cousin? Her own flesh and blood? That the brief affair resulted in her becoming pregnant? Should Sandra clue him in that she was a part of the devastating decision made to abort the pregnancy?

Sandra had lost relationships with both family and friends, all because she strongly believed that the love she so selflessly gave to Mack would someday be reciprocated. She believed that Mack loved her, but she knew that he wasn't in love with her, as she was with him.

Sandra needed more. Living her life around heartache was breaking her. "What have I done for you to constantly hurt me like this? If you can't love me the way I deserve to be loved, then let me go, Mack," she pleaded.

"Baby, do you think I'm out to hurt you? Do you think that's my intention? I would never want to cause you any pain. I know I haven't been there for you like I'm supposed to, and I know I'm putting you through a lot, but just hold on for me. It's going to get better, I promise." He walked up to Sandra, pulling her into a warm, tight embrace.

"When?...When?" She was no longer able to restrain her tears as she sobbed into his chest. "I can't take this anymore."

Mack created just enough space between them to cup Sandra's chin. He gently lifted her head until her teary eyes met his. "That's it. No more hurt. I can't stand to see you like this, baby. From now on I only want to bring joy into your life. That's what you deserve. Give me one more chance and I'll make your life so much better."

Mack ended his words with a gentle kiss to her soft lips. He wiped the tears from her face, kissed her cheek, which led to another kiss on the nape of her neck. Sandra closed her eyes, embracing the pleasure. Her body temperature rose and her breathing became heavy. Mack allowed his hands to glide against her smooth silk robe, coming to a stop once they reached her soft, full breasts.

"I'm so sorry, Sandra," he whispered between kisses. "I want you in my life forever...I love you."

Caught completely in the moment, Sandra gave in to any thoughts of resistance.

Mack led her to the bedroom. He took his time giving every inch of her body much needed and pleasurable attention, before making passionate love to her until day began to break.

Around mid-afternoon, the smell of French toast, scrambled eggs and turkey bacon stirred Mack out of a deep slumber. He went to the bathroom to brush his teeth and wash his face. Fully awake and refreshed, he followed the tantalizing aroma into the kitchen.

Sandra stood in front of the stove dressed in a sexy peach colored semi-translucent teddy and fur lined slippers. Mack slid up on her from behind, giving her plump, round ass a slap. She slightly jumped at the unexpected smack. He removed any space between them and softly kissed her neck.

"Damn, I'm the luckiest man in the world. I had desert last night and now I'm getting breakfast."

"Don't think you're out of the dog house so soon, Mr. Smooth Talker. You're far from it. We really have to talk and get an understanding. Can we discuss this over breakfast?"

"Are you serious?" Mack took a step back.

Sandra spun around, spatula in hand. "Damn right, I'm serious, Mack!"

He released a sigh of exasperation. "I think I better go take my medication." He went into the dining room, rolled a blunt, turned the wall mounted TV on and smoked while surfing through the channels.

Ten minutes later, the food was finished and Mack was feeling good because of the potent weed. His attention was on a developing CNN story when Sandra brought in two plates of food. She placed one plate on the table in front of him, and then sat down next to him with her food.

With an invigorated appetite, Mack tore into his meal. Sandra picked and nibbled at hers. Her mind was more on making an attempt to mend their severely strained relationship.

Unsure of how to begin, Sandra simply allowed her heart to speak. "Mack, our relationship can be amazing if we'd just put more time into it. All I'm asking for is your heart. Instead of you telling me how much you love me, I want you to allow your actions to do the talking."

"You're right, Sandra. I can't argue with that. I make a lot of bad choices, and I'm going to work on doing better."

She held on tightly to his promise. "I just want you to trust in me, and the love that I have for you. If we can..." Sandra's words trailed off into silence.

Mack's attention was suddenly diverted when he heard CNN's analyst begin to discuss recent trends in the stock market. The speaker talked about the top performing stocks of the month. Mack's eyes were glued to the television once he saw that Western Union was the number two top performing stock. To his amazement, the woman mentioned her interest in investing in bonds over stocks for the near future.

Mack jumped up from his seat, sped to the bedroom, and removed his iPhone from his pants pocket. He dialed Terry's number.

"Waddup?" Terry answered on the second ring.

"Yo, he was right!" Mack exclaimed.

"What are you talkin' about?"

"The ol' head from Starbucks. I was just watching the news and everything he said was right. I knew I should have put some money in those stocks."

"Come on, Mack. That was just a lucky guess. That old drunk couldn't tell his mouth from his ass. You need to be focused on this week coming up. The Cavaliers is playing the Sixers. That means it's going to be a big bump in business. Plus, we gotta call a photographer to take some pictures of Dynasty for the advertisement."

"Yeah, you're right," Mack conceded. But deep down he had a feeling that the drunkard knew what he was talking about. That feeling morphed into a desire to speak with that man again.

After hanging up with Terry, he used his phone and did a Google search. Mack remembered the man's first name but was having trouble recalling his last. He sat there brooding for a moment until the full name came to him. He keyed in: Marty Frankel.

Mack was astonished at what he saw. There was a picture of a fit, groomed and well dressed version of the man he encountered a few weeks before. He read the numerous articles that were published on Marty Frankel, amazed at how far the man had made it, only to fall to the depths of alcoholism and poverty.

For some reason, Mack had a strong feeling that the key to financial freedom was Marty's brain. Continuing his online inquiry, he searched for Marty's address. He found it. *Fuck it, I'm going to go with my gut and see where it takes me*, Mack said to himself while getting dressed.

He thought about Sandra and silently cursed for abruptly leaving her in mid conversation. "Sandra!" he yelled out. A moment later she walked into the bedroom. She said nothing. "Listen, baby. Something really important just came up. I have to go to New York." He slipped on his Gucci loafers and searched for his keys while talking. "I know we didn't finish our conversation, but when I come back we're going on a vacation. Just you and I."

"No, we're not," Sandra's voice was low. She stared at the floor shaking her head.

"Yes, we are. I promise." He finally found his keys.

"It's over, Mack. Everything in your life is more important than me. No matter what I say, or try, it's not going to change."

Mack turned around and saw her eyes welling up. "Come on Sandra, don't start that crying shit again. Why do you want to stress me out with all this drama?"

"I want you to get your clothes, guns, and everything else out of my house. It'll be better if you live your life without me in it."

Mack ran a hand over his face in frustration. "I'm not about to go through this shit with you right now, Sandra. As soon as I come back, we'll talk." Mack walked out of her room, and her house, once again, leaving Sandra alone.

———

The Flying Spur's navigation system led him directly to Marty's address in New York City. After finding a safe place to park, he got out and walked into the outdated building. While walking up the five flights of decrepit stairs, he began to second guess his ambition to reacquaint himself with Marty. He slowly walked down the desolate hallway, coming to a stop once he reached apartment 44. Instead of giving the door a gentle rap, he knocked hard in hopes of receiving a quicker response.

"Go away!" a voice shouted from the inside.

"Marty, this is Sabrie Mack. I need to talk to you."

"I said go away!"

"I drove all the way from Philly to make you rich again and I'm not leaving until I talk to you!" Silence consumed the hallway for a moment. Then, Mack heard the two dead bolts unfasten. The door cracked open as far as the interior chain lock allowed. A scruffy bearded man peeked a skeptical eye through the opening.

"Well, if it ain't the ding bat from Starbucks. You're going to make me rich? You couldn't come up with a hundred dollars if someone stuffed it into your pocket." Marty laughed and slammed the door shut. Mack could hear Marty's bellowing grow faint as he descended further into the apartment.

"Shit!" Mack swore. He banged on the door again. This time he pounded harder than the first. He heard footsteps as Marty stomped toward the door. He snatched the door open with an erupting attitude.

"What the..." his words were halted. His eyes were transfixed on what Mack held in his hand.

"I reached in my pocket and found this." Mack held a large, folded wad of bills. "This is five thousand dollars. You can have it if you give me thirty minutes of your time."

"Listen, kid. I don't know what kind of games you're playing, but..."

"I didn't drive this far to play games with you. Here." Mack stuffed the money through the door's opening. With lightning speed, Marty snatched the money out of Mack's hand, then slammed the door shut.

"I know this mutha fucka ain't tryin' to play me," Mack blurted out. Just then the door opened.

"Come in. You've got thirty minutes...not a second more."

Walking into the apartment, Mack looked around, repulsed at the foul condition Marty had become content with living in. "I'm going to get straight to the point. You gave me some good advice at the coffee shop. Had I listened, I would have been a little richer. I checked you out and you're official. After that scandal broke out at the company you worked for, you allowed yourself to sink. Call me crazy, but I believe that even though your spirits are weak, your brain still has strength."

"You think that just because you read a few articles about me that you can summarize my life? You have no idea what I've been through!" Marty was livid. He reached for a half empty bottle of cheap vodka, removed the top and chugged a huge portion. "I've been stabbed in the back by everyone in my life. I was loyal to all of them!" he ranted emotionally.

"You're right. I don't know you or all that you've been through. But you can't keep living in the past and you definitely can't keep drowning your sorrows in alcohol. Listen man, I'm no mentor. All I know is I have the financial ability to put you back in the game. I think you have the mindset to rise to the top again. But there's no way I'm going to invest in a loser. And keeping it real, right now that's what you are."

"Yeah? Well, I don't give a rat's ass what you think!" Marty took another gulp.

"I know you don't. You don't give a fuck about anything. Not even yourself. But the only way you'll have a chance at turning your life back around is if you start giving a rat's ass."

Mack's words seemed to effectively penetrate Marty's wall of denial. He remained humbly quiet as Mack continued. Marty slowly opened up and shared his crushing past with Mack, who listened intently. The release of his accumulated hurt, anger and disappointment actually caused Marty to feel a little better about himself. Mack understood that their conversation was the first step in a long journey, but it was a step that Marty willingly took. It signified that Marty wanted change. The question was if he was prepared for the change.

"Let me ask you a question," Mack said. "Do you think you can leave the alcohol alone?"

"The easy answer is 'yes', but the honest answer is 'it's possible'. I know deep down I can do it, but I know it's going to take a lot of hard work and commitment."

"In order to leave the liquor alone you'll have to make the decision to stop wasting your life and find your purpose."

"I agree."

"If I had fifty thousand dollars to invest in you, do you think you could turn a profit with it?"

"I didn't lose my career because I wasn't good enough, I lost it because of misguided trust and naivety. I was one of the best in my field...I still am. If you believe in me enough to invest fifty thousand dollars, I promise that I will make you a rich man."

"Alright. I'll invest the money into you and we'll split the profits three ways; between you, myself and my friend that I was with at the coffee shop. But this can only be done under one condition: you have to get yourself together. I have to know that you are going to be committed. You have five grand. It's yours to use any way you want. I just hope you use it to better yourself. I'm going to check up on you in three weeks. If you're straightened up and sober when I come back, then we have a deal. If you're not, then it'll show you never wanted change and we'll move on with our lives."

They sealed the deal by shaking hands. They conversed a little more, afterwards Mack left the apartment building and New York City...

CHAPTER 22

Jihad and Shawn sat next to each other on their flight from Miami, Florida, en route to Philadelphia. The argument Jihad had with Terry was never mentioned to Shawn. Jihad thought everything out clearly before reacting.

Terry was no longer the same person he had grown so close to. By sharing the common goals of overcoming adversity and ensuring survival, they had formed a seemingly impenetrable bond.

However, now that they had achieved and surpassed their initial goals, their second tier of goals were different. Because of this, it appeared that their lives were headed in different directions. The thread that held their bond together was beginning to wither away.

It was undeniable that their friendship had become distant. The only time that he received a call from Terry was to discuss business matters. Hanging out and having fun together had become a thing of the past.

While their friendship began to dissipate, Mack and Terry, steadily grew closer. After the argument it had become evident to Jihad that he was being used solely for the position he played in the SP movement. Terry had no intention to elevate Jihad's status, while, he and Mack, continued to rise in wealth and power. He thought about making an attempt to sit Terry down to try to hash everything out, but odds were it would prove worthless and damaging. Terry was an intelligent man who was well aware of the decisions he was making. Terry was knowingly removing himself from their friendship. Two best friends were on a fast track to become distant strangers. And in their way of life, strangers received neither love nor remorse. Accepting reality, Jihad pondered his options. The only way he could turn the odds in his favor was to increase his power while weakening Terry's. In the process of doing that, he could never be viewed as Terry's enemy. At least not until it would be too late for Terry and Mack. In order for his takeover to be a success he would have to recruit Shawn, who was

Mack's top soldier.

Jihad turned to Shawn, who was reclined in the plane's seat listening to music on his phone, and tapped him.

Shawn removed his left ear bud. "Wassup, cannon?"

"I need to holla at you about some real shit."

Shawn turned off his phone and removed the other ear bud, giving Jihad his full attention. "Talk to me."

"Let's say your homies was driving a car and you knew it was going to crash. You tried to warn them, but they wouldn't listen. Would you jump out, or take the chance of surviving the crash with them?" Jihad asked.

"What kind of question is that?" Shawn laughed. "You already know the answer. Come on, Jihad. You know you ain't gotta speak in riddles to me. Tell me what's on your mind."

Jihad paused for a contemplative moment. "Alright, but you have to give me your word that everything I say remains between us."

"You got my word. What's going on?"

"Terry and Mack is gon' end up getting knocked."

Jihad's revelation caused Shawn to sit upright, "What? Why you say that?"

"They're getting too hot. It's too much going on, and all fingers are pointing to them," Jihad explained. "Do you remember Tricia?"

"Yeah, you talkin' about the dark skinned chick you been smashing, right?"

"Yeah. Her uncle is a cop. He works for the narcotics unit. He told her that they're on to him," Jihad lied.

"Why would he tell her?"

"'Cause one day I was driving Terry's Benz and I stopped by her house. I guess he happened to drive past. He told Tricia he didn't want to see her get trapped off in his shit."

"Fuck! That means they know about us, too." Worry began to set in.

"Nah, they're not watching us, not yet. But if we keep on, we're definitely going down with them."

"We gotta tell them what's going on."

"You don't think I tried to put them on already? They're on some ride or die shit. Them niggas really think they're untouchable. Now, if I keep bringing this up and they end up getting knocked, who are they going to think snitched on them?"

"You." Shawn answered in a low voice.

"Exactly. At this point it's all about self-preservation, my nigga. I did all I can do. I'm puttin' you on game 'cause you a real ass nigga, and I fuck with you."

"Yo, that's wassup. I appreciate that."

"Now, there's a way that we can save ourselves, and come out of this with the money that we're supposed to have as well. Are you with me?"

Shawn thought about it for a moment. He looked Jihad in the eyes, and said, "I'm with you, my dude…"

CHAPTER 23

Terry and Mack were inside of Dynasty Luxury Rentals pouring over the company's records.

"Business is steadily growing," Terry commented, keying at his computer.

"We're definitely bringing in more customers. Our SUVs have been booked up for three weeks straight. It looks like we have to buy a few more." "Imagine how far we can take this company if we put our all into it."

Mack placed the portfolio he was reviewing down on his desk. "What do you mean? If we weren't putting our all into this place, it would have been tanked."

"Nah. We ain't fail because we're natural hustlers. What I'm saying is if we leave our other business alone, we'll have a lot less stress and more time to focus strictly on the growth of Dynasty."

"So, you're saying you want to go one hundred percent legit?"

For the first time, Terry looked away from his computer screen. His eyes met Mack's. "Yeah."

There was a light knock on their office door. Kerri, their secretary, poked her head inside. "Excuse me, Mr. Mack, Mr. Frankel is here to see you."

The name quickly registered to Mack. However, it was a complete shock that Marty not only found out about the rental company, but he also made the trip from Manhattan to pay him a visit. "Show him in, Kerri."

A moment later an impeccably dressed, clean shaven and vibrant, Marty Frankel, walked into the office accompanied by his reestablished comrade, Vincent. Mack slowly stood from his desk, surprised at the man who stood before him. Marty approached, displaying a pleasant smile. He extended his hand, giving Mack a firm handshake.

"Good afternoon, Mack".

"Is this really you? What are you doing here?"

"You said you'd be back in three weeks. It's been three weeks and two days, so I figured I'd come and check on you. I hope you don't mind, but I brought a friend with me." He turned to Vincent and introduced them. They shook hands.

"Marty, you remember my friend, Terry, right?" Mack asked.

"Sure." Marty turned to Terry. "How are you doing?"

Terry stopped typing on the computer long enough to look up. "I'm doing well. I'm sorry, but I can't think of where I remember you from."

"Remember the guy from Starbucks in New York who gave us the advice on the stocks?"

Terry studied the man's face more closely. "Oh, shit, that's him!" He quickly stood from his desk and walked over to Marty. He shook his hand. "You look like a new man."

"I am a new man. Thanks to Mack and Vincent…oh, I almost forgot." Marty reached inside his suit pocket, pulled out a white envelope and handed it to Mack.

"What's this?" Mack accepted the envelope.

"That's the five thousand you gave me, plus an extra thousand bucks. Within the past three weeks, I turned that five grand into thirty-six large." He then recited a line from *Coming To America*, "Mortimer, we're back!"

Mack, Terry and Vincent laughed. "I appreciate this, but I didn't loan you that money. I gave it to you. I'm just happy that you used it to get back on your feet." Mack gave the envelope back.

"I have always been a man of my word. I told you that I'd get myself together. I haven't had a drink since the day you left my apartment. Our conversation and the faith you had in me played a pivotal role in me taking the needed steps to get my life back on track."

"My words could only do but so much." Mack gestured for Marty and Vincent to take a seat, and resumed his place behind his desk. "It was your actions that created the change."

"Nice try at being modest and minimizing your role, young man. However, I'm not letting you off that easy. Like I said, I'm a man of my word. I told you that I'd make you rich. By the looks of this place, you're not doing bad at all, but I want to introduce you and your friend to generational wealth. Are you guys ready to play in the big leagues?"

Terry looked over to Mack, unsure of what was going on. "Mack, why didn't you tell me that you went to see Starbucks?" he asked, referring to Marty.

"Because you didn't see what I saw at the time."

"Well, I see this man standing in front of me, and I'll be the first to admit that he's a completely different version of the guy we met. It's obvious he knows what he's talking about, and we'd be fools not to listen to him for the second time."

"No question," Mack said, then turned to Marty. "Mr. Frankel, if it's okay with you, we'd love to become your students as well as investors and partners." All four men shook hands, solidifying their starting point...

CHAPTER 24

Terry and Mack had learned more than they had ever imagined about commodities trading since partnering with Marty and Vincent, who made it a priority that while under their tutelage they obtained knowledge along with wealth.

Vincent was an integral part of their operation because he was still employed by Goldman's. Marty's former mentor, Jack, had taken a liking to Vincent, which in Marty's eyes only meant that he would be offered as the company's sacrificial lamb if the need ever arose.

Now that Vincent was aware of Jack's cold-hearted, callous ways, he took advantage by absorbing valuable information and using it for his benefit. His inside access combined with Marty's uncanny knowledge proved to create a winning team. Marty's ingenious trading decisions were based on extremely complex mathematical algorithms to process data on market developments and execute trades rapidly.

In forty-five days, Terry and Mack's combined one hundred thousand dollar investment saw a nearly forty percent return and there was no sign of slowing down.

The lives they lived on the other side of the fence, however, proved to be much more difficult to maintain. Mack's relationship with Sandra had fallen completely apart. One day after buying her an assortment of gifts and flowers, he went to her house and found that Sandra no longer lived there. The house was vacant with a For Rent sign in the window. He tried calling and texting her. He even made attempts to contact her through Facebook and Instagram, to no avail.

Mack did his best to suppress his feelings, but reflections of the tremendous amount of pain he caused her, coupled with her constant pleas for him to change that went ignored, consumed him. Attempting to keep the multiple aspects of his life separate was becoming more and more difficult.

On his way to a business meeting, Mack received a call from Boogs asking him to

come over right away. The urgency in Boogs' voice made it clear that it was extremely important. Mack was forced to cancel the meeting. He drove directly to Boogs' house. Terry had made it there minutes earlier.

As soon as Mack stepped into the house he sensed tension. "Wassup?"

"Somebody broke into the stash house, setting it on fire. That shit has been on the news all morning."

Mack was fuming. "What? What the fuck you mean somebody broke into the house?"

"Whoever did it shot the dogs, took the work, and got out of the house before the police responded to the alarm," Terry said.

"What the fuck is going on? First, somebody robs Shawn for sixty stacks, now they're runnin' up in our houses?" Mack began to pace. "How much did we have in the house?"

"Fourteen bricks," Terry answered.

"Fourteen jawns? You're telling me it's a muthafucka out there with fourteen ki's of our coke? Hell nah." Mack shook his head in disbelief. "I don't give a fuck what it takes to find out who did this, I want them muthafuckas dead. Period!"

"Say no more," Boogs said, feeling his friend's pain…

CHAPTER 25

Mack and Terry decided to temporarily shut down their drug operation. Their objective was to find out who was behind Shawn being robbed and their stash house being burglarized. With the understanding that no one could be excluded from being considered a suspect, every high positioned member of SP was informed that a drought had come. They were told that the drought was expected to last a while.

Feeling the pinch from not having any drugs to hustle, Boogs kept his eyes and ears open. The streets not only watched, but they also talked. In time information would surface and whoever was responsible would pay for their actions with their lives. Everyone laid low and remained attentive.

To Boogs' relief, Reek had finally made it out of jail after the judge set his bail at seventy-five hundred dollars for the Felon in Possession of a Weapon charge. It pained him deeply to see his cousin in such a debilitated state. However, Reek's unyielding resilience left Boogs no other choice but to remain strong and optimistic for him. Three days out of the week, Boogs picked him up, and escorted him to the rehabilitation center. He remained by his cousin's side, encouraging him every step of the way. As Reek continued to grow stronger physically, Boogs grew more confident that he would eventually be back, or at least very close to normal.

Because of their complex schedule, Terry and Mack were unable to spend as much time as they would have liked with Reek. However, they made it their business to check up on him, and also to make sure he was fully taken care of financially.

Reek understood that he was involved in a very serious open case. He was also aware that Terry had been questioned by the same homicide detectives who attempted to interrogate him. With the understanding that it would have been foolish for them to remain in close contact with each other, they remained in touch while maintaining distance.

On a Wednesday morning, Boogs was preparing to pick Reek up when he got a call from Keith.

"Wassup, Keith?"

"Ain't shit. Watchu up to?"

"I'm 'bout to scoop Reek up and take him to the rehabilitation center."

"Oh, yeah? Damn, I ain't seen my nigga since before that shit popped off. Yo, I need a favor from you. I need you to take me to pick my truck up. I had to get the back end repainted. Some broad scratched my jawn up."

"Aaight. Be ready in about twenty minutes. I'ma pick Reek up, then come and get you."

"Good lookin'."

They hung up. Boogs got into his pearl white Cadillac XTS

191

and headed to Reek's place. Once there, he wheeled him to the passenger side, helped him in, folded the wheelchair up, and placed it in the trunk.

"Keith asked me to pick him up," Reek said, getting behind the wheel.

"Keith? I heard he was fuckin' with Mack and T-Lova."

"Yeah, the bawh been down with the team for a minute now."

"I don't know how that li'l nigga wiggled his way in." Reek shook his head.

"Wasn't that your li'l man?"

"I fucked with him, but I knew he wasn't loyal. He was dealin' with them grimey ass twins, and they was filling his head with a bunch of bullshit. He didn't give a fuck about the movement, it was all about him."

"I'm glad you put me onto his ass." Boogs pulled over in front of Keith's apartment, then called him on his cell phone letting him know they were outside.

Three minutes later Keith was out of the door. He trotted over to the Cadillac and hopped in the back seat. "Wassup, cannon?" Keith said to Reek, excitedly.

"I'm coolin'. Wassup with you?"

"You already know. I'm tryin' to make it happen."

"I hear you doin' big things now." Reek turned the upper, mobile half of his body so he could get a better look at Keith.

"Nah, I ain't doing it big, yet, but I'm finally getting my chance to shine."

"That's wassup," Reek responded, not particularly interested in what Keith had to say.

"Where's your truck at?" Boogs asked as he pulled away from the curb.

"Oh, it's at Impressions in South Philly."

"Aaight." Boogs headed in that direction. They engaged in small talk until he made it to the repair shop.

"Damn, Keith. The shop's not open yet," Reek said.

"Fuck! They supposed to be open. Go around to the back and see if they left my whip back there."

Boogs released a sigh of frustration, but did as he was asked. Once there, Keith scanned the area. His truck was nowhere in sight.

"Give me a second. Let me run to the back door and see if someone's inside."

Boogs threw the car in park and Keith bolted out. In a matter of seconds he was back. "Nobody's there."

"So, what you gonna do?" Boogs asked. He turned in his seat only to come face to face with a huge semi-automatic handgun.

Boom! Boom! Boom! Keith sent three rounds from his .45 into Boogs' head. The high velocity slugs shattered his skull. It's thick, red contents decorated the windshield, dashboard, and left side of Reek.

Reek sat there in complete shock, staring at the half-headed, bloodied corpse that was once his cousin. His ears were still ringing from the deftly loud gun bursts.

"Mack thinks you're snitchin'," Keith said. The raw words snapped Reek out of his state of shock.

"Nah, man. Mack know I ain't no rat...why you killed my cousin?" Reek couldn't stop himself from sobbing as the pungent copper smell filled the car. "You ain't have to kill him, man."

"Shut the fuck up!" Keith aimed his gun at Reek. "I don't give a fuck if you're tellin' or not. Both of ya'll gotta go. Your bitch ass ain't never want to put me on, but I got on anyway. Once you get back in the game, I ain't never gon' blow up."

"Keith, you ain't gotta do this."

"Fuck you, it's done." Keith fired two close range shots into the left side of Reek's head. The bullets exited the right side, causing a mixture of blood and brain matter to flow out of the gaping holes.

Keith quietly, but carefully, wiped down every section of the car that he touched, and then got out. He opened the driver's door, took Boogs' phone, and left the two bodies slumped in the car...

CHAPTER 26

After a long and strenuous night of work and less than six hours of sleep, Terry was reluctant to get up and remove himself from the comfort of his cozy king-sized bed. But he had no other choice. Unlike the street hustle where he created his own work schedule, in the legal field he had to abide by business hours; no matter how stringent they were.

The magnificent three thousand seven hundred square feet home he'd purchased begged for him to remain inside. Resisting the calling, he forced himself out of bed, and then washed up and got dressed. The anticipation of going to his office and reviewing the volume charts of his commodities stocks was the motivating factor. He could easily analyze them on his laptop or iPhone, but he had made it a part of his routine to wait.

Just as he stepped out of his home and deactivated the alarm of his Tesla, his phone vibrated.

"Hello?"

"T. Wassup, big bruh?" It was Keith.

"I'm coolin'. I just stepped out of the house. What's good?"

"I got something important to holla at you about."

"I'm on my way to work. Can it wait until I get off?" Terry asked.

"Nah, it can't. Stop by my crib on your way."

"Aaight. I'll be there in a half an hour." Terry hung up and cursed himself for answering the phone without viewing the *Caller ID* first. Deciding it was best to just get it over with, he drove directly over to Keith's house.

Terry pulled into Keith's drive way and blew the horn twice. It didn't take long before Keith came out the door and got into the passenger side of the car.

"I hope this is important." Terry looked over at Keith showing a hint of frustration.

"It is." Keith looked back at him. "I had to kill Reek and Boogs."

"What? Are you serious?"

"You know I wouldn't play with nothing like this."

"What the fuck is wrong with you?"

"The bawh Reek was workin' with the police, and Boogs knew about it." Keith defended his actions.

"How you know?"

"They told me this morning. That's when I hit 'em."

"Yo, you can't be that fuckin' stupid!" Terry pounded on the center armrest in anger. "Why didn't you just come and tell me?"

"Man, put yourself in my shoes," Keith said. "I just found

196

out that Reek was a rat. That nigga was tellin' on my man. Nobody was around. I had to do it, T."

Terry fought to suppress his anger and remain focused. "Listen, I want you to lay low for a minute. I don't want you doing nothin' unless me or Mack tell you to."

"Aaight."

"Don't you tell nobody about this. I don't even want you to fuckin' think about it too hard. You hear me?"

"I got you. I might have reacted too quick, but I did it for you. I ain't lettin' no nigga cross the fam. I don't care who it is."

"Aaight, kid. Just be easy. Do you need any paper?"

"Nah, I'm good."

"Remember what I said. Lay low and keep your mouth shut. Once this shit blows over we'll be back to business."

"I got you, T." He gave Terry some dap and left the car smiling inwardly. His actions brought him one step closer to achieving a top position.

Terry's mind was no longer on his legal business. He was too preoccupied with how to deal with the horrible information that was just relayed to him. There had to be more to the story. He did a masterful job of concealing his emotions in front of Keith, but the truth was his heart was crushed. Reek was a great friend. He had been there unconditionally for Terry. He placed his life on the front lines for the team. Terry never mentioned it to Keith, but he was positive that Reek didn't tell the police anything. He was sure because his personal attorney and Reek's attorney worked for the same law firm. Reek had never given any statement to any officer, and any discussion with the district attorney was conducted through his lawyer.

Two of his good friends, Twan and Reek had become casualties of wars created by him and Mack. Boogs, who had grown to be a great and trustworthy friend, had now lost his life too.

All of this weighed heavily on Terry's heart and mind.

Terry did his absolute best to switch roles and mask his emotions, pulling into the lot of Dynasty Luxury Rentals. He walked into the building and greeted his staff routinely. Making it to his office, he was relieved to see Mack inside at work.

"I know this ain't the time or the place, but I got some horrible news."

"I guess when it rains, it pours. I got some bad news, too," Mack countered.

"Reek and Boogs are dead," Terry's voice was low and course.

"That can't be true. I just talked to Boogs last night. He told me that Reek was doing good."

"Keith killed both of them this morning. He said Reek was snitchin' and Boogs was in on it."

"That's bullshit!" Mack shouted, as the burning anger consumed him. "We got all of his paperwork. He wasn't hot!"

"I know, but I didn't tell Keith. I just went along with what he was saying."

Mack jumped to his feet with his large hands clenched tightly into fists. "Nah, man. I can't fuckin' believe this shit. My mans can't be dead!" Mack shouted. He refused to believe the truth, as reality forced it's way in. Visions of both Reek and Boogs impeded his thought process, forcing him to take a seat.

They sat in their chairs in a contemplative moment of silence. "I'ma have to kill Keith," Terry said, finally.

Mack wanted nothing more than to make sure Keith was removed from earth, for unjustly killing his comrades. Just before he agreed with Terry, a thought came to his mind. "I may have a better idea."

"Wassup?"

"I was going to tell you that word just got back to me that Jihad and Shawn is still selling weight in North and West Philly."

Terry's eyes widened at the news. "Do you think they're the ones who broke into the house?"

"We kept that place a secret. They're the only ones besides me, you and Sandra who knew about it. Think about it; Shawn gets robbed earlier and he claims he didn't get to see their faces, then we get robbed for fourteen bricks…it's them."

The more Terry reflected on it, the clearer the picture became. The relationship between him and his long-time friend had withered away. The problem was he had become too consumed with working toward reaching his goals to realize it. While he pursued new ventures, Jihad remained content with continuing to use proceeds from selling drugs as his only source of income. The line was clearly drawn. They now stood on opposite sides.

"What's your plan?" Terry asked.

"We're going to kill three birds with one stone…"

CHAPTER 27

Since receiving the helpful information from the robber-turned-informant, Kevin, detectives Todd and Latrice began to utilize all their resources to compile as much information on Terry – T-Lova – Maddox and Sabrie Mack.

The more information that was gathered, the more convinced they became that those men were, if not responsible, at least capable of causing the deaths of the Simmons twins.

The detectives sat in Latrice's congested cubicle sipping poorly made coffee out of styrofoam cups. "So, what do you think?" Todd asked.

Latrice pushed against her desk, causing her chair to roll out a bit, then stretched her legs. "Well, we definitely don't have enough to arrest Maddox or Mack on the murders. There's absolutely no direct evidence. All we have is a statement from a thug with an extensive arrest record who wants to save his own ass from spending life behind bars."

"What if we bring them in for questioning?"

"That'll do more harm than good." Latrice batted down the option and took another sip of her bitter coffee. "When we brought Maddox in the last time, he knew exactly what to, and what not to say. He's not dumb by a long shot."

"Yeah, but it might be different with Mack," Todd said.

"Birds of a feather flock together. These guys didn't make it this far by being lucky. I don't even want to bring them in here until we have enough evidence to charge them."

The detectives racked their brains trying to figure out how to get Terry and Mack off the streets. Todd bolted upright in his chair when an idea came to him. "Terry is originally from Syracuse, right?"

"Yes."

"There has to be a reason why he left. Do me a favor, get me the number to Syracuse Police Department."

Latrice rolled her chair closer to her desk and began typing rapidly on her computer. "Got it."

Todd pushed the intercom button on her desk phone and pressed the numbers as she recited them to him. The phone rang a half dozen times before someone picked up. "Syracuse Police Department, Maggie Flemming speaking."

"Hello Maggie. This is homicide detective, Todd Reed, from Philadelphia. There is an individual that we are investigating. He's originally from Syracuse and we wanted to find out if he's raised any eyebrows there before coming here."

"Okay. I'm going to transfer your call to the lieutenant. He will be able to assist you."

"Thank you."

There was a momentary pause, then someone picked up.

"Lieutenant Schwartz," the voice bellowed through the phone.

"Good afternoon, Lieutenant. This is Detective Todd Reed of Philadelphia Homicide. We're investigating a suspect by the name of Terry Maddox. He goes by T-Lova. We know that he was a lifelong resident of Syracuse. We're trying to see if anyone in your department has ever investigated him, or has any helpful information about him."

"You said, Terry Maddox, right?"

"Yes, sir."

"The name certainly rings a bell. Hold on a sec." The clicking of computer keys could be heard in the background. "Ah...here we go. Terry Maddox, also known as T-Lova. I remember him now. I had a confidential informant who was working on a controlled buy from him."

"What was the outcome?" Todd asked.

"My CI was murdered before we had a chance to get to Maddox."

"Do you think that Terry was involved?"

"There was no way we could attribute the murder to him. During our investigation we found out that Maddox was out of town when the murder occurred. We concluded that his death was the result of a drug deal gone wrong. It was a side deal that my CI was conducting which we weren't privy to. The case is still open."

"Damn, another dead end," Todd said disappointedly.

"For what it's worth, detective, I've always believed that Maddox was somehow involved with the murder of my CI He informed me that the four kilos of cocaine recovered from his vehicle during his arrest belonged to Maddox. It's my belief that Terry found out the CI was working for us and had him killed. But, of course, it's just speculation."

The fact that Shwartz's informant was killed as a result of involvement with drugs caused Latrice to chime in. "Hello Lieutenant Schwartz. This is Detective Reed. The case we're working on involves drugs, as well. We believe the victims were killed in retaliation for a robbery which resulted in the death and severe injury of Terry's friends."

"Well, if you need our assistance for anything, just give us a ring."

"We appreciate your help, Lieutenant," Todd said, and then hung up.

The detectives looked at each other wearing the same dismal expression. Just then Latrice's cell phone rang. Whenever that phone rang they knew they would be coming in contact with a dead body. She answered the phone, jotted down the needed information, and ended the call.

"It looks like we're the proud owners of a double homicide. Are you ready?"

"Would it make any difference if I said no?" Todd questioned.

"Nope," Latrice exhaled and stood. She began to gather a few things from her desk. "Let's see what we have on our hands and pick up some real coffee on the way," she said in a frail attempt to lighten the mood.

The change into the spring season brought a beautiful and pleasing mood to the city. Budding leaves on the trees danced softly against the winds. It was an alluring day. Unfortunately, it was a day that someone was no longer blessed to enjoy. Todd believed that he would eventually become numb to witnessing the aftermath of a murder. But for both him and his sister, each corpse they encountered brought with it a feeling of loss. Their defense mechanisms were to force their minds not to think of the person or spirit that once occupied the body, or the traumatic loss of their father. Sometimes it worked, but for the most part it didn't.

The Chevy Impala crawled into the rear lot of Impressions Car Shop. They were greeted by the usual bright yellow crime scene tape, and forensic examiners milling about the scene. Latrice was the first to approach the Cadillac that contained the two bodies. They were both slumped over. The interior was splattered with drying blood. Slowly, she circled the perimeter of the car, peering inside the windows. She came to a stop at the driver's side and leaned in an attempt to get a closer look at the victims.

Todd walked up to the car, coming to a stop at her side. "You're not going to believe who's in that car."

"Who?" she looked to her brother for the answer.

"The one in the passenger seat was ID'd as Tyreek Simmons."

Latrice was slightly taken aback once the name registered. "I'm willing to bet my last dollar that all of these murders are somehow tied together." Her mind reverted back to the moment they went to the hospital to question Reek. He had lay in the hospital bed partially paralyzed, fighting for his life.

She went to the hospital room with the simple motive of questioning a witness. However, once she laid eyes on him and noticed his condition, she saw a young man who was swallowed by his circumstances. That same young man lost his battle for survival which he fought hard to win. The bullet laced body was the evidence of his defeat.

"I don't know if Terry and Mack actually pulled the trigger, but I'm almost certain that all of these deaths are linked to them." Her discomfort was clearly visible. "We have to get them off the streets..."

CHAPTER 28

Inside of a tinted, maroon Honda CR-V, Keith sat reclined in the driver's seat scanning the surrounding area. He focused on the white and gray duplex that was five houses away.

The task he was assigned was far from simple. He had to end the life of a man who was not only intelligent, but a killer himself. His nerves had been on edge ever since he began to follow Jihad ten days ago. So far Keith had been successful at keeping a tab on him from a safe distance.

To his surprise, Jihad moved to a remarkably routine schedule. Every morning, Monday through Friday, Jihad left his home by no later than eight-thirty, got into his Porsche Panamera, and drove to Starbucks. He always placed his order with the same cashier, a young, attractive Hispanic woman who never failed to provide a bright, flirtatious smile at the sight of him. Keith even noticed that his order never differed. About five minutes after entering, Jihad left the coffee shop with a large cappuccino and two blueberry scones. He never followed Jihad after that point. Doing that would highly increase the odds of him being spotted.

Every Saturday night, Jihad went to a different club or bar to unwind. Even then, he stuck to a specific schedule. He was out of his house by midnight. His only inconsistency was the time he returned home. He rarely brought a woman to his place, which meant some nights were spent at a hotel.

Keith contemplated breaking into his house and lying in wait, but even if he could get around Jihad's massive man stopping Presso Canario, there was no way he could disable the elaborate alarm system, including motion activated cameras.

With the uneasy feeling that he was pressing his luck by tailing Jihad for so long without being detected, Keith decided not to wait any longer. Being that it was ten o'clock on a Saturday night, he knew that Jihad would be leaving within two hours. He reached under the seat of the stolen SUV and pulled out his Glock 31. With a push of a button, the magazine fell into his awaiting lap. The clip was filled to it's fifteen shot capacity with massive .357 SIG bullets. After pulling the slide back and releasing it, which caused a round to be injected into the chamber, he placed the gun in his hand and waited.

———

Shawn gave Tisha directions from the reclined passenger seat of her Acura ILX. She made a right off Germantown Avenue, onto Mount Airy Street where Jihad lived. Cruising at a steady speed down the street, the CR-V caught Shawn's attention. It looked as if someone had been inside, but the windows were tinted and the dark skies didn't help pass any light. He brushed it off, instructed Tisha to pull over in front of a specific house, then removed his phone and called Jihad.

"Hello?" Jihad answered.

"I'm in front of your house. Come open the door. And put that big, dumb ass dog in the basement."

"How about I let him answer the door for me?"

"Stop playin'."

"Then don't call my dog dumb. He's put up. Come on in," Jihad said before hanging up.

Shawn gave Tisha a peck on the lips, then eased out of her car nicely dressed in a Givenchy striped sweatshirt, Paul Smith slacks and Jimmy Choo sneakers. He opened the metal fence, walked up the short flight of steps and into the moderately sized home. Jihad's house was well taken care of and furnished with great attention to detail.

He walked in and saw Jihad making a quick dash up the stairs. "Damn, cannon, you're not even dressed. I thought we was going out tonight?" Shawn didn't receive a response. A few minutes later, Jihad trudged down the stairs. After one look at Jihad's disheveled face, he knew their plans were cancelled. "Are you alright?"

"Hell no. I've been sick all fuckin' day. I think this bitch put something in my drink."

"Nigga, ain't nobody put nothing in your drink. That's all that bootleg Chinese food you be eating. Or you probably just ate some bad pussy."

"Yeah, whatever nigga. Do me a favor. Run to the store and get me some Tums."

"Aaight, but I gotta take your car, I thought I was being slick, I had my girl to drop me off so I could be chauffeured, but now you want me gettin' behind the wheel." Shawn complained. "Where's the keys?"

Jihad spun around and darted back up the stairs to the bathroom. "Kitchen counter!" He yelled, trying to hold back the vomit that was about to spew.

Shawn shook his head, walked to the kitchen, and snatched the keys off the counter. He wasn't too upset because he didn't mind taking the Porsche for a spin. He would have purchased one if Jihad hadn't beaten him to the punch.

He eased the four door coupe out of the garage and backed out of the driveway, heading down the street.

———————

Keith had just finished rolling his blunt. He grabbed his lighter and clicked it. The fire lit the weed, he took a deep pull, filling his lungs with the pungent smoke.

His eyes widened as he looked through the windshield. The Porsche Panamera had just drove past him. "Fuck!" he cursed himself as he started the SUV, threw the blunt into the ashtray, and adjusted the gun on his lap. It was now or never. He mashed down on the accelerator, pushing the CR-V to catch up to the Porsche.

———————

Shawn noticed the lights of the CR-V come to life and pull off only moments after he passed it. Once he made it to the end of the street, he made a right, then slightly reduced the speed. The Honda made the same right turn. Certain that he was being

followed, he removed his massive Dan Wesson fully automatic
.38 Super handgun from his waist. Fully loaded with twenty
one rounds in the magazine, he switched the safety off and
rolled the passenger window down, and prepared to fire his

weapon.

With one hand on the steering wheel and the other on his
gun, Keith steadily decreased the distance between the two vehicles. Odds were that he had already been spotted. If Jihad decided to flee there was no way the Honda would be able to keep
up. With few other options, Keith honked his horn and flashed
the high beams.

The Panamera pulled over to the left. Keith rolled down the
driver's window.

With nerves working on overtime, Shawn kept his finger
wrapped around the trigger of his gun. Leaning forward in an
attempt to see who was behind the wheel of the SUV, he relaxed
a bit once he recognized the driver. "Damn, li'l nigga. I didn't
know who you was."

Keith was shocked to see that Shawn was driving the car
and not Jihad. Being that he was next in line to be killed, Keith
figured he might as well get rid of him while the opportunity
presented itself. Without responding, Keith raised his Glock
and quickly fired three shots into the Porsche. The bullets narrowly missed their target. With lightning-fast speed, Shawn

aimed his gun and pulled the trigger, sending an army of bullets into the SUV. Keith fired several more rounds, and then pulled off. Astonished that none of the slugs pierced his body, Shawn pursued Keith fueled by rage. The pursuit didn't last long. The CR-V veered onto the sidewalk and crashed into a tree.

Shawn slammed on the brakes, and the Porsche came to a screeching halt. He jumped out, gun in hand, and ran up on the crashed truck. Blood trickled out of Keith's mouth as he raised his head off the steering wheel. He had been shot. He was alive, but in bad condition.

While looking into Keith's pleading eyes, Shawn raised his gun. "You should've stayed in your lane, li'l nigga!" The bombardment of slugs from the automatic gun ripped Keith's face apart. All that used to be in his head was now nothing more than a bloody mess splattered throughout the interior. Shawn hustled back to the Porsche and pulled off...

CHAPTER 29

Life had taken a tremendous upswing for Marty. With a rare opportunity to receive a second chance at success, he refused to allow failure to defeat him. With a tremendous amount of hard work, frugal spending and wise decisions, Marty had once again accumulated savings nearing seven figures. His focus was no longer on living in a prestigious home, driving the finest automobiles, and dressing in the most desired clothing.

Although his line of business called for him to be well dressed, and display an air of wealth, all that he had amassed was purchased with a newly found respect for money. He came to the understanding that the enjoyment of living a lavish life-style could only come after the hard work to secure financial freedom was put in.

Marty also learned to contain his emotions, which proved to be invaluable. Because he was back in the commodities trading business, he was forced to move among the same circles as some of his former friends and colleagues.

Marty and Vincent had been invited to a special black tie event. Although he wasn't interested in attending, he knew there would be high-positioned people present. With a little coaxing from Vincent, Marty agreed that not only would it be sensible to connect with them, but it would also be a good decision to allow people who witnessed or heard about his fall to see the clean, sober and ambitious new, Marty Frankel. He could not permit any harbored feelings to interfere with his ultimate plan.

Vincent observed his friend make a one hundred eighty degree turn for the better. The trust and faith that was shared between them allowed them to help one another in ways beyond their imagination. Marty's teachings helped him grow intellectually, becoming superior to all who were at one point on the same level.

They arrived at the event via limousine, decked in tailored black tuxedos. All of the other men in attendance donned the same colored suits with subtle variations. It was nearly impossible for one man to be distinguished from the other. The women's attire, however, was more enticing. They were casually dressed in expensive gowns and evening dresses of different colors and styles, along with exquisite jewelry.

The majority of the men and women at the gathering were egotistical, opportunistic snobs whose only concerns were personal gains. Because Marty was now aware of their motives, the advantage had shifted to his side.

There were a few people who shared whispers while cutting disdainful eyes at him. On the other hand, there were also men and women who offered pleasing smiles of approval and genuine handshakes. The varied reactions kept Marty edgy and tense. He did his best to conceal his nervousness as he greeted his peers. Vincent took notice of his brittle demeanor and pulled him aside.

"Marty, you have to relax."

"What do you mean, Vince? I'm okay."

"No, you're not! The confidence I'm used to seeing in your eyes isn't there. The way you're walking and talking is not assertive. Your handshakes aren't firm. Damn it, you have to show these people that you're not the drunk that everyone heard about. Hell, you're better than the Marty they knew before the scandal."

Vincent kept his voice low enough for only Marty to hear, but the intensity made his message very clear.

"You're absolutely right," Marty admitted, regaining his composure.

"You have a one up on everybody here. You've experienced life at both the top and the bottom. Now you're on your way back up. You have intelligence, passion and an understanding. Allow it to exude. Let them see the flame in your eyes!"

"You got it, Vince." Reinvigorated by their conversation, Marty pulled himself together. Within an instant he seemingly morphed into a confident, ambitious and energetic man of promise. The new aura he began to emit caused many who graced his presence to become intrigued by this man whom they'd heard about through gossip.

Vincent led Marty to a small congregation of powerful men. The man controlling the conversation was Andy Merola, the vice president of Global Financials, one of the top five trading firms and also one of Goldman's fiercest competitors.

After being introduced, Andy didn't hesitate to ask Marty for his insight regarding a debate the group was having concerning the fluctuation of crude oil prices. Resisting the urge to become repressed, Marty offered his opinion, which he backed by data he happened to accumulate while researching the same topic days before. All of the men, including Andy, were completely blown away by Marty's knowledge.

Seemingly out of nowhere, Jack Goldberg approached the gathering. "Good evening, gentlemen." He received handshakes from a few of the men. Marty and Andy, however, returned Jack's greeting with a nonchalant head nod. The tension was immediately evident.

Jack looked over to Vincent. "So, this is who you've been spending your time with? This can have a negative impact on your future with Goldman's."

Vincent refused to respond. People saw Jack as a business-oriented man of success. Marty, Vincent, and now Andy saw a back-stabbing, conniving, and manipulative man who knew no boundaries when it came to obtaining more power. "I must say, Marty, you look well. I'm glad to see that you've made a turn around," Jack said.

"Thank you," Marty responded evenly without displaying a hint of the anger that was boiling over inside of him. "I'm glad I made a turnaround as well." Marty's bright and confident smile displeased Jack.

During Marty's tenure at Goldman's he always went above and beyond protocol. Although he followed orders, he often did more than he was instructed to do. Any other supervisor would have seen Marty's loyalty and ambition for what it was, but not Jack. However, Jack viewed Marty as a potential threat to his position. This brought Jack to the conclusion that Marty had to be obliterated. All of his power needed to be removed. Jack devised a plan that stripped Marty of his job, money, home, and his reputation. Jack thought he had destroyed Marty, but he had returned like cancer.

Jack's companion strutted up to him carrying two flutes of champagne. "Thank you, sweetheart." He accepted one of the glasses with a slight grin.

"Gentlemen, this is my girlfriend, Kate. Marty, I'm sure the two of you have met."

This was the first time Marty had seen Kate since she abandoned him. His heart sank to the pit of his stomach. The love of his life had given her love to the man responsible for plotting his demise. Marty did his absolute best to contain his emotions.

"Good evening, Kate."

Kate was noticeably stunned. The last person on earth she expected to see at the event was Marty. She was told that he was nothing more than a homeless drunk, but he stood before her in opulence. Kate lowered her head as the realization set in that she was a simple pawn in a complex game.

"What's the matter, Marty? You look a little flushed. Would you like a drink?" Jack offered Marty the champagne glass with a devil's smirk.

"Thanks, but no thanks. I'm staying away from anything that's bad for me." Marty's words were a direct shot at Jack and his former wife. At that moment, Marty swore that he would not let either of them get away with their ultimate act of betrayal.

After accomplishing his goal of belittling Marty in front of the others, Jack grabbed Kate's hand and led her away.

The encounter threw Marty completely off balance. There was no way he could remain at the gathering knowing that Jack and Kate were there. He began to excuse himself from the others when Andy stopped him.

"Marty, I don't know everything about your past, but I do know that Jack orchestrated your downfall. I admire your courage to come back. If you ever need my assistance, just give me a call." Andy reached into his pocket and produced a business card. Marty accepted it.

"Thanks, Andy, I really appreciate it. You will be hearing from me..."

CHAPTER 30

"This shit is getting too far out of control. We don't know what Jihad or Shawn is thinking. What the fuck are we gonna do now?" Terry said, hoping that Mack would provide a decent answer. He drove through light Philadelphia traffic. Every occupant of every vehicle that he gazed at appeared to be starting their morning off wonderfully, without a care in the world. Some were involved in conversations, some were singing along to music, and others were simply living in the moment. This was not the case for Terry and Mack. The news of Keith being killed had both of them on edge. Their stress levels had dramatically risen to a peak.

"We don't have no other choice but to kill 'em ourselves." Mack revealed his thoughts, glancing at Terry who looked perplexed. "What else can we do, sit back, and play dumb while they rock us to sleep? We sent a fuckin' hit out on them niggas and they ain't dead. You think we can just go back to business

217

like everything's normal? I know Shawn and you know Jihad. They ain't stupid or scared."

"Yeah, you're right." The vivid image of Terry putting a bullet into Jihad's head sent a chill rushing down his spine. The wicked lifestyle of the streets had placed him in such a position that ending the life of his long time friend was now a likely option.

They made their way to Dynasty Rental. Both in deep thought and heavily burdened by their predicament.

Terry finally broke the silence, "There may be another option."

"What's that?"

"What if we give Jihad and Shawn the streets?"

"I don't get it."

"We've been kicking around the idea of leaving the drug game alone for a while now. We're making a ton of money with Marty, and the company is doing better than we've ever imagined. If we give them the plug on the coke they'll have what they always wanted and it'll give us a way out of the game."

"Give them the plug?" Mack asked in disbelief. "The only thing I'm trying to give them niggas is a big bullet to the head. We're in a quiet war against them and you're trying to give them the opportunity to make more money, which will give them more power. That goes against the rules of the game!" He stared blankly out of the parked car's window. "I'm not giving them the money and power to crush us."

"You're looking at it all wrong, bruh," Terry said. "First of all, we're going to limit what they can buy. Second, we're washing our hands with the streets. We're distancing ourselves from them. They won't see us as a threat."

"I don't know about this, T."

"We gotta get out of this game and this is the smartest way to do it. Look at all the legends of Philly that you told me about: Ace, Giovanni, the Junior Black Mafia. They made it to the top, but they didn't make it out. We have to learn from their mistakes." Terry looked over to Mack, who appeared to be in contemplation. "Every time you made a call that I didn't agree with, I went with you. That's because I trust you. I need you to ride with me on this one, bruh."

The momentary silence seemed to last forever until Mack spoke up. "Fuck it. I'ma ride with you. Let's do it."

Terry called Jihad, and Mack called Shawn. They were both given instructions to come to Dynasty Rentals right away. Illegal business had never before been conducted or discussed there, but it was one of the only places that everyone would feel comfortable meeting.

Terry and Mack rehashed their plan while waiting for their guests. Within an hour Shawn and Jihad showed up together, which meant it was more than likely they had already discussed the possibilities of why the meeting was called, and devised a plan themselves.

Jihad opened the door and they cautiously entered the private office. There was no denying the tension that lingered in the air like a foul stench.

"What's going on? Have a seat," Terry offered.

"Nah. I think we'll stand," Jihad countered defiantly.

"I know what went down with you and Keith, but don't come up in here like we got beef!" Mack spat and stood.

"I think we are beefin'!" Shawn erupted in a rage of his own.

"Nigga, who the fuck you talkin' to? If I had a problem with you, I'd just blow your fuckin' head off! Don't none of you niggas want a problem with me!" Mack was unable to contain his anger.

"So, what's up?" Jihad stood his ground, right hand close to his waist where a gun undoubtedly rested.

"Move your hand closer to your waist and we gon' find out who's the best," Mack growled. His hand in close proximity to his gun as well.

"Listen, we all know what we can do. But that's not why ya'll was called down here," Terry spoke up in an effort to diffuse the stand-off. "I'm losing too many of my niggas to this bullshit. We used to have to worry about the opposition knocking us off, now we got to worry about the ones closest to us. When I become weary of my own friends, that means something's gotta change. I know ya'll think we did some grimey shit. And, keepin' it a stack, we think ya'll did some snake shit. But the bottom line is I don't know, and neither do ya'll. So what I'm going to do is make myself believe that ya'll wouldn't cross us, and hopefully you two will do the same on our behalf."

"What, we're supposed to just put our thoughts to the side and act like everything's perfect? Keep it real, my nigga." Jihad stepped closer to the desk. "Shit has changed between us. We're not what we used to be. We've drifted too far apart to get back to where we were."

"You're right, Jihad. We have different goals now. I'm more focused on building a legitimate empire. You're still intent on controlling the streets. I'm definitely not knocking that. I'm...we're just moving in different directions."

"No matter what we're going through, at the end of the day we still got love for ya'll," Mack spoke up, after allowing his temper to settle. "That's why we called ya'll down here. We decided to leave the streets alone, and focus on the legit business. Instead of shutting down the operation and leaving you to fend for yourself, we wanted to see if you wanted to take over."

Jihad couldn't believe what he heard. "I don't believe you,

and I don't know if I can trust you." He took a step back and folded his arms across his chest.

"Listen, my nigga," Terry spoke in a direct tone, inadvertently showing a hint of impatience. "The only thing that changed is my game plan. This money ain't make me soft. I'm still that nigga. If I wanted to go to war with you I would do so, and I won't stop until blood is spilled – either yours or mine. But I know that all battles must be chosen wisely. I have the ability to choose my friends as well as my enemies. You're not my enemy. We're just on a different path. I'd rather for us to go our separate ways than for us to be out here trying to kill each other."

"So, you want us to believe that you're just going to give us the connect?" Shawn asked.

"No, I'm not giving you the connect," Terry responded. "I'm gonna make sure you get ten bricks a month. Nothing more, nothing less. I'm also going to put a ten percent markup on the back end. This is how it's going to be: Shawn, you have to drop the money off to Julio's garage. Jihad, a few days later Julio will give you a call to come and pick up the work. During both the drop off and pick up both of you are to be alone. I'll be calling you every month for my ten percent. If the money is ever off, or you deviate from the plan in any way, I'm shutting it down permanently. I want ya'll to be mindful that this thing is bigger than me. Don't allow greed to overpower your common sense. Your actions can impact your families."

The power of Terry's words jolted Jihad and Shawn. They understood that he was basically telling them that if anything goes awry, the Zeta Cartel would become involved. Nonetheless, the offer presented to them was accepted. All four men shook hands. Jihad and Shawn left the building knowing their lives were about to shift dramatically. The direction of that shift would depend on their decisions…

CHAPTER 31

As the weeks turned into months, Terry and Mack grew more comfortable in their decision to wash their hands of all illegal activity. Despite their retirement from the drug game, they kept a watchful eye on Jihad and Shawn. The stakes were simply too high. It was undeniable that they were smart hustlers, but they also had grimy tendencies. The relinquish of Terry and Mack's position of power was calculated. It was not given to Jihad and Shawn out of fear, nor love. The acceptance of this power was received with the understanding that there could very well be ulterior motives. Defense was being played on both sides.

When Terry and Mack broke the news that they were officially one hundred percent legit to Marty he was elated. He and Vincent began teaching them more about the intricacies of stocks and investing, which was now an integral part of their new way of life.

Terry and Mack decided to celebrate by throwing a huge and extravagant all-white party, representing purity…a legitimate life. This party was touted as an epic event on radio and social media. To ensure that only the *crem de la crem* attended, admission was two hundred dollars and five thousand dollars for VIP seating. Everyone from sports stars to celebrities to corporate executives were set to attend.

After two months of constant promotion, the night of the party had come. The African American Art Museum on Seventh and Arch Street was the place worthy of such an ostentatious celebration. The fall night held a comfortable temperature and produced a wind just strong enough to cause a few colorful leaves to dance along the sidewalk. The full moon along with a few stars radiated as they stood out against the backdrop of the cloudless dark blue sky like LED lights. Minute by minute, luxury cars began to arrive. Well-dressed men and women of many nationalities pulled up near the entrance, handed their keys to the valet, and headed into the building.

Shortly after eleven thirty, two rare, luxurious and beautiful automobiles pulled up directly in front of the building. The first, a pewter colored Bentley Mulsanne Speed, Bentley's flagship sedan. This opulent yacht on wheels dwarfed even the Mercedes S class sedan. The second car was a pearl white and silver Bugatti Veyron. A one point five million dollar, two hundred mile per hour work of art. After the automobiles came to a stop, two suited security guards left the sidewalk and placed four orange cones around the perimeters of the magnificent cars.

Mack opened the driver's door of his Mulsanne and stepped out donning a white tailored Brunello Cucinelli sport jacket, white silk-cotton blend button down shirt and pants by Alexander Wang. A light brown leather John Varvatos belt and matching Santoni loafers rounded out his outfit.

At nearly the same time, Terry opened the door of his Bugatti and eased out. He wore a Canali white sport jacket and Tom Ford white button down shirt and slacks. His outfit was offset by a charcoal gray and black checkered Louis Vuiton belt and gray Louis Vuiton loafers.

Terry walked up to Mack and gave him a hug. At that moment an overwhelming feeling of accomplishment engulfed them. They were two men from two different states, yet their ambitions were the same. Their loyalty towards one another helped to create an unbreakable bond. Both men had risen out of the bucket of despair and were now considered successful by anyone's standards.

"We did it, bruh," Mack said.

"Can you believe this shit?" Terry looked around at the museum with people steadily pulling up and making their way inside. "All of these people are here for us!"

"Yeah, we made it, T. We're game changers now. It's only one place to go from here…"

"That's straight to the top!" Terry gave Mack a pound and they prepared for their grand entrance.

Once inside, the legendary DJ Green Lantern's voice blared over the speakers as he saluted Terry and Mack. People greeted them with warm smiles and handshakes. Some were even recording and taking pictures with their phones.

All the well-dressed men and women complimented the upscale interior of the museum. One couple, in particular, stood off in a corner, casually bobbing to the music while simultaneously keeping visual surveillance.

"I spent my entire week's salary on this outfit, plus two hundred dollars for that ticket. It damn well better be worth it," Detective Todd said above the music, but just loud enough for his partner to hear.

"I'm a little upset about the two hundred dollars for the ticket, but not this outfit. This thing will be back on the rack at Macy's first thing tomorrow," Detective Latrice admitted.

Todd giggled. His smile instantly vanished as he tapped Latrice on the shoulder. She quickly zeroed in on the two reasons that she was there: Terry and Mack. They were responsible for large quantities of cocaine hitting the streets of Philadelphia, and multiple murders which came as a result of their drug operation. And there they were, smiling and shaking hands among the affluent without a care in the world. Latrice took a deep breath in an effort to subdue her rising anger.

Todd sensed his sister's shift of emotion. "We have to act normal or we're going to stick out like a sore thumb."

They walked to the bar and placed an order for an apple and a dry Martini. The two detectives sat on stools sipping their drinks while keeping a casual eye on their persons of interest.

Terry and Mack made it to their VIP section where chilled bottles of Ace Of Spades and Louis the Thirteenth awaited. After a few drinks, their moods were amplified. Terry looked out into the crowd. An older woman wearing a long, beautiful white dress was slowly weaving through the throng of people, heading in his direction. In a flash he jumped up from his seat and hurried toward the lady. He embraced his mother, Anita, with a strong, lingering hug.

"Ma, I thought you said you wouldn't be able to make it?"

"Shit, boy your bad ass used to lie to me at least three times a day. I can't lie to you once?" Her bright smile was infectious. Terry leaned in for another hug. Anita took a small step back and scanned her son from head to toe. "Look at my baby. You're so handsome. You were supposed to be a model. You look just like your father."

"Thanks, Ma." Terry began to blush.

"Speaking of your father, he stopped by the restaurant a few days ago. I told him that you were doing good and I mentioned your party. He begged me to ask you if he could come. I told him I'd ask you, but I didn't bother because I knew what your answer would be."

"Thanks for handling that, Ma. Our lives have been so much better without him in it. I lost my father when I was a kid. He chose heroin over us and he can never take that back."

"I know baby." Anita noticed the somber look on her son's face and immediately regretted bringing Terry senior up. "Forget that, baby. This is your special night. There's a lot of people here who wants to see you, so show them that perfect smile that you got from ya mamma. We'll have plenty of time to talk later."

"Okay, Ma," Terry responded, giving her a warm smile.

"I'm going to get a glass of champagne. And, I saw a fine man over there by the bar...let's see if Stella can get her groove back."

"Behave yourself young lady!" Terry kissed his mother on the cheek and she weaved into the crowd.

Terry turned around to come face to face with Jihad and Shawn. They were both dressed for the occasion and holding bottles of Cliquot in their hands.

"Congratulations, T-Lova," Jihad took a sip from his bottle.

"Thanks, yo." Terry gave them both pounds. "I'm glad ya'll came. How you been doing?"

"We're doing good. As a matter of fact, I need to holla at you and Mack. I need you to increase our order by five bricks." Jihad said just loud enough for Terry to hear over the music.

"I told you that the order won't increase. You're getting more than enough for you to stack some good paper...listen, this is not the time or the place to talk about that. Give me a ring tomorrow and…"

"Congratulations, Terry!" Vincent interrupted. "This turn out is absolutely amazing."

Terry turned his back to Shawn and Jihad to face Vincent. It was evident that he didn't want to introduce Vincent to them. "Thanks, Vincent."

"See what happens when you stop chasing peanuts?"

"Yeah this is a much different ball game," Terry responded. He could smell alcohol wafting from Vincent as he spoke.

"Oh yeah, I received a promising call today. I think it will be in your best interest to order an extra hundred barrels," Vincent looked Terry in the eyes and patted him on the shoulder. "You guys are making more money than the president. Welcome to the major leagues."

Jihad was inebriated but his hearing was crisp. He picked up on the bulk of the conversation between Terry and the elegantly dressed white man.

"Where's Marty?" Terry inquired, changing the subject.

"He's over there, talking to Mack." Vincent pointed a tipsy finger towards the VIP section. He looked bewildered after following his own index finger and noticing that the VIP section was empty. "I could have sworn"

Marty, who was accompanied by Mack, placed a hand on Vincent's shoulder. "How are you guys doing?"

"We're great!" Vincent exclaimed. "I was just telling Terry that he should seriously consider purchasing more---"

Unlike Vincent, Marty was completely sober. He quickly honed in on the two men who were within earshot. He had never seen them before. "I'm sure Terry would rather discuss that matter in a more private setting," Marty interjected. "Terry, it appears these two young men are waiting to speak with you."

He gestured toward Shawn and Jihad. "We'll have plenty of time to talk later. Congratulations on this wonderful event." After shaking Terry's hand, he escorted Vincent away.

"Who was that?" Jihad's thoughts manifested into words before he could catch himself.

"Just a couple of friends," Mack answered dismissively.

"Sounds like they're more than *just friends* to me." Jihad paused to take a swig of alcohol from his bottle. "I just asked T-Lova to increase our order and before I knew it, *El Hefe* comes up telling him to increase his barrels order."

Mack quickly put two and two together, which caused him to laugh.

"That dude mentioned barrels. It's only one thing that's coming in by the barrels," Jihad continued.

"Oh yeah? What's that?" Terry asked. He knew Jihad's answer would amuse them.

"Nigga, he's talking about heroin! Ya'll gettin' at that real paper, knowing we'd be satisfied with the scraps."

Both Terry and Mack laughed in their faces. Their nonchalant attitudes worked with the alcohol to anger Jihad.

"Ya'll laughin', but you know I'm right. Wassup? You gon' put a nigga on, or keep me as the low man on the totem pole?" The question was posed to Terry.

"Listen, Jihad," Terry spoke above the music so that he could be heard clearly. "We're one hundred percent legit, cannon. He was talking about a legal investment. We invest in commodities."

"Damn, you can look me straight in my eyes and lie to me now?" Jihad said, chuckling. "I guess it's official; I really don't know you anymore."

"I guess you never knew me, 'cuz if you did, for one, you'd

BEANIE SIGEL & JUMA SAMPSON

know that I don't fuck with heroin. And for two, you'd know the only mutha fuckas I gotta lie to is the cops and the judge!"

Mack noticed that Terry was getting agitated and a few heads were turning in their direction. "Man, we're all out of pocket for even discussing this type of shit right now. We're supposed to be enjoying ourselves. What Terry told you is true. It don't matter if you believe him or not. It is what it is. Now if ya'll want to discuss this some more, cool. But definitely not here and not now. Ya'll can either enjoy the rest of the evening or get the fuck out!" With that said, Mack and Terry left Jihad and Shawn standing alone.

"Come on, let's get the fuck outta here," Shawn tapped Jihad's arm as he turned to walk away.

Jihad jerked his arm away as if Shawn's hand was contaminated. "Now you got a mouth? You ain't have nothin' to say while both of them niggas was spinnin' me!"

"I ain't say nothin' because maybe they wasn't lyin'."

Jihad suppressed a giggle as he took a swig from his bottle. "Yo, you green as a fuckin' pool table. I don't know why I snatched you from Mack. I should have handled this shit myself." Jihad spun off on Shawn using his large frame to part the crowd of partygoers. He headed directly towards the door. Shawn stood in place amazed at what the alcohol caused Jihad to confess. He thought back to the moment they became allies, during the plane trip from Miami. Jihad deceived him, causing him to be at odds with Mack. But the game wasn't over yet.

"Did you get that?" Detective Todd asked.

"Every second of it," Detective Latrice responded while discretely tucking her iPhone back into her clutch.

"Whoever those guys are, the conversation didn't seem casual."

"I agree. We have to find out who they are. And those white

men as well." The detectives finished their drinks and departed...

CHAPTER 32

Two days had passed since the altercation between Jihad and Shawn at the African American Art Museum. Jihad made an attempt to make light of his words and Shawn casually dismissed it, blaming the liquor. Everything continued as normal.

Their shipment of cocaine was scheduled to arrive in three days. Shawn had a little over one kilo remaining, and the way his phone was ringing, he knew it would all be sold before the day was over. He was cruising down Broad Street in his blacked out Dodge Challenger SRT, zoning out to Meek Mill's new mix tape when the phone rang. The music instantly muted when he answered.

"Wassup?"

"Wassup, young bawh?" Abdul Malik's voice came through the car's speakers. He was an OG from Passyunk Projects who ran the streets with Mack's father back in the day. After serving

231

a considerable amount of time in federal prison, he was sent back to the same streets a lot older, and stigmatized as a felon. The only place that would be slow to discriminate and quick to hire him was the streets. Therefore, he returned to what he'd been doing throughout his entire life – hustling.

"Wassup, old head?"

"Man, I'm mad as hell. I went to get a pack of smokes and they turned me down 'cause I was short a quarter!"

Shawn picked up on the key word, which was quarter. That meant Malik wanted to buy a quarter kilo of cocaine. "Don't worry about that, I'll bring you a pack of smokes. Where you at?"

"I'm in Passyunk Projects."

"Aaight, give me fifteen minutes." Shawn hung up, drove to his apartment that was used to store his drugs, weighed two hundred and fifty grams on the triple beam scale, placed it in a plastic Zip Lock bag, grabbed his Taurus 9 mm, and left.

On his way to make the sale, he drove down Hartranft Street. Blake was standing in front of the corner store when he saw the Challenger heading in his direction.

He waved his hands in the air, getting Shawn's attention. Shawn abruptly pulled over once he noticed who it was. Blake owed him thirty five hundred dollars. He got in the passenger's seat and counted two grand for Shawn and promised to call him later to pay off the remaining balance. Blake got out of the car and Shawn pulled off, merging into traffic.

A Philadelphia patrol vehicle was a few cars behind, noticed the black Dodge Challenger pull into traffic without using its signal. The officer also noticed that the driver wasn't wearing his safety belt. He activated his flashing lights. The two cars in front of him pulled over immediately. The officer sped up until he was directly behind the Challenger.

"Fuck!" Shawn cursed after looking in his rear view mirror. He saw the bright whir of lights. His first instinct was to fasten his seatbelt and put the 707 horsepower engine crammed into his Challenger Hellcat to the test. Shawn had a valid driver's license and his new car was properly insured. After reasoning with himself, he pulled over.

Coming to a stop behind the Challenger, the officer slid out of his patrol car, and walked up to the driver's side of the muscle car.

"Can you please turn your car off, sir?"

Shawn did as he was told. "Is there a problem, officer?"

"License and registration, please." The officer gave the request, ignoring Shawn's question.

As Shawn reached over to the glove box to retrieve the car's registration, the officer placed his hand on his holstered firearm. He watched cautiously as Shawn grabbed the registration, and then dug into his jeans pocket to remove his driver's license.

The officer looked from the license to Shawn – from Shawn to the license. He concluded that it was in fact his picture on the license. "You pulled away from the curb and into traffic without activating your turn signal. You're also not wearing your safety belt."

"I'm sorry, officer. I was in a rush to pick up my uncle from work."

"Sit tight while I run your information." The officer returned to his vehicle.

Shawn sat inside the car, doing his best to calm himself. He knew he didn't have any warrants, so the most the officer could do was issue him a few tickets and send him on his way.

Within five minutes the officer was out of his car and walking back towards Shawn. By the time he made it to the door of the Challenger, another patrol car pulled over in front of it. "Sir, can you step out of the vehicle, please?" It was more of a demand than a request.

"Did I do something wrong?" Tiny beads of sweat quickly formed on Shawn's forehead. His throat tightened.

"You have a felony drug conviction, you're in a car that costs over sixty thousand dollars, and you just pulled off from a known drug area. That gives me probable cause to search you." He lied. "Now can you please step out of the vehicle?" The officer who was now accompanied by another, kept his hand on his weapon. His hawk-like eyes were lasered on Shawn. He was prepared to react if any sudden movements were made.

Shawn's heart began to beat like African drums during a ceremony. He looked at the two imposing white policemen and knew that he had no chance of escaping.

The drugs and gun were tucked under the passenger seat. He had nothing on his person. He opened the door and eased out of the car as calmly as possible. The officers, who were seasoned, observed Shawn's outward appearance. Nervousness and anxiety were clearly evident in his demeanor.

They escorted Shawn to the rear of his car. "Place your hands on the trunk and spread your legs, sir." Shawn did as he was instructed. While conducting the pat down, the officer removed a large sum of money from his front pockets. "This is a lot of money. How much do you have here?"

"Umm...I have around nine hundred in my left pocket, and...two thousand in my right," he said, after recalling exactly how much Blake gave him.

"What are you doing driving around with so much money on you?"

"I had a good night at the casino this weekend. Is it illegal to have money?"

"Not at all, but when I find someone to be in possession of large amounts of money, and the majority of the bills are in small denominations, it gives me reasonable suspicion to believe it's drug money."

"Well, that ain't drug money."

"Zartman, search his car," the officer said to the other one.

"You can't do that. I didn't give you permission to search my car!" Shawn began to turn around to face the officer.

"Place your hands behind your back!" He commanded after spinning Shawn back around.

The will for survival took precedent. Shawn used his weight to push the officer back, then took off.

The officer quickly regained his footing and gave chase. "Freeze… Stop mother fucker or I'm going to shoot!" He radioed for backup.

The officer's threat was ignored as Shawn rapidly threw one leg in front of the other. He dodged cars as he ran across the street, darted between two houses, heading toward the rear. There was a metal fence that was chest high about thirty feet in front of him. He mentally prepared to jump it as he quickly became closer. Shawn placed his hands on top of the fence, but before he could hoist himself up, a powerful force slammed into him, knocking his tired body to the ground, and the wind out of his chest.

The uniformed officer delivered a barrage of punches and kicks to Shawn's face and body. "Stop resisting you son of a bitch!"

"I'm…not…resisting!" Shawn screamed in between blows from the relentless assault.

Out of breath and gasping for air, the officer turned Shawn

over. He dropped a knee into his back, twisted his hands behind his back with such force that Shawn thought his arm was broken. He then slammed the handcuffs over his wrists, securing them tightly. Shawn screamed in pain while being pulled to his feet by the cuffs. The officer radioed in his location and informed the other officers that the suspect had been detained.

"What the fuck you beat me up for?" he asked, taking in huge gulps of air.

"Shut your black ass up. You're lucky I didn't feel like doing the extra paperwork or I would have blown your fucking head off, you piece of shit! It's not like anyone would have given a fuck." The back-up officers met them as they were coming from the rear of the house.

"Looks like he took a fall," one of the officers said with a smirk, noticing Shawn's busted lip, along with his blood and grass stained shirt.

"The asshole took a swing at me," he lied.

"You're lucky it wasn't me," the black officer stated. "If it was, the coroner would have been coming to pick your ass up." Shawn was taken back to where the incident occurred and placed in the rear of a patrol car. A few minutes later, he was escorted to the police station and taken to an interview room. It was small, with nothing but a table that had a single chair on one side and two chairs on the opposite side. It was evident that the eggshell white walls hadn't been painted, or even cleaned, in years. There was also a tiny camera nestled in the upper corner of the wall.

Shawn sat in the uncomfortable chair inside the cold and unwelcoming room for nearly an hour, long enough to allow the depth of his situation to sink in. He thought of all the things he should have done differently to avoid being in the position he was in. Finally, he heard the sound of a key unlocking the door. When the door opened, a young, Hispanic man dressed in an inexpensive button down shirt, tan slacks and brown leather loafers walked in. He carried a cup of coffee and a file. After placing the items on the table, he introduced himself.

"Hello, Shawn Robinson. I'm Detective Melendez with the Philadelphia Special Investigation Unit."

"How you doin'?" Shawn responded dryly.

Detective Melendez snickered. "A lot better than you, I'm afraid." He watched as Shawn's head sank, then continued, "Look, my man, I'm going to be honest with you. You're in a shit load of trouble. You're being charged with illegally possessing a firearm, possession of two hundred and fifty grams of cocaine, resisting arrest and assault on an officer."

"Man, I never hit that cop. He's lyin'!"

"I never asked you how you're pleading to the charges. And to make matters worse," Detective Melendez opened a brown file and fingered through a few pages, "you have a prior felony conviction for drug possession and assault." Melendez shook his head in disappointment, placed his hands flat on the table, and looked Shawn directly in his eyes. "I don't give a rat's ass if you're lucky enough to hire the best lawyer in the United States, you're still going to prison for a very long time. And if we hand this over to the feds, which will more than likely be the case, you'll be charged as an armed career offender. With these charges, you'll get life.

"At this point you have two options: Either you can ask for a lawyer, at which point I will leave this room, and you will never take another breath of free air. Or, you can help yourself out of this situation. If you decide to help yourself, the only chance you'll have at getting your freedom back is if you have something really big to offer. Either way, it's up to you…"

CHAPTER 33

Vincent inhaled deeply as the crisp morning air shot into his nostrils, filling his lungs. He slowly exhaled while walking into the prestigious Goldman's building, and mentally prepared himself for the tedious day that lay ahead. He made his way to the elevator and pushed the Up button. A moment later, the doors whisked open, and he entered. There were five other people aboard. He gave a courteous head nod, which for the most part went ignored by the people who were lost in their own world. He pressed fourteen, and then stood motionless.

Vincent had been on this elevator more times than he could count, and the awkward feeling never failed to present itself during the brief ride.

Everyone stood in an uncomfortable silence like horses in a starting gate, anticipating the opening of the door, so they can speed to their destination. Once the elevator reached the four-teenth floor, it issued a light chime, and the door opened smoothly. Just like the others, Vincent scurried off.

With one hand clutching his black, leather Marc Jacobs briefcase, he used his free hand to unbutton his wool pea coat, maintaining his stride. He shared curt greetings with those he passed en route to his office. Once there, he unlocked his door and entered, placing his briefcase on his desk and hanging his coat on the standing rack, and then took a seat behind his desk. Before he had a chance to turn his computer on, there was a knock at his door. "Come in!"

Vincent's secretary, Marylin, walked in carrying a steaming cup of coffee, placing it next to him. Marylin was forty three years old, with a light tan, and sandy brown hair. She had hazel brown eyes that were filled with expression, high cheek bones and an admirable body that she dedicated one hour a day in the gym. She stopped aging ten years ago. "Good morning, Vin-cent."

"Good morning, Marylin. Thanks for the coffee."

"Don't thank me just yet. I may have to make you a fresh cup. Jack just called. He asked me to make sure that you go to see him as soon as you step in. He said it's urgent."

"Have you noticed that everything around here is urgent?"

"Yeah, everything except a pay raise," Marylin responded lightheartedly, and then left.

Vincent got up to leave, but before exiting, he retrieved his cell phone from his coat to take with him. Once again, he boarded the elevator and was struck with the same cumber-some feeling being cast off by a different group of people. Like them, he had become preoccupied in his thoughts.

Since the encounter at the black tie event, their conversa-tions had become limited. Vincent understood that Jack held the power, and a wrong move on his end, or a simple decision by Jack, could derail his future at Goldman's. Therefore, he had begun to prepare for the worst, and walked lightly in the process.

The elevator came to a rest on the twentieth floor where Jack's office was located. He was greeted in the reception area by Lois, Jack's secretary. "Good morning, Vincent. Jack is in his office. He's expecting you."

"Thank you." Vincent casually made his way to the large mahogany wood door and knocked.

"Come in, Vincent." The barrier muffled Jack's voice to a barely perceivable sound.

Vincent walked in and saw Jack in a tailored gray suit sitting behind his large and unquestionably expensive polished mahogany desk. His piercing eyes settled on Vincent, never wandering away as he neared. "Have a seat." Vincent sat down in a leather chair in front of his boss. "I would like to ask you a few questions."

"Go right ahead, sir." Vincent felt like he was back in college having an uneasy conversation with the dean, as butterflies churned in his stomach.

"Do you like your position here at Goldman's?"

"Yes, sir. This has been my dream since high school."

"There's no question that you have a knack for what you do, but I'll be honest with you. Everyone who works in this building has talent. Relying solely on your skills set can only get you so far. Is your ultimate goal to ascend the ladder, or are you satisfied with remaining complacent?"

Vincent shifted slightly in his seat. "Of course, I would love a higher position."

"Well, that can only be done if you have the backing by the right people...people like me. And, in order for me to make that recommendation, I have to feel confident that your ultimate goal is to make sure that this company continues it's legacy of being profitable. You must understand that the position you attain will come as a result of the role you play." Jack's words trailed off into silence. He wanted to be sure that Vincent digested them completely before he continued. "Are you ready to play a more pivotal role here at Goldman's?"

"Sure."

"Fine. Here's your first task. I want you to sell eighty percent of the company's shares of Schumblinger."

Vincent was very familiar with Schumblinger. It was an oil company that had been receiving a lot of attention over the past few weeks. "But Jack, why would you sell eighty percent of those shares? Schumblinger is preparing to merge with oil field equipment maker, Carmen, in a deal that's valued at eleven point six billion dollars. This will make them the world's largest oil field company. The Schumblinger shares jumped forty two percent at the news that both companies approved the deal. The shares are going to rise another thirty-four percent, at minimum, before the close of the day."

"No, Vincent. As of right now, those shares are valued at fifty nine dollars and ninety three cents. By the end of closing, I'll be surprised if they're worth eight dollars."

"With all due respect, Jack, what you're saying doesn't make sense. Goldman's will make millions of dollars because of this merger."

Jack leaned forward in his chair, resting his elbows on the desk and interlocking his fingers. "Listen to me, son. The board of both companies did approve the deal, but the transaction is still subject to Carmen shareholders' approval, and regulatory approval. There will be a meeting today and by the end of this evening it will be announced that the deal did not go through."

"How could you be certain that this will happen?"

"Maybe one day you will work yourself up to my position and you will align yourself with allies as I have." Jack leaned back in his chair. "For your work, I will issue you a two hundred thousand dollar bonus and approve a ten percent annual raise."

"Is this the same way you lured Marty Frankel into destroying his career?" Vincent asked, locking eyes with Jack.

"What in the hell are you talking about?"

"This is insider trading and you know it. You also know that I'm cleared to trade those stocks, so if the shit hits the fan it'll blow in my face while you stay squeaky clean!"

"Let me tell you something, asshole," Jack's voice boomed like a father when scolding his son. "Marty made the decision that destroyed his career. He began as a team player, then during the middle of the game he wanted to change the rules to suit himself. That's not how it goes! Do you think that what I'm doing is groundbreaking? No, it's not. Insider trading builds money, which builds power, which is the foundation of this company. Goldman's is a juggernaut. Neither one of us can stop its growth. Hell, Jesus can't stop it. Now I suggest you get off your moral high-horse and get with the goddamn program, son." Jack's voice dominated the room.

"I believe you plan on destroying my career the same way you sabotaged, Marty's. But, what you don't realize is that you failed in destroying Marty's spirit. And I won't give you a chance to ruin the reputation that I've worked so hard to build. I quit, Jack."

The laughter that bellowed from Jack's gut was so immense that it confused the entire situation. "What do you think your resignation will do? You can't stop the world from turning.

Only money can. There's a line of young men and women praying that you quit so they can assume your position with no questions asked. As a matter of fact, now that I see you're unfit to be under this company's employ, I'm relieving you of your position effective today."

Unable to find the perfect words to combat Jack's, Vincent stood up, and turned to leave. Before his hand grasped the shiny brass door knob, Jack yelled out, "By the way, if any of this conversation gets out, I'll show you how much power I truly have!" He released another deep, hearty laugh.

"We'll see who has the last laugh, Jack!" he shouted before exiting the office.

On the opposite side of the door, he removed the phone from his pocket, hoping the recording app worked properly. He turned the phone off and replaced it in the inner pocket of his suit jacket.

Vincent's heart felt as if it was going to beat its way out of his chest. Perspiration seeped out of the pores of his armpits, chest and forehead. He couldn't believe what he had just done. He had challenged King Kong in his own jungle. His body moved on auto pilot while his brain raced to put everything into perspective and figure out what his next move would be.

Before he knew it, he was back in his office, pacing back and forth. Time was of the essence. He called Marty and explained what had transpired. Marty gave Vincent a few instructions before they hung up.

There was no one Marty wanted to experience the feeling of having everything taken away from him more than Jack. The same man Marty admired as a friend and mentor had single handedly shattered his life. Not only did he strip him of his life's accumulations, he also stripped him of his wife. Marty knew that Jack didn't love Kate. He simply kept her as a trophy for his accomplishments.

They made their decisions and Marty had made his. He was going to do everything he could to bring *Jack The Ripper* down. He was aware that this battle would be bigger than David versus Goliath. For him to dethrone Jack, he needed the blessings of God, luck, and every other imaginable force on his side. Balls the size of grapefruits, too.

Marty scrolled down the numbers stored in his phone until he came across the name he had been searching for: Andy Merolla.

On the third ring Andy picked up. "Hello?"

"Andy, how are you doing? This is Marty."

"Marty?"

"Yes, we met at the black tie event."

There was a slight pause.

"...Oh, yes. Marty Frankel from New York City. What's up, pal? How are you doing?"

"I'm doing well. Listen, at the event you told me that you heard about what happened to me as a result of placing my trust in Jack."

"Yes. I've known Jack for a very long time. I hate to say it, but what he did to you is not out of his character. We are his main competitor. I'm well aware that he would love to bring me down. But I've been fortunate enough to stay a step ahead of him."

"Well, he now has an enemy who's hell bent on destroying him. I'll be honest with you, I have a little dirt on him, but it's nowhere near enough to topple him. I'm not sure if, or how, you can help, but any assistance you can provide will be greatly appreciated. And, you have my word that *nothing* will come back on you."

There was another pause. This time it was longer. Finally, Andy broke the silence. "The enemy of my enemy is my friend. I have something that may help you. Give me a safe and secure address and I will send you what I have on a flash drive..."

CHAPTER 34

Jihad wrapped the thick, blue rubber band around the final ten thousand dollar stack of money. He placed it on the table next to the others and looked at the bundles of currency approvingly. There were twenty-five stacks in all for a total of two hundred and fifty thousand dollars, enough to purchase ten kilos of cocaine.

The money was supposed to be dropped off to Julio's garage by Shawn. However, Jihad had been calling and texting Shawn since the day before but had not reached him. *Fuck it,* Jihad thought as he began to drop the stacks into a green book bag. *If that nigga ain't serious about this money, then I'ma get it all.*

Jihad then called Terry. He told him that he needed to speak with him right away, and that it was concerning their *arrangement.* Terry informed him that he was at Dr. Denim on South Street and to get there within the next fifteen minutes. He grabbed the book bag containing the money and left.

During the drive to meet Terry, Jihad's phone rang. "Hello?"

"Wassup? Where you at?" Shawn asked.

"Nigga, where you at? I been callin' you since yesterday!"

"Long story. I'll explain it to you later. Did you put your half together?" Shawn asked, referring to his one hundred and twenty five thousand to purchase five of the ten kilos.

"Bruh, you're too late."

"Watchu mean?"

"I had to take everything to Julio earlier," Jihad lied, "that's why I was blowin' your phone up."

"Aaight, well I'll give you back your bread that you put in for me."

"I didn't have all the money. I had to call a couple of niggas and tell them to give me their money in advance. Now I have to give them theirs off the top. I wouldn't have to do that if you would've picked up ya fuckin' phone," Jihad's frustration was apparent.

Shawn couldn't believe what he was hearing. He had made a deal with the Philadelphia Narcotics Unit to give them a bust within a week. His plan was to purchase the five kilos and use one of them to set up an unsuspecting buyer. Now his plan seemed to be unraveling and he couldn't afford for that to happen.

"Listen, bruh, I can't wait for the next time. I'm counting on this. You have to give them their bread back."

Jihad grinned at the sound of desperation in Shawn's voice as he drove through the Philadelphia streets. He had to put an end to this conversation because he was approaching Dr. Denim where Terry awaited.

"Man, you know I can't just take them dude's money and not bring them what they're expecting. What I'm gon' tell 'em, that the work didn't come through? Then what's gon' happen when they find out I got work?

I ain't no sucka, but I gotta respect their gangsta. That's asking for trouble. I'll tell you what, I got five of my own. I'll sell you two."

"Two?" Shawn spat. "What the fuck am I-" Shawn fought to hold his tongue. "Alright. I'll holla at you tomorrow. He hung up before Jihad could respond.

Fuck it. I'll have eight birds for myself. Jihad thought. *If this nigga slip again, I'm gon' cut him all the way out.*

As Jihad drove down South Street, he spotted Terry's Mercedes, and parked in front of Dr. Denim. Terry was inside his car. Jihad got out of his SUV and into the passenger side of the Mercedes.

Jihad explained to Terry that he understood the protocol was for Shawn to drop the money off, but he hadn't heard from him in days. He asked for Terry's permission to make the drop this time. Terry grudgingly consented, then called Julio and explained that he would be seeing Jihad on two occasions: both the drop off and the pickup. Jihad thanked him and left. He returned to his SUV feeling exuberant. He headed to Julio's garage to drop off the money.

TWO DAYS LATER

At 7:16 a.m., Jihad was dressed and prepared to leave his house. He was expected to be at Julio's garage no later than 8:00

a.m. He had been up for over an hour anticipating the transaction. For the first time, he would have eight kilos of cocaine to himself.

He figured he'd sell Shawn two ki's...this time. But, Jihad had been questioning his partnership with Shawn. He had used Shawn to get as far as he could. He was no longer needed. On the next purchase, Jihad had decided he would take everything, including Shawn's life.

One of the garage doors to Julio's shop was raised, and Jihad pulled his Grand Cherokee inside. As soon as he killed the engine, one of the servicemen lowered the door.

Julio was leaning inside the raised hood of a Ford F-150 tinkering with the engine when Jihad approached.

"Are you sure you know what you're doing?" Jihad quipped. His generous smile negated the intimidating appearance of his large and solid frame.

Julio straightened up. "If I don't then I've been lucky for a really long time. How's it going?"

"Everything's okay. Nothing to complain about."

Julio gave Jihad a curious look as if to say: Are you sure? Jihad noticed it, but didn't comment. "Mr. Lajas called this morning," Julio said. "He wants Terry to give him a call from a secured phone right away. He said there will be no more business until they speak."

"Alright, Julio. I'll be sure to let him know."

"The Cherokee is ready," Julio stated, then leaned into the F-150's engine bay again.

Normally, they held a small conversation, but this time Julio was short on words.

Jihad didn't push the issue. He walked back to his SUV and hopped in. He turned in his seat and gave a quick glance behind him. On the floor in the rear was a black book bag. Jihad smiled, knowing that ten kilos of quality cocaine was inside. The door raised and he backed out of the garage.

While driving down Broad Street, Jihad thought about the brief conversation he had with Julio. Not only did Mr. Lajas, the connect, want to speak with Terry, but Julio's demeanor wasn't the same. He was distant. Maybe Terry wasn't fulfilling his obligation with the cartel. Jihad had been working on establishing a relationship with Julio in order to somehow slide in and eventually cut Terry out. He hated being told how much cocaine he could buy, as well as paying Terry and Mack an extra percentage on each shipment. Jihad was having second thoughts of selling Shawn those two ki's just in case things dried up for a while.

He came to a stop at Broad and Erie Avenue. A black cargo van came to a screeching halt directly in front of Jihad's Cherokee. Men wearing all black poured out from the rear of the van, swarmed the SUV with handguns aimed at Jihad. His heart froze with fear as he thought: *It's a hit! I'm dead!*

After about three seconds – which felt more like ten minutes – without the crackling sound of gunshots, he focused on the assailants enough to notice gold badges hanging around a few of their necks. His brain then allowed him to register the words being shouted at him.

"Police! Keep your fucking hands up!"

Jihad rapidly swiveled his neck left to right, his wide eyes frantically searching for an escape. There was no way out. Unmarked cars were positioned behind him. A minimum of eight police officers yelled aggressively with their guns trained on him. One false move and his life would come to a brutal and bloody end. He put the Cherokee in Park and raised his hands toward the roof.

Two burly officers snatched the driver's door open. Each

one grabbed one of Jihad's raised hands, pulled him out of the SUV, and slammed him violently to the ground. He was handcuffed, searched, and placed into the rear of a black unmarked police car. No one said a word to him. He watched in dismay as they began to search his SUV. An officer removed the black backpack, unzipped it and peered inside. Jihad watched his eyes light up. The officers began giving one another high fives and pats on the backs.

Everything felt surreal to Jihad. He couldn't believe what was happening. He dropped his head into his chest, struggling to come to grips with reality.

He was driven to the Thirty-Fifth Police District and escorted into the interrogation room where he sat for hours. During this time, Jihad raked his brain in an attempt to figure out who was responsible for informing the police on him. This was not a routine traffic stop. Who was behind it? There were only four people who knew the date and time he would pick up the drugs: Julio, Shawn, Terry and Mack. He was in the process of weighing the possibilities of each person being involved when the door opened and Melendez walked in. He dropped a thick folder onto the table and sat down. There was no introduction.

"Jihad Wilson, you are being charged with Possession of a Controlled Substance for ten kilos of cocaine that was recovered from your vehicle. The Narcotics Unit has just secured a search warrant for Julio's garage. Depending on what's found you may face additional charges, chiefly, conspiracy." Melendez thumbed through the paper work inside the folder, shook his head, and then chuckled. "You are so finished. I sure hope you enjoyed your last piece of pussy because you'll never get any more. Well, better you than me."

"Man I…"

"Wait, before you say anything, let me read you your rights." Melendez recited Jihad his Miranda Warning rights, advising him of his right to remain silent, right to have an attorney present, and the fact that anything he said could and would be used against him in a court of law. "Do you understand your rights?"

"Yeah."Jihad answered.

"Good. It doesn't take a rocket scientist to figure out that you'll never enjoy your freedom again. If you do happen to avoid getting a life sentence, by the time you get out you'll be too old to wipe your own ass after you take a shit. There's only one way for you to get out of this, big guy. Either you can help yourself or you can spend the rest of your life rotting in a cell."

Jihad sat in silence as Melendez's harsh words bore down on him like a heavy weight. In the streets, he had used his intellect and his gun to get him out of life altering situations. Now, for the first time, he was in a position that he couldn't shoot or manipulate his way out. Jihad made direct eye contact with Melendez. "If I can tell you about three murders, can you get me out of this?"

"Son, you can tell me who killed Biggie Smalls and I won't be able to wipe this clean. If you have information that can lead to the arrest and conviction of three people for murder, I'll talk the judge into giving you no more than eight years for your charges."

Jihad weighed the options in his mind. It was either stand up and face his consequences like a man or scurry away like a rat. *Fuck that shit*, Jihad thought. *My loyalty has been gone.* "Okay, I can tell you who's responsible for the murders of Keith and the twins Kahdeem and Quadir."

Melendez wrote the names down. "Tell me something the cops don't know."

"I know where the gun that killed Keith is at, and I witnessed the twins' deaths."

"Alright, let me find out who's investigating these homicides." Melendez closed his folder and stood.

"Before I go any further, I need you to make sure that I'll get no more than five years," Jihad said, lowering his potential term of imprisonment.

"I'll look into it right now." Melendez took his folder with

———————————

him, leaving Jihad alone.

The next day, Detective Todd Reed entered the precinct and made his way to his cubicle. After getting himself comfortable, he turned on his computer. He checked his emails, quickly skimming through the unimportant ones, until he opened the email from Detective Melendez. He read that Melendez had a suspect in custody who claimed to be a direct witness to two unsolved murders, and had compelling evidence on another murder that he was actively investigating. If the suspect proved to be legitimate, this meant that this person would positively identify Terry and Mack as the killers.

He snatched the phone up and called Latrice. She hadn't checked her email, so he broke the great news to her. After hanging up with her brother, Latrice called Detective Melendez. He briefed her on all that he knew, including the name of the potential witness and the possible deal that would be given to him if he could produce all that he said. Latrice thanked him, then called the precinct and arranged for Jihad to be escorted to an interrogation room. She was told he would be there within ten minutes

It wasn't long before there was a knock on the interrogation room door. Detective Todd opened it. Jihad was wearing dark blue pants and a light blue top. The detectives directed him to an empty chair and Jihad took a seat.

They reviewed their recorded footage dozens of times. He was one of the men who appeared to be in a heated discussion with Terry and Mack.

After introducing themselves, they got right down to business. Jihad was questioned for over two hours. During this time he gave the officers in depth statements on Terry, Mack and Shawn, implicating them with drugs and murders. After signing the statements, the detectives took their information directly to the courthouse and secured four search warrants. Terry, Mack and Shawn were officially wanted for murder...

CHAPTER 35

Detectives Todd and Latrice had no time to waste. They weren't attempting to apprehend the average street fugitives. Terry and Mack were seasoned criminals who had built a multi-million dollar empire from drugs and murder. Although Shawn was on the lower level of the totem pole, he was just as guilty and dangerous. The thugs needed to be removed from the streets before they knew warrants had been issued for their arrests.

Todd and Latrice spent all evening briefing the Warrant Unit on their targets. At nine o'clock the next morning, twenty specially trained officers sat in a large unit that resembled a school's classroom. The projector displayed blueprints of dwellings.

Shawn, whose cooperation with authorities led to Jihad's arrest, and the subsequent domino effect, had been brought into custody minutes ago. It was now time to take down the two heads of the operation.

"We're being divided into three groups," Sergeant White said. "You all know which groups you're in. Group A will be raiding Terry's last known address." He clicked the hand-held remote and Terry's face appeared on the large screen. "Group A, you should now be familiar with the layout of this house." He clicked the remote once again and the blueprint reappeared. "Any questions?"

The room was silent.

"Group B, you guys will be raiding Sabrie Mack's house." The screen showed Mack's face. "Just the same, you should be familiar with the layout of his home. Questions?"

No one spoke.

"Group C, we'll be raiding Dynasty Rentals. These men are expected to be armed, and we know that they will use their weapons. Remember, safety first. If a life has to be lost, it better not be one of ours. Move in fast and efficiently. Secure every area and get the bad guys into custody." He looked around to his men whose eyes were trained on him. "Okay, time is of the essence. Let's go get 'em!"

Everyone had risen to their feet, double checked their fire-arms and protective equipment, and then headed outside to the awaiting vans.

Because it was likely that Terry and Mack would be in their office during that time, Todd and Latrice were in group C, along with Sergeant White. Everyone loaded up into the vans and departed. During the ride, there was light conversation re-garding everyone's assignment, but the potential danger of what lay ahead created too much tension for casual talk.

Ten minutes later, Sergeant White said, "Get ready. It's show time!" The van came to a stop at Dynasty's entrance. The platoon of officers stormed out and quickly entered the building.

Kerri was on the phone with a customer arranging for the pick up of a sports car. By the time she looked up to see the source of all the commotion, there was a police officer pointing a gun at her, ordering her to get off the phone. Scared witless, Kerri quickly complied.

She was removed from her office desk and told to sit on a couch where Sergeant White questioned her.

It took less than twenty seconds for the entire building to be checked and secured. Terry and Mack were not present. The company's computers were being removed for evidence. Todd and Latrice searched the owners' office. To their dismay, there were no weapons or drugs found. Latrice had grown upset at these monsters' good judgment and caution. All she wanted was direct evidence to tie them to the criminal lifestyle, she was certain they were involved in. She searched carefully through the file cabinets. Nothing. She stood up and exhaled a sigh of frustration when her brother yelled over to her.

"Hey sis, come here for a minute. I might have something."

She walked over to the desk he stood at with a ledger in his hand. After examining it, they concluded that large increments of money were being invested in stocks and commodities, with entry dates as recent as three days. There was one name that appeared regularly throughout the ledger: Marty Frankel.

"What do you think?" asked Latrice.

"I think this may be something big."

"Alright, log it into evidence and we'll look into it when we get back to the office."

After confiscating everything considered evidence, questioning Kerri, who had no information of value to give, the officers departed. Kerri was noticeably shaken up. The once beautiful interior of the company was left in complete disarray. Dynasty Luxury Rentals was closed down.

Back at the precinct, Todd and Latrice were informed that neither Terry nor Mack were at their suspected homes and nothing illegal was recovered. According to the officers it didn't appear that they searched their everyday residences.

Todd did his best to stifle his emotions. Not only were these street gangsters cunning and calculated killers, but they also moved intelligently. It was too late for any subtleties. The button had been pushed. If Terry and Mack didn't know at that moment that they were wanted, they would be aware of it very soon. It was now time to apply pressure in hopes that they would panic and make a mistake. All they needed was one slip.

"Did you check into the name that was in the ledger, yet?" Todd asked.

"Marty Frankel? No, I'll do it now." Latrice typed the name into her computer's NCIC database. Within seconds a picture of Marty appeared along with the information regarding his plea of *no contest* to the charge of embezzlement. She studied the face on her screen. She had seen Marty before, but where?

"Sis, isn't that the guy who was talking to Terry at the all white event?"

Her recollection became clear. Although his mug shot was slightly different from the man she discreetly recorded conversing with Terry and Mack during their party, there was no doubt that it was him.

"I knew I saw him before." Latrice reclined in her chair pondering the possibilities of her discovery. "Yep, I'm willing to bet we're on to something big, bro. I'm going to have to call in for a federal favor on this one."

"I'm going to do a little more digging. Let me know how things turn out."

"Alright." Latrice picked up her phone and dialed the number to Jake Elzy, a federal agent from New York City. She worked on a case with him a few months ago. Noticing their chemistry, she felt an attraction to him. Despite her feelings, she did not pursue a romance. For one, they lived in two separate states. And two, she was completely committed to her job, which left little time for dating or a relationship. However, they remained in contact.

"Hello?"

"Hi, Jake. This is Latrice. Are you busy?"

"No. Not at all. What a nice surprise. I've been having a crappy day. Just hearing your voice is making me feel better."

Latrice offered a soft giggle. "Flattery will get you everywhere. Now, I'm feeling bad that this call is business related."

"It's cool. What's up?"

"I need a really big favor from you."

"Oh? What's that?"

Latrice took her time and explained everything regarding Terry, Mack and Marty Frankel. She then asked if it was possible for him to question Marty about his relationship with Mack and Terry. Perhaps getting him to admit to laundering money.

"So, you want me to hunt this guy down and squeeze him until he confesses to washing money for a pair of drug dealing killers? If I do this, what's in it for me?"

Latrice bit down on her lower lip, rushing to come up with

a suitable answer. "Well, if everything goes the way I expect, you will be able to take over the money laundering case."

"Nice try, but seeing that money laundering is a federal offense, odds are that this case will land on my desk anyway. I'm sorry, but you're going to have to do better than that."

"Okay, Mr. Negotiator, how would you like to be compensated for your time and diligent work?"

"I want the honor of taking you out for dinner."

"Jake!"

"I deal with the worst of the worst every day. Is it wrong to want to enjoy the presence of one of God's most beautiful creations?"

"There you go again, Cassanova." Latrice was blushing.

Jake sensed it. "I'm coming to Philadelphia this weekend. Do we have a deal or not?"

"Yes, Jake. We have a deal."

"Great. I'll get on it right away and will call you once I'm finished."

"Thanks a lot…Hey Jake, why were you coming to Philly this weekend?"

"Because I have a date with you." The line went dead, leaving Latrice with a bashful smile.

———

Jake's day had been quite boring. Unlike his colleagues, he didn't enjoy the quietness between the chaos. He loved to stay busy. Latrice's call was welcomed. He would have assisted her without the promise of a date. But knowing that he would enjoy the company of a beautiful and intelligent woman with similar qualities and interests as his was a welcomed bonus.

Jake utilized both the federal database and the Internet to gather as much information as possible on Marty. Once satisfied that he was armed with enough background information, he left the federal building, and walked to the parking lot where his government issued blue Ford Explorer awaited.

Marty was inside of his home office, logged online reviewing his investment portfolio when, he heard the chime of his doorbell. He reluctantly pulled himself from the computer desk and walked into the living room where the intercom was located. "Who is it?"

"FBI Agent Jake Elzy. I need to have a word with you."

Marty saw the tall, clean shaven man wearing a navy blue jacket with the federal logo on the front through the color monitor. "May I see your badge, please?"

Jake removed his credentials from his inner jacket pocket and held it close to the camera. Satisfied, Marty pressed the buzzer allowing the agent to enter the building. Marty made a quick dash to his office and returned before the agent made it to his door. Once Marty heard the knock, he opened the door and stood in the doorway.

"Good afternoon, Mr. Frankel. I'm Agent Jake Elzy." Once again, he removed his badge and identification and held it out for Marty to visually inspect in person. "I would like to talk to you about Terry Maddox and Sabrie Mack."

Marty's face conveyed concern once their names were mentioned. "Sure, come in." He stepped to the side and allowed Jake to enter. He closed the door and remained in the entryway.

Realizing that he would not be invited any further into the

residence, Jake dived right in. "Warrants have been issued for the arrest of Terry and Sabrie on charges of murder."

The news rocked Marty back on his heels. "There has to be some sort of mistake."

"There's no mistake, Mr. Frankel. There's enough evidence to charge these men with second degree murder."

"Well, if that's the case, I think this is something you should talk to their attorneys about. Not me."

"I'm here because additional charges may be filed against them, and if they are, you may be included."

"Me? What in the hell are you talking about?"

"I'm talking about charging you federally with money laundering and embezzlement."

"That's ridiculous!" Marty scoffed at the allegations. "I've done nothing of the sort."

"Don't stand in front of me and act like you're a saint. Your hands aren't clean. You don't think I'm aware of that insider trading scandal you went down for?"

"I was never found guilty of that!" Marty countered.

"Were you involved in insider trading?"

"No."

"Were you, or were you not involved in that huge scandal at Goldman's?" Jake pressed.

"Listen, Agent," Marty took in a deep breath and released it in an attempt to calm himself. "Yes, I did take a tremendous fall for that company, but it wasn't because of my wrong-doings. Someone at that company took advantage of my kindness…my loyalty. Although, I'm the face of that scandal, I was never involved in it. The greedy, heartless monster is still out there and now he feels unstoppable."

"According to my records, you lost everything, Mr. Frankel.

Now you're living in a beautiful apartment in the heart of Manhattan, and from what I've gathered, you are – should I say – financially stable. Did you hit the lottery?" Jake asked sarcastically.

"I did forfeit all of my assets. I was given a check for fifty thousand dollars by Goldman's. I nearly squandered it all before I got my bearings back, and returned to what I do best – investing."

"So, how did you get involved with Terry and Sabrie?"

"We met at a seminar in Philly and we've been close ever since. They're legitimate owners of a car rental company. I convinced them to take a shot at commodities trading. They are really good young men. I've never overhead them talk about anything illegal, or lose their tempers. What you're saying about them is a shock to me." Marty mixed his lies with the truth.

"I can believe that you may not know about the murders, but what I don't believe is that you weren't laundering money for them."

"Agent Elzy, I will make my records available for you, the IRS, and anyone else to inspect. I began investing with a little under five thousand dollars. I have never known Terry or Sabrie to invest any illegal proceeds into commodities."

With Marty adamant about his defense, there wasn't much more for Jake to ask. "Thank you for your time, Mr. Frankel. I'm sure I'll be talking to you again, soon."

"Yes, I'm sure you will," Marty responded. Jake turned toward the door. "Detective Elzy, I believe you dropped this."

The detective turned around to see a flash drive in Marty's hand. "No, that's not mine."

Marty threw him an incredulous look. This could be very valuable information." He extended his hand and Jake accepted the flash drive. He couldn't mask the puzzled look on his face.

After securing the flash drive, Agent Elzy left and Marty closed the door behind him. He couldn't avoid the triumphant smile that materialized…

CHAPTER 36

Terry woke up in Maria's bed to the pleasant smell of breakfast being prepared. He and Maria, a flight attendant, had been dating for the past six months.

After gathering his thoughts, Terry walked over to the chaise where his pants lay, removed his phone from the pocket, then returned to the bed. He was supposed to be at Dynasty and he knew Mack was going to chew him out for being late.

The moment he turned his phone on, it began to vibrate non-stop. There were dozens of texts from both Kerri and Mack. The first message, from Kerri, caused his heart rate to accelerate at a rapid pace. It read: *Dynasty was raided by the police. They're looking for u and Mack!* Panic struck him like a bolt of lightning. He read through a few more texts in disbelief. Every text from Mack simply said: *Call me right away!* He dialed Mack's number.

"Hello?" Mack picked up right away.

"Wassup?" Terry asked.

"Come to the Cool Out right now. Don't waste a second!"

The line went dead. Terry rushed to get dressed, and then darted downstairs. He walked into the kitchen where Maria was busy cooking.

"Baby, I can't stay. I gotta go."

Maria turned around to see Terry fully dressed and in a panicked state. "What's wrong, Terry? You're scaring me."

"I'm not sure what's going on, but as soon as I find out, I'll let you know."

"Are you okay?"

"Don't worry. Everything's going to be fine." Terry kissed Maria, then turned to leave.

"Terry, I'm…" Maria paused as soon as Terry turned to face her and they locked eyes.

"Wassup, Maria?"

She lowered her gaze. "I'm…I'm going to stay up until you call me and let me know everything's okay."

"Alright. I'll call you."

Terry rushed out of her house, into his car and made his way to a secluded house in King of Prussia, Pennsylvania, thirty minutes away. Terry and Mack used the house to get away from everything and to relax. They nick-named their place the Cool Out.

During the drive, Terry's mind raced to cover the possibilities of why he was wanted. He had left the streets alone, so it could only be something from his past coming back to haunt him. In thirty minutes he made it to the house. The moment his car came to an abrupt stop he was out of it. Mack, who was on high alert, opened the door and ushered him in.

"What the fuck is up, Mack?"

"These muthafuckas got murder warrants out on us!" Mack shut the door behind Terry.

One look at Mack's stress laden face and he knew their situation was real. An overwhelming surge of emotions plagued Terry as he realized the seriousness of their predicament. "What are we gonna do?"

"I talked to my lawyer. He said the warrants are for the murders of the twins."

The dreadful news seemed to consume Terry's energy. He plopped down on the couch. "Fuck!" he screamed in frustration.

"That's not it," Mack continued, "Jihad got knocked with ten bricks yesterday and they ran up in Julio's garage. They found like thirty ki's and a bunch of money. I think Shawn got knocked, too."

The information poured out like running water. Just the night before, Terry couldn't have asked to be in a better position. Now he had been thrown into a hole that continuously grew deeper and darker. He hoped that Jihad's arrest didn't result in the raid of Julio's garage. If so, that would be a detrimental blow.

"I have to call, Juk." Terry removed his phone and scrolled through his phone book.

"Who the fuck is Juk?"

"That's my man who introduced me to the cartel connect. If anything's wrong, he should know." After dialing the number, a computer-generated voice announced that the number was no longer in service.

"Something's not right," Terry said.

"Why you say that?" Mack asked.

"Juk's phone is disconnected. He would never change his

number without letting me know."

"I need to smoke." Mack took a seat on the couch next to Terry, who pulled out a small bag of high grade Indica and passed it to him.

"I have to call the connect. That's the only way we're going to know what's up." Terry found the number in his phone and pressed the call button.

"Hello?" Alfredo Lajas answered.

"Mr. Lajas, this is Terry. I..." The line went dead. Terry looked at his phone with a bewildered expression. He tried again and again. Each time the voice mail was instantly activated.

"What happened?" Mack asked anxiously waiting for a response. He finished rolling a healthy blunt and reached for the lighter on the coffee table.

"Yo, we got big fucking problems."

"No shit." Mack lit the blunt and took a pull.

"Nah, you don't understand. The connect answered the phone and hung up once he heard my voice."

"So, what does that mean?"

"That means he ain't got nothin' to say. He must think I'm responsible for Julio's garage getting busted."

"Man, fuck him!" Mack stood and removed his Glock 17. "If he want war, then war it's gon' be!" Mack took another pull from the blunt.

"You don't understand the power of the Zeta Cartel, bruh. These muthafuckas are serious. I'll bet he already sent some Mexicans up here to hunt me down."

"Listen, cannon, we're in this together. However they want it, they can get it. I'd rather take my chances with them than to turn myself in to the police. I ain't goin' out like that." He passed Terry the blunt. "We can't live our lives runnin' from the cops and the cartel. I'll tell you what, let's just lay low until we find out what the police have on us. They can't have no direct evidence. The most they can have is somebody snitchin'. We also have to find a way to clean this mess up with the cartel."

"We can't stay in Philly." Terry took a pull from the blunt, filled his lungs with the potent smoke, and then released it.

"Maria's mom left her a house in Newport News, Virginia. No one knows about it. We can stay there for a minute."

"Aaight. I'm with it, bruh. I got a little over two hundred grand." Mack pointed to a duffel bag on the floor.

"We're going to need more than that, in case we have a change of plans and need to bounce. I got three hundred grand at my other house. Let's pick that up, get the keys from Maria, and get the fuck outta here."

Mack grabbed his duffel bag of money and they left. He backed a late model Chevy Impala out of the garage. Terry then pulled his Mercedes into the garage and joined Mack.

The paranoia was hard to subdue as Mack cautiously navigated through the streets. They were now wanted on both sides of the fence. The sight of every patrol car they passed created tension. And the thought of an unfamiliar vehicle pulling alongside them and spraying their car with a barrage of bullets caused their nerves to remain unsettled.

Mack pulled the Impala into the driveway of Terry's second home. "Hurry up, T. We gotta get the fuck outta here."

"Aaight. I'll be in and out." Terry dashed out of the car. He had the key ready, so it took no time to unlock the front door. Once in the house, he moved with a purpose, pushing the glass coffee table to the side and rolling up the Oriental rug. He began to remove the wood panels revealing a large in-ground safe.

Terry keyed the combination into the electronic keypad when the sound of a cocked gun froze his movements.

He looked up and couldn't believe who was standing over him. "Juk...what's going on?"

"How could you fuck this up, T?" Jukwon asked, pointing a .357 Magnum at his head.

"Juk, listen to me. It wasn't my fault. I..."

"It was your fuckin' fault! You gave the plug to ya mans. You didn't have the authority to do no shit like that. You know what I had to go through in order to introduce you to the Zetas. I should have never done it."

"Juk, you gotta understand, I was easing my way out the game," Terry said, still on his knees.

"Mr. Lajas gave you simple rules. One of the rules was don't bring any heat on him. Because you violated his rule, and I introduced you to him, he's making me take care of the problem."

"Juk, you're my fuckin' brother. Just let me go and I promise you'll never hear from me again," Terry pleaded.

"You really don't get it. These muthafuckas is like gods. How do you think I knew you were coming here? He told me that if I don't take care of you personally, my brother, wife and son will share a grave with me."

Terry could not see a way out. The cartel had directed Jukwon to end his life. His failure to do so would result in the murder of him and his family. They were both placed in an unattainable situation.

"Can you do me a favor?" Terry asked.

"What?"

"Give this money to my mother. And tell her I love her." Terry pressed the remaining combination numbers into the keypad, opened the door, and exposed neat stacks of cash.

He noticed that Jukwon was no longer pointing the gun at him. With no other choice, he seized the opportunity and barreled his shoulder into Jukwon's mid-section, knocking him to the ground with tremendous force. The impact caused the revolver to fall from his hand and slide across the floor. With Terry on top, Jukwon threw a hard punch to his rib cage, and then another punch that hit him in the face. Terry absorbed the blows. He wrapped his hands around Jukwon's throat and squeezed with all his strength, restricting the flow of oxygen to his windpipe. Jukwon scratched, clawed, and kicked. Terry's arms were too long for Jukwon to reach his face.

"I'm sorry, Juk." Terry's eyes welled up while he continued to apply pressure. Jukwon's resistance grew weaker. "Aaaah!" Terry screamed at the top of his lungs in pain as Jukwon reached down and grabbed Terry's balls with a vice-like grip. He squeezed and twisted until Terry was forced to relinquish his choke hold. The air burned Jukwon's larynx as he took in a deep breath of oxygen. There was little time to recover. He kneed Terry hard in the groin causing debilitating pain. Jukwon pulled himself from under the weight of Terry's body and crawled toward the gun that lay a few feet away.

He reached out and grabbed Jukwon's boot, pulling his body back closer to him and away from the gun. Jukwon turned his body over so that his back was on the floor. He used his free foot to stiff kick Terry's face. Blood erupted from his nostrils. He released his grip. Again, Jukwon made a frenzied attempt to get to the weapon. Terry quickly stood and charged Jukwon. Jukwon's hand wrapped around the gun. He spun around, squeezing the trigger two times. The roar of the .357 echoed through the house. The first slug tore through Terry's waist, shattering his pelvis. The second drilled into the center of his chest, dropping him like a dead weight.

Jukwon struggled to his feet and went over to the safe. He

was going to honor his friend's last request.

The sound of the door crashing open startled Jukwon. He clutched his gun and looked up simultaneously. The sound of rapid gunfire forced him to release two rounds, and then run for cover. A multitude of bullets were still being fired in his direction, crashing into walls and furniture inches away. He scurried into the kitchen and out of the rear door.

Mack was about to give chase, but the sight of Terry's motionless body lying in a large pool of blood stopped him. He kneeled down next to his friend and slightly cradled his head. "It's okay, T. I'ma take you to the hospital." Terry's eyes fluttered slightly. "Who was that?" Mack asked.

Terry struggled to get the word out. Blood seeped from his mouth followed by a single word, "Jukwon."

"I'ma find him, T. I'ma find him and I'ma kill him. Don't die on me, bruh. We gon' make it outta here!"

"G-go!" Terry's final word eased out. His body completely relaxed. His eyes rolled to the back of his head. His life was gone.

Tears fell as Mack looked down at the corpse of his best friend. He used his fingers to gently close Terry's eyelids. The distant sound of sirens broke Mack out of his trance.

———————————

An unmarked car had been parked several houses down from Terry's home. The officer had been assigned to keep surveillance on the suspect's residence since that morning.

When the Impala pulled into the driveway, he notified Homicide Detectives Todd and Latrice. They called in the Fugitive Task force and wasted no time arriving at the scene fully prepared for whatever lay ahead.

———————

"I promise I'm going to kill, Jukwon." With one final look at the body of his comrade, he picked up his Glock, bolted through the living room, and out the door.

"Mack, put the gun down!" Todd ordered. He, Latrice and several officers had their weapons aimed directly at him.

Mack's eyes darted around. There were at least twelve police officers prepared to fire. "Fuck you!" Mack tightened the grip on his semi-automatic.

"It's not worth it," Latrice reasoned, keeping her firearm trained on him. "You can't win that way. Put the gun down."

Mack's mind raced. He could go out shooting with the hopes of taking a cop or two with him, or he could live to fight another day. The vision of Terry's body, along with so many others that he encountered, flashed through his head. He had much more living to do before the time for him to die would come. Mack released the grip on his gun, allowing it to fall to the ground, and raised his hands above his head. With Todd covering his sister, Latrice placed Mack's hands behind his back, and secured them with handcuffs.

"Damn, it feels so good to put these on you. You're under arrest for the murders of Kahdeem and Quadir Wilson."

Mack looked Latrice directly in her eyes. "I want to see if you have that same look on your face when I beat the charges..."

EPILOGUE

Marty Frankel had just taken a morning shower and was headed towards his bedroom when he heard a light rap on his door. He wrapped himself in a thick cotton robe and answered the door. It was the doorman. Marty paid the doorman extra to bring him three specific newspapers every day. After taking the papers, he decided to have a seat on the living room sofa. He went directly to the *USA Today's* money section, which was his normal routine. He nearly jumped out of his skin when he read the headline of the cover story.

<u>100 Million Dollar Trading Scheme Unraveled</u>

He continued to read:

> *On Tuesday, federal authorities unsealed charges against international traders and computer hackers who allegedly reaped more than one hundred million in illegal profits by gaining access to pending corporate announcements and trading on*

the news before it was made public.

FBI Agent Jake Elzy, who spearheaded the investigation, led to charges being filed against two hackers from Ukraine and the traders, Jack Goldberg of Goldman's and Kate Mills Frankel, who is an associate of Jack's. The American defendants were arrested Tuesday and the others remain at large overseas.

"Check mate!" Marty screamed with excitement. He grabbed the phone to share the news that the notorious *Jack The Ripper* had been toppled.

Not long after hanging up with Vincent, Marty's phone rang.

"Hello?"

"Marty, it's Mack."

"What's up, pal?"

"I got some bad news. I'm in the Roundhouse in Philly. They charged me with murder."

Marty sat up on the end of the sofa. "Do you have an attorney?"

"All of my assets have been frozen. I need your help, Marty."

"Listen to me carefully. I wouldn't be in the position I am today if it weren't for you. All of my resources are at your disposal. We're going to get you the best lawyers in the goddamn country!"

After talking to Marty, who promised to remain by his side and help him in any way needed, Mack returned to his cell. He faced an extreme uphill battle. He also made a promise to T-Lova that he would kill Jukwon, and he intended to keep it…

THE END?

CPSIA information can be obtained
at www.ICGtesting.com
Printed in the USA
LVOW03s1554100118

562548LV00003B/502/P